A MOST INCONVENIENT LOVE

A Most Inconvenient Love

Ruth Logan Herne

Dedication

This book is dedicated to Mary Eichas Gavigan, a woman who forged her way forward in a time that didn't necessarily encourage women in business or politics. She set a strong and wonderful example for the children she taught, especially the girls… and for all of the women in the Western New York Eichas family. While the names in the story don't reflect any particular person, they honor a family of faith, hope and love. Aunt Mary… This one's for you.

"Let the morning bring me word of your unfailing love, for I have put my trust in you. Show me the way I should go, for to you I entrust my life."

~ Psalm 143:8

Chapter One

SEBASTIAN WARD DIDN'T GROWL, AND he felt good about that.

He wanted to, and he would be well within his rights if he did. While he expected the 9:03 train to deliver a massive load of planed wood from his father's Minnesota lumber mills, he wasn't expecting an illegitimate brother as part of the deal.

The five-year-old, tear-stained boy standing in front of him said otherwise. And when a wet stain branded the front of the little guy's trousers, Seb realized something else.

He'd need a new, smaller seat in the necessary.

He couldn't head east and throttle his father, despite the temptation to do just that. It was late August and the push of westward migration was in full swing. That made a trip back to Minnesota quite impossible, a fact Cedric Ward most likely counted on. Homes, barns, and businesses were breaking ground and a new granary was being built just up the railroad line, built with load after load of Ward lumber.

Two new retail buildings were half-constructed on Main Street, and two more were just begun on Harrison Street, named for the president that recently signed South Dakota into statehood. And on scattered claims throughout the area, Ward lumber was being used to change the face of the

American landscape forever.

What in the world was he going to do with a kid?

He's not a kid. He's your brother, and he's little and he's scared. Kindness first, Sebby.

His mother's voice, the dulcet tones of the nicest, kindest gentlest woman he knew. What a shame that she was married to a rich, cheating scoundrel of a man.

Kindness first.

He sighed, motioned to his crew that he was leaving, and lifted the boy's bag. "Let's get you cleaned up and fed, all right?"

The boy stared up at him. Just that, nothing more, a wide-eyed stare that said so much more than words. And then he gulped.

Seb's heart pinched.

What was the matter with his father? What sort of game was he playing? Seb didn't know, but he'd figure it out soon enough. In the meantime, the boy needed some looking after. And from the lightweight feel of his bag, he'd need clothes.

When I was hungry, you fed me. Naked, you clothed me.

Seb wasn't a church-going man. He'd never seen the sense in wasting time when the Lord had given him a perfectly good outdoors that seemed steeped in prayer. But that verse came chasing back to him now. Once he had the boy cleaned up and changed at his somewhat Spartan apartment attached to the mill, he walked him over to Hattie McGillicuddy's sewing shop. One way or another the child needed clothing, and Hattie would know exactly what to do. She always did.

The big inner door stood open, but Levi Eichas had fashioned a screened door for Hattie. Levi was a fine carpenter. He built solid wagons and carriages, the work of a true tradesman. When someone needed a fancy this or that, Levi used the winter quiet to make it for them. Of course his wife's aversion to bugs most likely bumped that screened door to the top of Levi's work list. Nellie Eichas worked at Hattie's shop, and Levi liked keeping Nellie happy. Marriage seemed to suit the woodcrafter.

Marriage wasn't in the cards for Seb. He'd watched Cedric Ward treat his wife as an inferior being. His father had run the gamut of rook deals to build his business, and kept the pretense of an illustrious lumber baron by keeping his wife and daughters in fine style. While cheating on the side, of course.

No, he'd seen enough of marriage's dark side. Single and focused was fine by him. As he and the boy approached the sewing shop, the quick rise and fall of women's voices made him hesitate.

He didn't want to get caught in the clutches of nattering old hens, not when there was work to be done, but as his shadow darkened the entry, the first woman turned.

Something inside him might have rolled to a stop, or kept right on going. Either way, her beauty was enough to make Seb square his shoulders.

"Seb! Come in, come in!" Hattie's voice beckoned him from behind the other two women, and of course going in was about last on his list of things to do with three women mixing it up, but what choice did he have?

None.

He swung the door wide, ushered the boy in and stepped in behind him. "Morning, ladies."

"Mr. Ward!" Nellie looked delighted to see him, but she generally looked happy so he wasn't sure if he should be pleased or complacent. "Nice to see you! And who is this?" She bent low to the little guy.

Eli shrank against his leg, and the child's mix of fear and trust made Seb feel bigger and stronger. That was downright silly because he'd been big and strong for quite some time. And how was he supposed to introduce his father's love child? If he mentioned the word brother, someone was sure to get wind of it back in Minnesota. Which meant he'd add lying to his list of infractions, and Seb Ward never lied.

He did today, at least to buy some time. "A young friend. Elijah. He's come to stay with me awhile."

"Lovely!" Nellie looked quite pleased. Then she turned an off-shade of green like new lumber, poorly cured. She went off like a shot, out the door and down the steps.

"Is she all right?" he wondered, turning back.

Hattie came his way. "She will be in a matter of months. Seb, give me just a moment to finish up with Rachel here..."

He didn't have a moment, but he couldn't say that. He couldn't say that the reason his lumberyard was making money and others had bellied up was because Seb wasn't afraid to make things happen in a timely fashion after years of drought and money loss had pushed other wood lots to call it a day.

The other woman took a step back. "Hattie, I'm waiting on Solomon and Ann to ride back to the farm, and they'll be a few minutes, yet. Go ahead and see to Mr. Ward's order."

Kind.

Gentle.

And downright lovely, he realized when she lifted her gaze to his. No, not just lovely, with oak-brown hair pulled back in an old-fashioned bun and ivory skin the color of his mother's old lace table covers... hazel eyes, the color of mixed autumn leaves, all green and gold and bits of brown.

Regal.

He was taken with the word and the tall woman's appearance and Seb couldn't remember the last time he'd had time to even think of a woman. That meant he'd been working too hard and too long for a father who clearly thought of women too often.

He swallowed a sigh because it wouldn't do one lick of good to expel it. "That's very kind, Miss—"

"Eichas. Rachel Eichas. I'm Nellie's sister-in-law. And if our young friend here is going to be in town for a while, perhaps you'd like to sign him up for the fall semester of school?"

School.

Of course, a boy almost six would be starting school.

Seb hoped he didn't look as flummoxed as he felt. It was all well and good to learn these things a step at a time, but to have the boy unceremoniously dropped on his doorstep went beyond surprise and straight to confusion.

That wasn't the lad's fault. He looked from her to Hattie. "I expect that's a wise idea."

"Rachel has graciously accepted the proposal of the school board to take on the fall session after Mr. Blount's misfortune."

"I heard he went back east." Seb grimaced. "It's hard enough to make it out here without an ailment, that's for certain." He addressed Rachel more directly. "No offense meant, but are you able to handle the mix of classes? Those bigger boys gave Blount a hard time and caused his eventual downfall, didn't they?"

She tried to hide the flash of uncertainty, but Seb saw it.

What kind of school board put a woman in charge of a classroom full of earnest students, certain to be pestered by a band of rowdy boys who had roughed up the former teacher?

But then she surprised him more than a little when she said, "I expect they'll listen with some encouragement from me. And possibly my sister's homemade cheese and Ann's bread."

"The way to a boy's and man's heart. I do declare you might be on to something, Rachel!" Hattie came around the counter. "Seb, are we looking for things for you or young Elijah?"

"For Eli," he told her. She whipped out a measuring tape, and within a minute had jotted down lengths of this, that and the other thing on a slate board with a handy piece of twine going from side to side. Then she hung that little slate on a wall with several other slates, all holding orders. "You're busy enough, then?" he asked.

Hattie laughed. "And then some, and most confounded with my helpers getting married one right after the other. Fortunately they've all settled hereabouts and are still willing to work as they're able. Rachel, I'll have your two teaching frocks done by Wednesday next, and Seb, I'm going to bump Eli's clothes to the front of the line for you."

How did she know? Did he look desperate?

Probably so. "I appreciate that, Hattie, but I don't want to be rude."

"Not a spot of rudeness about it, a boy needs a few changes of clothes by mere merit of being a boy and the preponderance of puddles we'll be privy to once the autumn rains hit. Three shirts, three pants and I know Ginny got some new suspenders in over at the mercantile. Her prices beat the catalogues."

"Shopping local is what builds a town," he agreed. "Then we're set?"

"Come by Monday, I'll have enough ready to get you by. I'll finish the rest with Nellie during the following week."

"Monday, then." He tipped his hat slightly, and turned to Rachel. "A pleasure to meet you, Miss Eichas."

"Mr. Ward."

She didn't say it was nice to meet him, because it most likely wasn't, but for a moment he wished things were different. He wished he was nicer, friendlier, more open.

He was none of those things and shrewd business skills had been his falling out with a few locals. In a small town like Second Chance, a reputation was a hard thing to build up and fairly easy to bring down, so he practiced doing neither. He swung the door wide and stepped out. The boy followed, still quiet.

Was that normal?

How would he know?

He'd been a quiet youngster, but ambitious and forward-thinking, so maybe Eli was like that.

He turned to let the door swing shut softly.

Rachel was watching the boy with a look so tender and sweet that Seb's heart stirred once more. His mother had looked at him like that, long ago. Funny, what a man remembered and what he chose to forget.

Rachel lifted her gaze again. When she met his, time paused. She didn't drop her eyes the way proper young women did back in the city, and he'd met his share before coming west to set up shop. She studied him as if reading his features meant something.

It didn't because no matter what she surmised, Seb Ward let few people see the tired soul within the ambitious businessman's body. That's the way it had always been. That's the way it would stay.

Rachel Mary Eichas had just met her match.

She knew it.

She felt it.

And while she'd seen Sebastian Ward in passing now and again, her family had been like so many others the past several years. They'd worked three seasons, night and day, building not only their triple-claim north of town, but her brother's wagon-making and smithy business at the corner of Second Avenue and Main Street.

Rachel watched him walk away.

Tall. Square-built, with broad shoulders. Slate gray eyes set in a firm face beneath dark, almost shaggy hair which meant he didn't take time from work to visit Clem for a cut.

Business first.

That's how she'd describe Seb Ward, and she'd been

raised by the narrow-minded constraints of a work-first father. At his death she vowed no man would ever run her life with that kind of iron fist again, and she'd meant every word.

So why did her breath haul up short and her ribs feel tight when she faced the lumberman in close proximity? And now, with this unexpected opportunity to stay in town for the next several months, she'd be living almost next door to Ward's Lumber. The lumbering operation sat directly across the road from her set of rooms attached to the carriage shop. The lumberyard was bordered on the south side by the train tracks that put Second Chance on everyone's new map.

"Rachel, I know you've got the gold-and-brown floral that your brother commissioned for Christmas last year."

"With Nellie's hand for tucks, yes." Her brother had surprised all three Eichas sisters with a custom-made dress when Nellie had come to town. Their father believed in dressing plain, and by plain he meant austere... A plain farm, plain land, plain clothing. But when the embittered farmer had died two years before, the three Eichas sisters began to see the light. Not the light of faith, they had that love tucked securely in their hearts... but the light of freedom. And free choice. The right to wear what they chose, when they desired. Like butterflies emerging from a dull chrysalis, they'd begun to blossom at Christmas and here was Rachel, stepping off the farm to take on a new job as the local schoolmarm.

"What about if we go with a nice, serviceable blue and perhaps a cheerier yellow calico?"

Rachel's chest pinched. Her hands clenched and her fingers buzzed.

She'd been serviceable all her life. She, Miriam and Esther had worn work-friendly frocks from the time they could walk. They'd only started coming into town on a regular basis this past year.

So, no.

She didn't want functional. She'd had her share of that, thank you very much. For the next four months she'd be living in town, teaching the school children, and living on her own.

Serviceable was fine for farm work, cleaning and cheese-making, but for this time in her life, Rachel looked across the counter to Hattie's pattern pictures and pointed. "Hattie, I'm going to say this to you only, woman to woman."

Instantly intrigued, the matronly seamstress drew closer.

"I don't want to hear or say the word serviceable for the rest of this calendar year. All right?"

Hattie laughed out loud. "Head around the corner to the mercantile, and pick out material with Ginny. If Nellie's over her bout of sickness, drag her along with you and bring me back a dress length of both colors, and enough white cotton for a proper underpinning. A lace inset collar would be nice, too. Muslin has its day." Hattie wasn't disinclined to explain as a general rule, and today was no exception, but her frankness and integrity earned her a highly regarded reputation throughout the town. "But some styles are best paired with fine cotton, and that's all I'm going to say about that!"

"I'll find Nellie, make the purchase and be back before Solomon and Ann are ready to head out to their claim." Her widowed cousin Solomon had come west with his two small children the year before, then won the hand of Hattie's last helper, a widow named Ann. "And Hattie?"

The middle-aged seamstress met Rachel's gaze straight on.

Rachel wasn't sure how to explain herself, so in the end, she kept it simple. "Thank you for understanding."

"Understanding and approving," Hattie declared. She added a few notes to the measurements she'd already made and hung Rachel's slate on the wall. "The chance to see you wearing stylish clothing as you walk back and forth to that school the next few months is something I should have thought of myself. I'm surprised I didn't," Hattie admitted. "But I'm certainly glad you did, Rachel."

Is that what she'd done? Rachel wondered.

Did she step into deep waters because she saw that light of appreciation in Seb Ward's eyes? Did she see this time off their busy and expanding claim as her one chance to be seen? At twenty-four-years old, she didn't feel aged, but she couldn't call herself young, either. Thinking back, Rachel wasn't sure when she'd had the freedom to be young. Once her stepmother had left, Rachel was expected to assume a matriarchal role, and she'd done it with no questions asked. Maybe being meek and mild was her undoing. She'd learned better, though, and the woman about to run the Second Chance schoolhouse was quite different from the young woman who stepped into a role to help her family on their prairie claim years before.

She walked out the door, walked down Second Avenue at a good clip, then turned the corner, nearly plowing into Seb Ward and Eli.

"Just the person I wanted to see."

That voice. Those words.

Oh, land sakes! For all that was plain and brown on a dust-swept prairie, the notion that Sebastian Ward would have this effect on her was a bitter pill that didn't seem all that bitter.

She knew better. More than anyone, she knew that kind of man from grim experience. She drew a breath, pretended her heart wasn't skittering in her chest, and kept her tone level. "You needed me?"

"For this." He thrust a small sack of items her way. "I asked Ginny what Eli would need for school when it starts next week, and she suggested what you see here. Is there anything I've overlooked, Miss Eichas?"

Oh, she was silly, all right, assuming he'd been thinking

of her the way she'd been taken with him.

Silly enough for her cheeks to flame and her hands grow tight. She checked out the parcel and nodded. "I think you're fine, Mr. Ward. Eli will be in the first primary class. I'm aware of only two children sitting that class. My cousin Solomon's boy Ethan will join Eli. They're of the same age and I expect they'll get on well together."

"A playmate."

"Well, we do take education seriously, but of course, there will be playtime at recess. Children do better with a built-in free time."

"No, you misunderstand."

He sounded brusque, and Rachel had entertained brusque from her father for two decades. No more. "Did I?" She sent him a cool look, unoffended, and thoroughly unimpressed. "Perhaps you can explain yourself, Mr. Ward?"

He glanced over her head to the lumberyard. The shrill notes of a train whistle had him grabbing his chin as if in deep thought. "I have to get back to work, and for poor Eli, he has to come with me because there is no instant recourse with matters like this."

"Matters like...?"

"A child. A lad, a boy in need of a playmate. Listen, can we meet and talk about this, because—" the train whistle sounded again, long and insistent. "I've got to get over there and meet this supply train. Later today, perhaps?"

"I'm leaving town to go back to our farm and pack my things, but I'll be moving into my brother's now vacant apartment tomorrow."

"Attached to the smithy?"

"Yes."

"Then we'll talk tomorrow." With the boy's hand tucked firmly in his, he strode off, a man with a purpose, intent on work and barely polite.

The boy half-jogged along, trying to keep up.

She turned and kept walking toward the mercantile,

determined to shrug off her first-impression fantasy. She'd let Sebastian's firm gaze and good looks muddy her brain. By rights she was a sensible woman. Everyone said so, so why did the flash of interest in Seb's eyes render her quite insensible? She knew his type too well. And yet...

"Come unto me, all ye that labor and are heavy laden, and I will give you rest."

Matthew's words from the Gospels, a simple invitation, freely given.

And in that verse lay her answer.

Sebastian Ward was heavy laden. He hid it well, like she did, but she sensed the internal struggle in him, perhaps because it reflected hers. She'd been set on a course of action years ago, with no end in sight. That all changed when the local school board put a teaching contract in her hand.

Rachel was ready to begin anew, starting with a couple of pretty dresses. And if she happened to catch a single man's eye over the next few months, that would be more than the last five years had wrought.

She spotted Nellie chatting with Levi, grabbed her sister-in-law's arm and steered her toward the shop. "Nellie, dear?" She tucked the vibrant young seamstress's hand through her arm, and left her brother standing there as she pulled her away. "Come and help me find material suitable for a teacher and an independent woman ready to make her mark in this world."

Nellie paused their progress, looked up at Rachel and offered a 'what took you so long' kind of nod. "And possibly find a man along the way, eh?"

Rachel laughed, because once Nellie had joined the family, frank conversation became the rule, rather than the exception. "God willing. But first, the dress. And nothing drab or plain, all right?"

Nellie hugged her arm, because she understood more than most what Rachel's father had been like. "I wouldn't dream of it, sweetie. You leave this to me and Hattie. By the time you walk to that school next week, Seb Ward and any other eligible bachelor around town will sit up and take notice. You have my word on it."

Nellie meant it, too, and when they'd picked out a delightful blue to couple with an inset white bodice, and a rose and tan calico trimmed out in gathered lace, they carried the yardage back to Hattie's and deposited the goods onto the back table.

Solomon called her name just then. She said quick goodbyes and hurried to the wagon. Tonight would be the last night of cooking for the family for some time to come. Tomorrow she'd be living in the little rooms Levi and Nellie had just vacated. The young, expectant couple had relocated to the prairie farmhouse to await the birth of their first child. Miriam and Esther would step into Rachel's chores, and that wasn't without its own amusement.

Miriam made great cheese, but couldn't boil water without the pot going dry and Esther was more at home fixing fence and riding herd than mashing potatoes.

And Nellie, bless her heart, was so down with morning sickness right now that food was the last thing on her mind.

But the cool evenings and the surprise offering of the school board suggested change was at hand, and at twenty-four-years old, Rachel Eichas figured it was long overdue.

Chapter Two

"MISS EICHAS."

I will not react to the amazing and wonderful deep timbre of his voice. I will not.

Rachel turned, determined, but the moment Seb drew close her breath hitched and she was pretty sure death was imminent. She forced herself to look down at young Eli. Seeing the sadness of the boy's sweet face fixed her breath and her heart in quick order. "Eli." She bent low and smiled gently. "How are you on your second day in Second Chance?"

"I miss my mommy." Tears flooded out of his eyes, a storm, unleashed. "I just miss her so much."

She gathered him in and held him close. She had no idea if it was the right thing to do, but it felt right and that was enough for Rachel. She angled a look of question up to Seb. His serious demeanor and the slight shake of his head said enough.

She let the little guy have his cry, then straightened. "Mr. Ward."

"Sebastian, please. Or Seb," he added, as if in afterthought. "We're neighbors now, and it would be easier all around to be on a first name basis."

Except she hadn't offered any such thing, nor was she inclined to do so at his direction.

She ignored his request and laid a hand on Eli's shoulder. "I know you mentioned yesterday that you'd like a playmate for Eli, and our Ethan might be ideal, but I was wondering if we could come to a different arrangement for today. Would you allow Eli to help me tidy up the school room?"

Seb Ward looked like a drowning man who had just been handed a lifeline. "You don't mind?"

"I'd be delighted by the help, and it would give Eli and me a chance to work together. And give him a chance to get to know his new teacher."

"Miss Eichas..."

Rachel made no attempt to offer her given name as an option, but the lumberyard owner didn't seem overly concerned.

"That would be a wonderful thing. There's nothing he can do at the lumberyard, and there's danger lurking around every corner. A boy's propensity for climbing makes stacked lumber most attractive, but I don't want anything to happen to him."

"I concur." She tipped a smile up to him, then down to Eli. "I could use the extra help, so I think we have a lovely solution."

"I'll gather lunch for both of you and bring it by a little after twelve, if that's all right?"

"For Eli, yes, that would do well, but—"

He took her hand.

Did he know what that simple, sincere gesture did to her? She looked at him, and when he covered her hand with his second one, Rachel felt feminine and petite for the first time in her life. "Allow me to do this if for no other reason than your kindness is giving him a chance to be a boy and me a chance to get work accomplished."

Her hand, wrapped in his. His gaze, sincere, and something else, something deeper, she thought, and then scolded herself internally for thinking such a thing. An appreciative note warmed his voice.

"I'll have lunch done up at the hotel and bring it by, and if you both don't mind, I'd enjoy taking time to eat with you."

"Taking time from work?" Rachel didn't soften her note of surprise.

"Children need time as much as adults need to work," he replied. "Eli and I barely know one another, and thrusting him off on someone else isn't an ideal situation. So lunch would be a treat."

"I don't like liver sausage." Eli found gumption enough to deliver those five words.

"Me, either," declared Seb, smiling. "Miss Eichas, I'm heading back now before you think to rescind your generous offer." He touched his hat, then stooped low to meet Eli eye-to-eye. "And Eli, I'll see you in a few hours, all right?"

The boy swallowed hard. He dipped his head in a slight nod, clearly uncomfortable. But when she took his hand, he breathed deep and didn't sob. As Seb walked up the shallow incline to the lumberyard property bordering the rail bed, she held up a key.

Eli peered at it, suspicious.

"This is the key to the schoolroom," she whispered.

He didn't look too impressed by that declaration.

"You and I are the first ones to see it this term."

That revelation sparked a little more interest.

"And you and I need to see what is in the schoolroom, and what we'll need to have on hand in a few days."

"Maybe cookies?"

Such a normal thing for a child to want.

She smiled and gripped his little fingers in hers. "We might be able to find a tin that holds a biscuit or two. Or cookies, if you will."

"I like them so very much." He held tight to her hand, as if the familiarity of a woman's touch felt good and right.

A train whistle sounded from miles east, fighting to be heard over the steady western breeze, and she thought of Sebastian Ward, suddenly showing up with a child in tow.

Was Eli his child?

He hadn't said, nor had he made mention of a wife that she'd ever heard, but the frontier was not always a place women embraced. Not every man came west with his wife.

Not all children are born of marriage.

She'd read the look Seb shot her before he'd gone back to work. The boy's mother was gone, that much was clear. That was a too-common occurrence on the prairie. If a little fellow like Elijah felt better holding snug to her hand, Rachel was of the mind to let him do just that. They strolled to the single story white building nestled west of the lumberyard. The school stood on a shallow hill just above her new apartment. Pastor Barber's church stood not far from the school lot, and his house lay diagonal from both. The whole arrangement created a cozy effect of church and school. Ginny at the mercantile had contributed pencils and a large slate board for the front of the room. Two of the big boys had broken the last one in a fit of temper, ending the spring term on a sour note.

She unlocked the door, and swung it inward.

Old air rushed out, and as she threw the four windows open, fresh air poured in. Clean prairie air filled the room. In no time at all the new breeze had pushed old scents on their way.

She drew a bucket of water from the well and started scrubbing desks. She handed a small wash rag to Eli, and he joined in. They scrubbed and rinsed, and scrubbed again, and by late morning, the room looked better. It smelled of clean wood and oil soap, and while Eli wasn't really much help, he happily worked his rag across desks and floor and then the floor again.

He was a mess.

Rachel was a mess.

But the room was clean, if a little shabby.

Rachel had been raised in a plain house, by an austere man. Threadbare wasn't necessarily a bad thing, and Rachel had every intention of keeping the students busy enough that the word shabby would never have a chance to cross their minds.

She busied Eli with a small shovel from the tool shed as she weeded the narrow gardens around three sides of the school house. The gardens hadn't been tended in a long while, but she had sprouts she could plant for spring, and bulbs, too, brought from Minnesota. She'd planted them years ago, and there were hundreds now. With time and a firm hand, the school house wouldn't have to look forlorn. The faded building needed what everything craved, love and care, and Rachel meant to deliver both. Of course, if they didn't re-hire her for the spring term, she'd be back on the farm, but the bulbs would welcome others after a long, cold, prairie winter.

"Hello."

No.

Rachel heard Sebastian's voice, felt the warmth of mid-day sun, but still wanted to deny the moment. Seb Ward had gotten here already, and Rachel was pretty sure she'd never looked worse in her life. She glanced up at the mid-day sun, then him.

"It's not noon yet. Is it?" She sounded desperate, and Rachel never sounded desperate, but fifteen minutes and a good washing would have been nice.

"Ten of at the hotel, and I didn't want things to get cold."

"What a thoughtful gesture." That's what she said, but her head was yelling for a chance to meet a wash bucket face-to-face. She reached a hand to her hair, and the few remaining pins fell forward.

Her hair obscured her face, which was just as well because the last thing she wanted to see was Seb laughing at her.

Or pitying her. That would be worse.

"Gentlemen." She shoved her hair off her face as Eli dashed around the corner of the schoolhouse, and didn't dare think of how dirt-smudged she must be. "I'm going to freshen up, and Eli, I'd like you to do the same. Clean hands and face at the table, look as pretty as you're able."

"That rhymes." Eli grinned up at her. "My mommy told me about rhymes and she said cat rhymes with hat."

"And rat."

"And fat." He grinned and reached for her hand. "You're a good rhymer!"

"As are you." She took his hand and wished she didn't have to face Seb, but what choice was there? "Eli and I will be right back."

"I'll get things ready," he told her. He wasn't laughing at her exactly, but she did seem to be a source of amusement. Marvelous.

She refused to sigh because this was her own fault.

Why hadn't she stopped a quarter hour before? She could have been neat and tidy when he strode up to the school. Instead, she looked like a—

She didn't know what she looked like, in actuality, because most women on the prairie wouldn't let themselves get caught looking this bad in town.

Living on the claim was different. Everyone worked on a claim, it was the only way to put in five years and avoid starvation. But town life was set apart. Enterprise, businesses, schools and churches set a different tone, more educated and better situated. And she'd managed to greet the handsome business owner smudged, tattered and work-worn.

She came back with Eli a few minutes later. Seb had moved inside with the small food basket. As they approached, he was studying the thinly supplied school room. She tried to read his expression, but failed. "Did you go to a big school, Mr. Ward?"

"I didn't." He turned her way, musing. "Small, like this. I worked by my father's side and went to our one-room schoolhouse until I'd grown enough to apprentice in the wood. And once I knew the lumber business, you couldn't have paid me enough to sit in a classroom again."

"You love it."

He raised one absolutely gorgeous brow in question.

"Working with wood," she went on. "You love what you do."

He opened the small basket the inn owner had packed and mulled her statement as he set out food. "I enjoy running a business. But I miss the hands-on working with wood. When there's time, I like making things. Creating things. Fine carpentry. Bringing out the beauty of wood like your brother does in his shop. But." He didn't look sad, nor pensive, either, but a hint of regret flattened his tone. "There hasn't been time for that in a long while."

Ripe smells filled the air. Eli's tummy growled. So did hers, but she pretended it was Eli's again because she'd already been humiliated enough for one day.

"I love fried chicken, Seb!" Eli clasped his hands together and grinned. "It's my favorite chicken, ever!"

"And you, Rachel?"

His gaze rested on hers.

"It is an absolute treat, Seb."

He smiled then, and it wasn't the cool, distracted smile she'd seen before.

Genuine warmth deepened the curve of his mouth and added a twinkle to his eyes. "You've done well in here. It smells clean. I expect it was a little musty when you opened that door."

"It was." She buttered a hunk of bread for Eli. He sat at one of the smaller desks up front, and her heart opened wider when Seb strode forward and brought a small desk back to her and put it alongside the table against the back wall.

"It's more fun to eat together, isn't it, Eli?"

Eli nodded, chewing quickly, and hurried back to them.

"It sure is!"

His little face searched Seb's. Looking for what? Rachel wondered. Pride? Acceptance? Love? All the things a child should be raised knowing, but Rachel understood the serious lack therein. Not all parents blanketed their children in loving emotion.

She would.

If God saw fit to bless her with a husband and a family, they would know her love every single day, regardless of circumstance. Even children on a tight budget benefitted from hugs and stories and kisses.

"Gentlemen."

Eli had taken another big bite, Seb had filled the plate from the hotel kitchen, and handed one to her. "Yes?"

"Did we forget to thank the Lord?" She was pretty sure he'd scoff because while her church attendance had been scarce because of her father's reticence, she'd never once seen Seb darken the church door, and that had set more than one tongue wagging.

Eli frowned.

Seb didn't. He set his plate at the table and didn't fold his hands. He spread them wide, preacher-style, and Rachel Eichas got her second surprise of the day.

Seb Ward prayed a quick, gentle prayer of thanksgiving as if he did it all the time.

Or he's an accomplished actor, her conscience warned.

Was he?

She didn't know, but when he didn't simply sit, when he drew out a chair for her, and waited while she sat, the quiet gesture set her heart fluttering in her chest all over again.

A silly reaction. Almost childish. As if she was a young girl, searching for romance.

She wasn't young, but the thought of romance lured her. The reality squashed the allure when she considered the setting, her appearance, and the mystery surrounding the sweet child swiping his sleeve to his face. "Eli." She handed

him a thin napkin she'd packed in her own lunch sack.
"Use this instead."

He rolled his eyes, dashed the cotton square across his
face, and managed to eat two pieces of chicken, the hunk
of bread, a small apple and a cup of water in an amazingly
short period of time. Then he was up and out of the small
desk like a shot. "Can I go play?"

"Stay close, and don't go anywhere near those railroad
tracks," Seb warned.

"I won't! I promise!" He raced outside and around back.

"I gave him one of the smaller shovels to dig with,"
Rachel explained. "While I was working on the front
edges of the yard, I let him dig in the back. He's a good
digger," she admitted, smiling.

"And he's not being a nuisance? Or too much of a nuisance," Seb amended.

"Not one bit, and it's good practice for me to be around
a little one before I step into my role next week."

His look sharpened. "You've not taught before?"

"Only my siblings."

"Then let's talk again about the rowdy boys from Cutter's Crossing."

She didn't want to talk about them. She knew they'd
raised trouble with the former teacher. He'd gone back
east with a broken arm, some bangs and bruises and no
thought of coming back. That's how she'd secured the job.
They'd closed the school for the remainder of the spring
term, and now hoped to re-establish education in Second
Chance. "I mean to apply reason and love of education to
keep all the students motivated."

He didn't soften his stare and Rachel refused to squirm.
"You doubt me, but I am quite effective in a quiet way."

"Those boys are trouble."

She knew that, so why belabor it?

"They don't just want to get out of school like so many
kids. They want to disrupt the school. It seems that was

their sole reason for attending."

"And if they do, I'll send them on their way."

"You know what they did to Mr. Blount?"

"Yes." But she also knew Mr. Blount from personal experience. He'd shown interest in her sister Miri two years before, and had proven himself to be a disagreeable, wormy sort of man. When Miri refused to go walking with him, he'd pouted and sneered.

What form of man behaved like that? And if he behaved like that while trying to win the favor of a young woman, what kind of behavior did he bring to a classroom of scholars?

"Blount was a fool."

She blushed because Seb read her mind.

"But he was also a man and they took advantage of him. I don't want them to do the same with a woman."

"I'm no shrinking violet."

He got up, moved to the window and leaned out to check on Eli. When the boy answered his call, he turned back to her. He stood there, tall and strong and firm. Her father had stood like that, too, only his demeanor had been curt and stern.

Seb's was neither. Concerned, yes. Harsh? No. "Promise me this." He locked his thoughtful gaze with hers. "If there is trouble, send Eli across to the lumberyard. If he should suddenly appear in the middle of the day, I'll know it's a call for help and I'll come running."

She didn't want to talk about this. Talking about trouble with those teenage thugs meant it was a reality. They'd been sent on their way once. They wouldn't dare come back. Would they?

And yet, could she deny them the right to education, a right she cherished?

"Rachel." He moved close. So close. So close that when she stood, her face was a hair's breadth from his. Delicious scents teased. Something warm and spicy mingled with fresh lumber and fried chicken and something else... something distinctly male and delightfully strong.

"Promise me you'll send Eli. Please."

She shouldn't be standing so close to him, or him to her, but truth to tell, she'd like to be closer yet.

She lifted her gaze up.

Those eyes. Deep and still, storm-cloud gray, under dark brows and darker hair.

He held her gaze. She was pretty sure he didn't breathe for long seconds. She knew she didn't, but then she stepped back to break the moment. "Seb, I—"

"Promise." He didn't touch her. He folded his arms and stood strong and silent, watching her. "I can't send Elijah into a dangerous situation without some sort of back-up measure, Rachel. Promise me, please. For the children's safety, if not your own."

The boy.

Of course he'd want to protect Eli, and teenage thugs with man-sized fists could wreak havoc quickly. Their quiet town had found that out during the former term. "You make good sense, and I'll do as you ask."

Her words relieved him. "Good."

"But if by chance Eli is unable to come, I will train Ethan on what to do."

"The clear message being that if a young boy comes tearing into the lumberyard, I should take heed."

She nodded. "Yes."

"Thank you." He started to put the dishes and silverware back into the basket. "That's one worry off my back."

"Taking on the care of a youngster is a grave responsibility." She left it at that on purpose, hoping he'd open up.

He didn't.

Was she willing to ask outright?

No.

Nellie would have.

She would have bored in, leaving nothing to chance and

little to thought as she delved. Rachel had admired her open manner and sunny nature from the time they first met. Having Nellie as part of the family had given them all a glimpse of a non-reticent life.

But Rachel hadn't accomplished that feat as yet. She hinted and waited, wondering what to do in given situations, but one way or another, she was going to learn to be more open like Nellie. She'd had enough of silence and secrets growing up.

This was a new day, a new time, and Rachel had every intention of moving forward on a path of her own choosing. And that was that.

Chapter Three

STUBBORN.
  Beautiful.

Hard-working.

Seb came right back around to stubborn, because what kind of woman didn't jump at the chance to be protected? Rachel Eichas, for one.

He spent the afternoon checking in lumber and checking out orders as wagon after wagonload of sawed wood headed to claims and building lots. The solid financial year had put some folks in a good situation. New arrivals came with money in their pocket, buying claims and then lumber for those claims. And each order of precision-sawed boards made his father a little richer and more powerful because Seb's lumber came from Ward Mills in Minnesota.

He checked the mail one more time, thinking Cedric Ward might have sent something asking about the boy. About his son.

Nothing.

Which shouldn't surprise Seb because until you were old enough to be worth something to the company, his father pretty much ignored his boys.

It was different with Seb's sisters. He'd indulged Cecily and Althea like a pair of pretty pets from the time they were born. And despite his mother's attempts to inspire a more level-headed demeanor, their father's over-indulgence had left its mark. Cecily had become less attention-seeking as she matured, and he had hopes that her gentle nature would win out eventually, but Althea...

Seb winced as he directed two workers on where to put the newest shipment of 2" x 6" lumber.

Althea had the fetching look of their mother and the self-serving streak of their father, a rough pairing. But they were in Minnesota, living a well-heeled life in Minneapolis, while little Eli was banished to the treeless prairie.

It wasn't fair, but Seb had figured out the inequities in life a long time ago. He'd been blessed with a great mother and a rich, careless father, but he had life, he had livelihood, and a fresh start here in Second Chance, away from the rigors of being Cedric Ward's son.

"Seb!"

He spun around when Eli called his name. The boy spotted him. Eli waved eagerly and came running at the very same moment one of the men swung the near end of a chained six-inch beam.

Seb's heart stopped. He could see the outcome and do nothing to stop it from where he stood. "No!"

He screamed the word, and he wasn't even sure to whom. The boy racing his way, unmindful of the imminent danger?

Or to Ben Harroway, a strong, trusted worker, doing his job with no thought to a small child underfoot?

Ben looked up, surprised.

Eli kept coming, arms out, waving in childish innocence.

And then he was gone. Out of sight. As was the beam for one split second before reappearing on the near side of the yard. The beam swung as it was supposed to, Ben's partner caught his end, and together they laid it on the waiting wagon.

And there was no Eli, running his way.

Seb's chest heaved.

He jumped off the stacked lumber, darted between the rows, having no idea what he'd see when he got to that juncture.

His heart pounded hard and hollow against his chest.

His breath caught tight between each beat.

And when he turned the corner, hands fisted, ready to punch someone, anyone, because there were too many children lost in a world that took them for granted, he came to a dead stop.

There was his little brother, on the ground, snug in the arms of the school teacher. The boy looked rightly surprised, and very much alive, and Seb wasn't sure whether he should laugh or cry, but grown men didn't cry. Ever. He moved forward, numb with overwhelming gratitude.

Rachel sat there calm as could be, as if accustomed to saving small children from imminent disaster. When she spoke up matter-of-factly, her composure helped in more ways than she would ever know.

"Well, that was a fright."

Eli stared up at Rachel and gulped. "You knocked me right down, Miss Eichas!"

"It was that or bury you," she offered mildly, and started to get up as Seb raced their way. "Rescue won."

"Are you all right? Rachel? Eli? Are you okay?"

"I am but my arm is a little hurt," Eli told him with all the swagger of a western boy. "But *just* a little," he assured Seb with miniature male bravado.

"You saved him, Rachel." He grabbed hold of her, then the boy, then her again. "You saved Eli."

"I had limited options, but we might want to revisit that whole 'Eli comes to get me if you need help' idea, at least until Eli knows to not cut through the lumber yard."

"You could have been killed, Eli." Seb hugged him close and buried his face in the little guy's hair. Old images mixed with new, and the smell of lumber and little boy tunneled him twenty years back to a different boy and a different day. "I'm so glad you're okay." He held the boy close, probably too close and tried to calm himself with a breath.

It didn't work.

But Eli was all right, and Rachel...

With Eli held tight in his left arm, he reached out and hauled Rachel in for a hug.

It was an unseemly thing to do with a woman he barely knew,

and a woman who would be teaching school, besides. Small towns thrived on gossip, and a woman's reputation was an important thing, but Seb cared for none of that right now. "Thank you." He whispered the words, wishing he could say more. Do more. "Thank you so much."

"Boss, is he okay?" Ben appeared at the end of the row. If he was surprised to see Seb holding Rachel and Eli, he didn't let it show. "I didn't hear or see him coming. Not a lick."

"I know. I'll school him on where to walk, Ben. But I guess we all need to keep a better look out now that there's a boy on hand."

"I will, Boss. I sure will."

Thomas Mason came around next to Ben, and the relief on his face when he saw the boy rivaled Seb's. "All's well that ends well, but I might be tying a cowbell around that youngun's neck. Give a body some warnin'."

"That might be a sound idea." Rachel stepped back. A gaping hole in the side of her dress ran from her sleeve to the bodice.

Seb made a worried sound when he saw the long tear. "You've ruined your dress."

"An old one, fortunately, but it is quite ruined."

"I'll replace it, Rachel."

"No need, as I said. I wore it to clean today because it is old. While serviceable, it needed replacing."

He moved closer as Ben and Thomas returned to the

loading dock. "You saved my boy. You risked yourself and your clothing. I believe that puts me deeply in debt, does it not?"

He raised one hand to her chin and when she winced, so did he. "You're hurt."

"A scratch." She shrugged. "Nothing for a prairie girl to fret over."

"A nasty scratch and brush burn." He didn't touch the raw skin, but grazed his thumb along the unhurt patch of cheek and chin beyond it. "I'm sorry you're scraped."

"Well. Thank you."

He studied her, her gaze, her face and the growing flush on her cheeks.

And then her mouth, her very pretty mouth.

She wasn't having a fit, she wasn't raging about a torn gown, she wasn't lamenting her losses. Her concern and humor had been for Eli's benefit.

Her price is far above rubies…

The old Proverb came to mind, but it wasn't Rachel's possible ability to spin and weave that put him in mind of kissing her right there and then. It was her heart and her willingness to sacrifice for others, but he'd seen the looks she gave him before.

She didn't trust him, and she was joined by others, and that was a Ward legacy if ever there was one. A legacy that a private man hadn't bothered to contest because why would he? He'd kept himself separate purposely. At the moment, he wished he'd made more of an effort to mix with the town before now.

He stepped back because the stacked lumber at her back prevented Rachel from moving. "I'll have Hattie make a new gown. It's the least I can do. Solomon stopped by the yard today and said Eli could come visit his wife and the two children tomorrow. That will keep him out of danger's path for another day."

He half-scolded the boy with his tone, and he should

scold him, he knew it, but he couldn't. Not right now. He would, however, set firm rules to keep Eli safe, and if needed, he'd take him to the woodshed for not minding. When dangerous equipment and heavy, stacked lumber stood at every turn, a child's life could be snuffed out too readily. Seb knew that better than anyone.

"He'll enjoy that." Rachel slipped to the side now that he'd moved back. "Eli, you be careful, all right?"

"Rachel."

She'd turned to go but now swung back. "Yes?"

He wanted a reassurance that she was all right. He wanted to go on talking to her, and thanking her. He wanted to take a soft clean cloth to her cheek and offer comfort and care.

He had no right to do that, so all he said was, "Thank you."

She didn't blush again. She didn't look away, either, in fact she looked at him as if she longed for the very same thing he'd just denied himself. And then she bobbed a narrow curtsy between the stacked boards. "You are quite welcome, Seb."

She left and he carried Eli inside to tend his scraped arm.

The boy's brush with disaster had been a close call.

Too close.

That meant he needed to do some reconfiguring. Yes, he had to work at the lumberyard, but he didn't need to exacerbate the situation by making his home there.

He could build a house. Or have it built, with time running short this late in the season. Then if Eli visited the yard, he'd make sure he came the safe way, away from the lumber operations. But when he was home, the boy would have a place to play and run, out of harm's way.

He made the decision, then and there.

He understood that Eli might be snatched away at his father's whim, but that would mean acknowledging the boy as his own. Seb's father was unlikely to do that. And

Seb could look into making the boy his own legally. Giving the boy his name, the Ward name, a name he deserved but had been denied.

What would his father say to that? Nothing, most likely. Cedric was quite good at putting himself first.

Resolved, Seb got the little fellow cleaned up, and stopped by the sheriff's office on his way to the hotel for dinner. Sheriff Tucker would know when the circuit judge would be around to answer questions. The sheriff's brother had started a realty business on Second Avenue, just past Hattie's shop. He could stop by Jake Tucker's land office and order Rachel's dress at once.

Was he being foolish?

Maybe.

But real estate investment wasn't a dumb choice, and seeing to Eli's future was prudent for both of them. Sure, the town would wonder about a single man, taking in a child and giving his name.

He slowed his steps for the boy's benefit, and then his own.

Rachel would wonder.

He swallowed hard, because it wasn't a stretch to imagine what she was thinking. Many men fathered children across the wide open west, often disappearing out of their children's lives. He wouldn't do that, he couldn't do that. He'd seen the outcome of disinterested fatherhood, and if he ever became a father, he'd be a sight better than his father had ever been to him.

But he was currently shackled by convention.

He couldn't explain the boy to others because his mother might get wind of it. Too many local settlers had once called Minnesota home, and the Ward name was well-known there.

He was sworn to silence, a silence that could label him a fornicator. In a land sometimes governed by lack of self-governance, many would likely believe it. What should he do?

Protect the boy's heart.

The command came as if from God himself, and Seb agreed. This time a Ward son would be cherished the way he should be.

Graham Tucker stood outside the small sheriff's office facing Main Street. He was scraping down the twin window ledges for a fresh coat of white paint when Seb and Eli approached. He set down the scraper and folded his arms, then aimed a stern look down at Eli. "So you've caught me a desperado, Seb? One of those rail-routin' bad guys, holding up trains crossing the prairie?"

Eli's eyes went wide, and Seb was pretty sure the little guy thought he might be really going to jail. "Naw, this is one of the good guys, Sheriff. He's in town to check out some land deals with your brother."

The sheriff wiped a hand of pretend relief across his brow. "Then I don't have to lock him up. Phew. And it just so happens that Mrs. Thornton sent over a few cookies from the bakeshop at the inn, so if you'd like to dash inside and grab one, I can talk to Seb. Deal?"

"I can go into a jail? For real? All by myself?"

"Well, there's no prisoners right now, so yes. But only with my permission," Graham reminded him. And when Eli dashed inside, Seb took the narrow window of time to ask about the circuit judge.

"He's handled more than a few adoption cases lately, with orphan trains bringing kids from the east," Graham told Seb. "I've heard some haven't worked out well, and that's a shame in a God-fearing land. But I expect this one will be the exception." He indicated the little boy inside with a sideways nod. "There's a fee, but the rest is pretty cut and dried, Seb. Shouldn't be a problem taking care of it when he rolls into town later this fall."

"Thanks, Graham. I wasn't sure if you'd be familiar with the process, but I knew you'd know the circuit schedule."

"Just in case we need it," Graham answered. "Although this has been a quieter year than last," he noted. The year before, the railroad and the local settlements had been plagued with a series of robberies and mishaps caused by a rogue group of thieves. The circuit judge had sent two of them to prison, and the rest had run off, leaving Second Chance and the surrounding areas in relative peace.

"Quiet is good," noted Seb.

"To a degree, until the town decides they don't really need a sheriff." Graham sent him a rueful look. "But I've been able to keep busy building for folks, so it's worked out all right."

Graham was a skilled hand with tools and when he put his skills to a building, it came out right. That was a trait Seb admired in anyone. "I'm going to talk with your brother about buying a piece of land. Building a place. If you're not booked, Graham, I could use a hand seeing it through with as busy as the lumberyard is."

"I'll make time, Seb." Graham indicated the adjacent street with a thrust of his chin. Raw gold lumber stood proud and tall beside painted facades, and the sounds of building and growth echoed from multiple sides. "That's the only way to build a town on this wide open prairie. Make time to help one another." He clapped Seb on the back as Eli came back through the door, happily chewing a cookie.

He thanked the sheriff, met with his brother Jake a few minutes later, then stopped by Hattie's.

"Well, this is a delightful surprise." Hattie bustled forward. "And most Providential, too, because I've got Eli's first shirt done, and I'd like to try it for size. Do you have a minute, Seb?"

"We do."

"Excellent." She took a miniature shirt from a hook near her machine, slipped Eli's shirt off and helped put the new one on. "A mite long in the sleeve, but honestly, Seb, I'd leave it because boys are guaranteed to do three things. Eat, grow and get into mischief. What is your opinion?" Hattie offered him a frank look from her spot on the stool.

"My opinion is that I should defer to your opinion in this matter."

She laughed and slipped the shirt off the boy. "Well, said. Who'd have taken you for a diplomat, Seb Ward? Not I, but then in the years you've been here, I don't believe I've heard too many speeches come out of your mouth, so my opinion is based on scant evidence which is never a good measure." She paused, stood and re-hooked the shirt. "I'll continue with these, and his trousers. And the fresh cut on his arm tells me I may be called on to mend and repair from time to time, because children do like to get into scrapes."

"Miss Rachel saved my life," Eli boasted. "Tom said I woulda been a goner if it hadn't been for Miss Rachel, didn't he, Seb?"

Hattie shot him a more interested glance. "And so it begins. Although this is not surprising news, gentlemen."

"It's not?" Eli's eyebrows shot up because he seemed to consider being saved fairly surprising.

"No?" Seb lifted a single brow.

She shook her head firmly as she re-hung the shirt. "Rachel's quiet but she acts quickly, and she's a problem-solver, not an instigator. That's why I think she'll do all right at the school, because she's not looking for trouble. She's looking to spread opportunity."

"You think that's enough to keep all contingents in hand?"

Hattie braced her hands on the broad, wooden counter. "I think it *could* be enough." Her glance down at Eli said she understood not speaking in a more direct fashion. "We shall see."

"Speaking of Rachel."

Her smile went wide when he spoke Rachel's name.

"We were, weren't we? Yes?"

"I need a dress for her."

"Excuse me?" Hattie was a fairly modern woman, she kept a modern shop and had all kinds of thoughts on women's rights and voting and many other things, but when he requested to commission a dress for his neighbor, even Hattie looked a little old-fashioned concerned.

"Miss Rachel's dress tore bad when she rescued me," Eli told her, and that schooled Seb on another thing. When one has a child around, thoughts of privacy no longer existed.

He sighed and pinched the bridge of his nose between his thumb and his forefinger. "That is exactly what happened, and although she protested the age of the dress, it must be replaced. I thought since you were already making other things for her..."

"That I can add an additional gown to the work."

"Yes."

"And well I can, and I think we should make this a surprise, don't you?"

Did he? How would he know? He'd never surprised a woman in his life. He stared at her, then thought... why not? "Surprises are nice."

"I love them so much!" Eli was in favor and that clinched the deal.

"I'll pick material that is different from the other two, but not too fancy or formal. Rachel prefers simple, but not plain or ordinary, either."

All this talk of dresses made him squirm.

Skip that.

All this *talk* made him squirm. In his years of running the wood yard he hadn't ever needed to talk to this many people in such a short span of time. It felt out of character, but then he thought of giving Rachel a new dress, and that felt odder yet. But good, too. "Let me know when things are done and I'll settle up. Unless you'd like money down now?"

"At pick-up is fine, Seb. You're not going anywhere, nor am I and the town is sprouting up around us. Makes me glad I hung my shingle here. I expect you feel much the same."

"We held on through some rough patches, didn't we?"

"Fires, blizzards, grasshoppers, droughts. To name a few."

"It feels good to be on the rise again." He turned and opened the door. "Thank you, Hattie."

"It's my pleasure!" She laughed lightly when the door clicked shut behind them, as if their visit brightened her day.

What a difference a child makes...

Seb saw it, plain as the sun rising daily in the east.

Eli's influence on *him* changed Seb's effect on those around them. Two days ago he'd been plodding through life in the exact same pattern he'd followed for years.

A bore. A hard-working, well-established bore.

Then a kid showed up and suddenly he's talking with schoolmarms, buying clothes, changing homes, ordering dresses and buying people lunch.

As a student, he studied cause and effect long years ago. Displeasure in Europe brought many people to America, seeking a new way, new advances. And the result had been a broadening of peoples throughout the land.

And now he saw how in one day, the addition of a single child had its own far-reaching consequences.

He walked Eli to the hotel. He'd have to apply to the state for adoption, and the required fee would cement the deal, but that would all be for another day because he'd discovered another fact. Hungry boys grew cranky, and when Eli started dragging his heels, Seb knew it was time to eat.

He was learning and re-learning old lessons of childhood, and while he was surprised by some, others he recalled like it was yesterday. A boy will be a boy, all of his days.

Chapter Four

L EVI CROSSED THE NARROW TRAIL separating the church from the school yard and grabbed Rachel's arms on Sunday morning. "Who hurt you, Rachel? Did those rough boys come into town? I told you this was an imprudent idea. Why didn't you listen?"

She should scold her brother, but his genuine concern was a compassionate gesture. "The boys had nothing to do with it, I fell with young Eli and got a bit of a scrape. That's all."

"She saved his life is what she did," said Nellie. "Little Eli told Ethan and Ann all about it, and we may have chatted the outcome on the way into town this morning. Rachel, are you all right? For certain?"

"I am, and so is Eli and that's the main thing."

"And here he comes," added her sister Miriam as she stepped down from the wagon. "And a child shall lead them," she quoted softly from the book of Isaiah. "Seb Ward appears to be coming to church."

"Don't stare. For pity's sake, shall we go in and not embarrass ourselves?" Rachel turned to move up the stairs, hoping they'd follow.

Her cheeks went warm.

Her palms grew damp.

She didn't want Seb to think she was waiting for him at

the base of the steps. She might be on in years by prairie estimations where girls of eighteen were often wed, but she was not desperate for a man's attention.

And even if she was, it wouldn't be his.

Would it?

A few days before she'd have never thought the possibility, but it teased now. She pushed it out of mind as she moved to a church pew.

Henry Eichas kept up his children's prayers, but they were mostly done at home. They'd rarely come to town, and when they did, it was Levi who'd conducted business. The girls were generally kept on the prairie, working together, building the claims.

Things were different now. She and Miriam and Esther were different. Levi, too.

But change took time, and she wasn't about to humiliate her whole family... or have them do likewise to her... over a man. And yet her cheeks flushed the minute she saw him, which meant she'd more than likely mortify herself.

When Pastor Will Barber concluded the service quickly to go tend an injury on a claim east of town, she lingered inside, purposely.

Will's busy wife crossed her way, plunked a toddler into her arms, and said, "Rachel, hold him, please! I've got to tend his little sister. I'll be right back." She dashed outside, and there was Rachel, snugging little Will Barber in her arms.

What would she do if he cried?

She had never in her life held a baby or been around one since her sisters were born, and that was a long time past.

Nellie swept in the far door of the church just then. "Oh, who do you have, Rachel? Hello, baby Will Barber, how are you today, sweetums?"

The little boy grinned wide and flapped his arms. "Ah, ba, ba, ba, ba!"

"Oh he's talking, bless his heart! Rachel, isn't he adorable?"

"He's quite amused with himself, and he seems to maintain a sunny disposition," Rachel agreed.

"He maintains a sunny disposition?" Nellie burst out laughing, then clapped a hand across her mouth. "Oh, don't take offense, it's just the sweetest way of saying that he's a good boy. In Rachel-speak."

"I think she spoke plain enough."

Both women turned when Seb's voice interrupted them. Nellie smiled and hummed softly, as if music were required. Rachel's heart paused, then raced, bringing on the same malady she'd faced before the service. Pink cheeks and damp palms.

She turned to face him, determined to take charge.

Did he know she'd stayed inside to avoid him? Was she foolish or was this a two-sided attraction? And even if it was, the whole thing was quite impossible.

Seb moved forward.

Nellie put out her hand. "Mr. Ward, a pleasure to see you again. And your little fellow was quite well behaved during services. It was nice that you brought him."

"The shortened length due to Will's emergency might have been our saving grace from ill manners. Eli wasn't exactly sitting still by the time we got to the final hymn." He turned more toward Rachel. "You seem to have a knack for finding children."

"Or they find me," she said. The baby patted her cheek as if pleased with her voice. "How is Eli doing after his scare?"

"Of the two of us..." he moved closer. "I was the more shaken up, I believe. In which case Elijah is doing quite well, and I'm looking for new quarters to live in to keep him alive."

"It is a weighty responsibility, isn't it?" She looked down at the baby's rounded cheeks, his chubby legs, and his almost bald head. "To care for a new life, from beginning to end."

"Or a unique opportunity to nurture a God-given gift and should be considered as such."

A poet's words to describe a fairly prosaic experience of fathering a child. She studied him a little more closely. "It would be wonderful if all fathers felt as you do."

His wince made her realize what she said. She'd pretty much accused him of being Eli's father. And if he was the boy's father? Then what of a mother? And did a woman steeped in Sunday school lessons toss aside the Ten Commandments because of sweet attraction? Or did she abide in the Good Book, as her father commanded all those years?

Macy bustled back into the small church just then. "Rachel, thank you for taking him. Little Maggie needed to be changed quickly and Cheekie was off to help Will at the Stuckey claim. I found myself quite out of willing hands. Seb, how are you today?"

Seb bowed slightly. "Quite well, Mrs. Barber."

Macy laughed. "If you continue to call me that, I'll feel so very old. And a mother of three has no time to feel old, so I'd appreciate being called Macy. Although." She scolded him with a look as she took Little Will from Rachel. "I do believe I've made this request a number of times, only to be ignored by my nearest neighbor."

"Macy, then. I should get back. Solomon is watching Eli and Ethan outside, and I expect Eli is hungry. Again." He turned back toward Rachel. "You're getting on all right after the scrape up the other day?"

The brush-burn had become a nasty scab, but Rachel understood health care the best of the three girls. "As long as I leave it be, it will be fine in a few days. Nothing serious."

"Well." He nodded to Macy, then Rachel. "I'll get on." He walked out, and the sound of firm, broad feet sounded on the outdoor stairs.

"Rachel Eichas." Macy planted a kiss on Little Will's head and grinned. "I do believe you're smitten, and I'm pretty sure the feeling is mutual, but there are some serious questions in need of answers concerning my hard-working neighbor."

"But not of our concern," Rachel suggested softly.

Macy disagreed. "If you have no interest in building a relationship with Sebastian Ward, then I'd agree. But it's best to wade into waters knowing where the drop-off lies rather than being unpleasantly surprised by a sudden dunking. And if there is scandal afoot, it's best to tread with care."

"And if there's not?"

"Then I welcome you to the neighborhood." Macy laughed, then sobered. "But I did already hear Taylor Beam wondering about the boy, and once he got a burr under his saddle, he had a group of folks wondering at the sheriff's office early yesterday."

"We both know it's become common to send children away from the cities, to find new homes in the west," Rachel reminded Macy as the three women crossed to the open church door. "I'm willing to assume a deed well done, myself. Until I hear otherwise."

"You're right." Macy followed Rachel outside. "There have been orphans brought out to a couple of families looking for help, I've seen that, too. But I'm a mother, Rachel."

Rachel paused and looked at her. "Yes?"

"And a mother sees things a little differently. Yes, there are orphans being sent out of New York and Chicago and Pittsburgh every day. But rarely do they bare such a solid resemblance to their caretaker."

Rachel had noticed the likeness, too. In her mind, you'd have to be blind to miss the resemblance of Eli to Seb, but then lots of little boys had dark curls and brows. And his eyes were a lighter gray than Seb's, with hints of blue around the pupil. It could be resemblance, and maybe it was. Or it could be coincidence.

"Just be careful. I'm not warning you off, and it's not my business, but now that you're living on your own in town, it's important to see things from many perspectives."

"Or the town gossips will have their day at sweet Rachel's expense," noted Nellie. "I had my share of that in Pittsburgh. It was neither fun nor fair."

Macy agreed. "Yes. And you don't deserve that, Rachel."

She didn't deserve that, but a great many folks endured things they didn't deserve on a daily basis. A little bit of gossip wasn't a welcome thing, but it wasn't the end of the world, either. Still, Macy was correct. "Thank you, Macy. And I'll take heed, but if there is one good lesson I learned from my father's years, it was to forge my own way and fight my own battles. Mostly because he left no other choice. But I do appreciate the warning and the wisdom."

"Well, I'm right across the street from you," Macy said, "and if you've an arm for rocking one baby or the other, I'd never say no to a bit of company. With Will doctoring again, and still conducting services, I'm on my own quite often and could use someone to talk with. I will be glad enough of a new pastor in town, and maybe two with how fast we're growing."

The thought of having another woman her age so close was a comfort. "I'd love to visit, Macy. It's lonely on my own, with both sisters back on the claim. And Nellie there, now, too."

Nellie hugged her arm in commiseration.

"This is a good change." She glanced around the town as they walked toward the parsonage. "But it *is* a change and a little company would be a welcome thing. If you're sure it won't be an intrusion?"

"Oh, Rachel." Macy set a hand on Rachel's arm as Violet Cooper approached from her porch, carrying Macy's infant daughter in her arms. "Every now and again Miss

Violet and I sit and knit and talk and we'd give anything to have a third person sit in."

"Then I'm honored to accept." They parted ways at the edge of the parsonage driveway, and Rachel continued on, more at ease. Her family was waiting just ahead, and when they asked... as she knew they would... if she was doing all right, she could now say yes.

Honestly.

Seb, Ben and Tom loaded seven wagons full of lumber before noon on Tuesday.

Seb was pretty sure they were going to set a record for daily sales. He hung on to Eli's hand as he crossed Main Street and forked left on Second Avenue. Jake Tucker met him halfway.

"Seb, perfect timing," the real estate broker declared. "I've got the plat map on my desk. Let's have a look-see at what's available and what's planned."

"Perfect."

The two men scanned the proposed town map together, and when Jake pointed out the available plots, Seb frowned. "These measure small, Jake. If I'm making the move to a house, the house need not be grand, but the yard needs size. I want a place for Eli to run and play." If his words made Jake wonder how long Eli would be around, the agent didn't let it show, and Seb appreciated that.

"We have a park planned for here, just north of the school." Jake set his finger on a blocked-out area that was nothing but prairie grass at the moment, and dull, dry prairie grass at that.

"A park that won't be a park for some years. But if I were to buy three connecting plots." Seb pointed to the lot adjacent to the park and the two abutting it, with the creek running along one border. "The three together would suit nicely."

"All three?" Jake looked excited, and why wouldn't he? He'd had more sales in the past six months than in his first two years. "I'll write up an offer."

Seb suggested a price.

Jake made a face. "It's low, Seb, but there's nothing wrong with coming in low and allowing room to move."

"If I am buying three lots in one deal, the size of the sale deserves a discount. And I'm not leaving room for price to move, Jake. I'm offering a chance to clinch three sales in one advantageously priced deal."

He sounded like his father, and Seb didn't like sounding like him, but in this respect, his father's example of shrewd business served him well.

"I'll submit the offer."

"Good." He turned to go, then paused when Eli tugged his arm. He looked down. "Yes?"

"Say fank you."

Seb paused. So did Jake, from his side of the desk.

"My mommy always made me say fank you because you're asposed to." Eli looked from him to Jake and back. "I fink she was right, Seb."

Manners. Courtesy. Habits he'd lost as a grown man, alone and intent on staying that way. He lifted his gaze from the earnest boy and shifted it to Jake. "Thank you, Jake. I am much obliged."

Jake smiled at the boy before he nodded to Seb. "You're welcome. It is a pleasure doing business with you."

It wasn't much of a pleasure because he cut hard deals with great purpose.

Seb knew that, and he recognized his part in it, but it seemed that Eli was destined to change that, too.

They walked back up the street. Two buildings were being raised on Second Avenue, to add to the two that had been erected in early summer. It was becoming a street now, with shape and size and boardwalks. Just north of Second Avenue, more streets were plotted out, including the one holding the three lots he offered on.

Growth was mushrooming in Second Chance, and with growth came opportunity. But how was he to work properly with a child to care for? And as soon as he thought that, he wondered about the child's mother. Had his father provided for Eli? Or had she tried to balance working and raising the boy on her own?

His next thought sprang to his father's long list of indiscretions. Were there more children out there?

His temples throbbed at the thought. His mother, such a good, caring woman, always ready to help others. Did she suspect his infidelity? Did she care? Or had Cedric used up her sympathy over the years?

He looked up as they reached the corner. He paused, drinking in the sight before him. Rachel Eichas was talking to Nellie outside her brother's wagon shop.

Simple beauty.

Nellie's good looks flashed with her quick moves, her blond hair and bright dresses.

Rachel's beauty shone in its more demure fashion, like the morning star. Not "notice-me" sharp, but warm and enticing. Peaceful.

She caught sight of him, watching her.

Fingers, long and tapering, went to her throat, as if unnerved.

She swallowed, and when Nellie followed the direction of her gaze, she smiled wide, as if surmising.

But there was nothing to surmise or expect. He knew that. He understood what wasn't said. He'd set a name for himself in this town, he'd kept himself apart with grave intent, and the image he'd put forth was done with purpose. A businessman couldn't be successful and easy-going. If he was, he didn't stay in business long, especially in the cut-throat business of lumber these days. Tens of millions of board feet of lumber came out of Minnesota, with thousands of loggers cutting year-round. It was a business

enjoying a huge upswing, but that upward arc of the pen-
dulum wouldn't last forever. Rising trends never did, and
Seb had to be prepared for not only the seasonal rise and
fall in sales, but the annual fluctuations. And now, a boy
that looked just like him, added into the mix.

"Miss Rachel!" Eli slipped his grip and raced for his
school-teacher friend. "I missed you!"

"Well." She smiled down as the boy grabbed her around
the legs, and if she was put off by the lad's enthusiasm and
show of ill manners, she didn't show it. "I've missed you,
too, Elijah. And I expect you've been most busy since I saw
you on Sunday?"

"Very!" He peered up at her, anxious to share every tid-
bit of their lives, no doubt.

"Eli, do we need to tell everything which occurs in our
lives to everyone?" He leveled a look meant to quell in the
boy's direction.

"Only if it's like real good stuff," Eli explained in a most
earnest tone, absolutely unabashed. "My ma said if you
say nice fings, everyfing is brighter." He reached up and
grasped Seb's hand in a tight hold. "I f-fink she was right,
don't you? 'Cause mas are always right, aren't they?"

Rachel spared Seb a response when she squatted to look
Eli right in the eye. "They are, Eli. Mothers want what's
best for us, all the time. And that is a wonderful code of
honor. Spreading joy and sunshine is what God wants for
us, too. To be good and gentle and kind."

"Well, God is pretty smart, I guess."

"I agree." Rachel stood back up and faced Nellie and
Seb. "The wisdom of children is a gift we often overlook."

Seb was learning that and a great deal more in his new
role. "Lack of reticence possibly being less of a gift."

"He is quick to share, that's for certain." Nellie palmed
the boy's head, then changed the subject. "I saw your post
on the mercantile board, Seb. Have you sent word to other
areas for a nanny?"

"A nanny?" Rachel looked from him to Nellie and back.

"This surprises you?" He swept Eli a look, then the lumberyard and the town before lifting a brow. "I can't keep him safe on my own. It wouldn't be prudent to think a boy this age can be happy in a small apartment, unminded. I've posted for help because it seems that keeping small beings alive takes vigilance. But so does running a business."

"You're right, Seb, I can't imagine Levi trying to run the smithy and the shop with Sol and mind a child at the same time. It's impossible. Surely there are some young women in want of a position."

"Sooner than later would be good. But right now Eli and I are going to my office to do paperwork, and then tomorrow he starts classes with Rachel, and that will keep him busy for some time. Are you excited to start?" He turned his attention to Rachel and kept it there.

"Excited and nervous." She clutched the small bag she was carrying a little tighter, then eased her grip. "First day jitters for teacher and students, I expect."

"If you need anything, ring the bell," Nellie told her. "Levi and Sol will come running."

"As will I."

Chapter Five

SEB WOULD COME RUNNING?
Oh, her heart. His words, his tone. Why did they call to her? Why from a man so stuck on business as to be *in* the town but not of the town? A man who wore pride like an expensive suit?

She lifted her eyes as he said the words.

Three simple words, softly given, but in those words and that gaze lay a pledge like none she'd ever seen before.

She despaired her lack of experience.

She railed at her thin knowledge of men. Years of being pretty much out of sight had left their mark. When other young women enjoyed flirtations, she'd been raising two sisters and working a claim.

Her heart sought to know him better.

Her head reminded her of her father's austerity, his iron-clad rules and lack of humility. She'd thought it normal, then. Only since his passing did she realize that not everyone shunned the world around them, and there was no way she'd let herself fall into that trap again. Yes, Seb was being friendly now, but only because he was forced into pleasantry by virtue of the boy, and Rachel knew how quickly that could dissipate.

She broke the connection and lifted her bag slightly. "I must get on, I've a few things to do to be ready for tomorrow. Nellie, thank you for bringing food by. I've been too busy to think about cooking as I prepare lessons for five separate grades that I know of. And thank you for bringing the extra jug, as well. It will be of necessity, no doubt."

"Have you checked the school's well?"

"I've been told it's good, but I'm checking it and the pump today. Eli." She leaned down slightly and extended her hand. "I'll see you tomorrow. You and Ethan will have seats right up front, by me."

"Fank you!" He hugged her legs again, and oh... what a sweet feeling that was, the joyous hug of a child. How many times had she let herself wonder the past few years if she would ever know the fullness of marriage? The love of a man? To become someone's beloved wife?

"You are most welcome. Be good today, all right?"

"I will!" The pair walked off, and at one point, Seb reached down and lifted the little fellow up, into his arms. He pointed up, and when Rachel and Nellie followed the direction of his hand, they saw the moon, on the wane, hanging quiet in the daytime sky.

"A man who takes time to teach has a good heart."

"Whether he does or not is not my concern."

Nellie rolled her eyes. "You keep telling yourself that, and I'll busy myself with baby clothes and planning a wedding. I've always longed to plan a wedding, so this will be a delightful way to spend some time."

"Stop."

"I'll stop, but only because your red cheeks give you away," Nellie teased. "Although I for one don't know what's stopping you, Rachel. You're both available, you're smitten with each other at least to the point of decided interest, and how can you not think that Sebastian Ward is a catch? Because darling," she snugged Rachel's arm in hers as they walked toward the schoolhouse. "He is."

"Dogged for business, keeps to himself, barely shows himself around town and a shrewd head for dealings favoring himself."

Nellie shrugged. "Lots of folks are private. And he seems far less private with the boy's arrival."

"And yet another reason to keep distant." Rachel moved forward and unlocked the schoolhouse door. "A head for business is a wonderful thing, but if one only has business in mind, then the family is left to either drag along or be ignored."

Nellie wasn't smiling now. "Levi has told me about your father. I didn't realize how separate he kept you girls until Levi explained it."

"And Seb keeps himself separated in much the same way." She grasped Nellie's hands and hung onto them. "I can't go backwards, dear sister. I look back at our years on the farm, rarely being allowed to come to town, not allowed to worship with others, or to wear the clothing other women wore, and I realize I've much to learn. I have no experience in the ways of the world, in women dealing with men. Having Levi bring you home has been the best change to our family, for you've experienced a great deal. And your love for God, for your family and your work shows joyfully in all you do. And that's what I want to bring to this job."

She released Nellie's hands and indicated the room around them. "I want these children to see the beauty of life and learning that my mother passed to me, the skills I shared with my sisters once I was old enough. So for now I must put the job first, and see if I can do what I truly long to do."

"Isn't that what you just found fault with concerning Seb? Putting work first?"

"It's different," Rachel explained, but then she had to ask herself why it was different?

"I don't think it is." Nellie took the material in her hand and began tacking the curtains into place along the first window. "I think you're feeling your way in new things, and so is he. And if you both weren't somewhat stubborn, you'd quick-step into a delightful romance and give this coming baby some cousins."

"Nellie!" Rachel laughed, then clapped her hand across her mouth because she'd never been allowed to speak of such things. Even as the animals produced their young, the mysteries of human reproduction weren't referenced in their home.

That all changed when Nellie grabbed hold of Levi's heart last Christmas, and now the thought of new life, under Nellie's joyful tutelage, made a difference. Such a difference.

"It is delightful to see young families coming up and about here," Nellie went on as she pinned. "Macy and those adorable children, Ann here now to help Sol raise Ethan and Sarah and there are two young families on claims just east of town, and one to the north. We're rising up nicely, and there are even seven single men who are either working a claim, or building a business in town. And two widowers. One way or another, I intend for you, Miriam and Esther to be noticed. And if it embarrasses you to talk about it, I won't, but..." she aimed a smirk toward Rachel as Rachel set out school supplies. "I'm keeping a sharp eye out. As is Hattie. Now that you girls get off the farm on a regular basis, there's no time like the present to cast an eye."

Nellie was half-kidding. Rachel knew that.

But as soon as she said the words, a vision of Seb and Eli filled Rachel's head. The big man, hauling the boy up, and showing him the wonders of the moon. The look in his eye when he touched her brush-burned cheek. The calm strength she read in his gaze.

She didn't want to cast her eye any farther, but that could be maidenly foolishness.

Her father had attracted two women. Her mother, a kindly, warm, happy soul whose joy seemed to fade with time. She'd perished after Esther's birth. Rachel had been just old enough to remember how her mother had been, and what she'd become. A sadder, more inward version of herself. And then she was gone.

It wasn't long before Henry Eichas remarried a happy woman named Sylvia.

Sylvia wasn't a bad stepmother. She appreciated pretty things. She dressed well and seemed to like children and challenges. She could cook and take care of the house and the four young children. She actually seemed to enjoy it. Rachel remembered those days of that marriage being filled with a quiet but sweet expectation.

But then things changed. Sylvia wasn't allowed to go to town. She wasn't allowed to wear pretty clothes. She had the same drab gray material that Rachel and her sisters had worn for years.

Sylvia changed, too.

She wasn't happy any longer.

She didn't teach the girls.

She sat in a chair by the far window, watching the days fade away.

And when their father had brought the whole family to the prairie, even before the railroad and the town, Sylvia had walked away and they'd never heard from her again.

Miriam and Esther had been too young to understand, or even to remember Sylvia all that well, but Rachel remembered, as did Levi.

Henry Eichas had drained the joy out of two women.

Rachel might not be schooled in the ways of men, but she was pretty sure that her father hadn't shown his true colors during courtship and there were plenty of Biblical stories that talked of deceit.

She refused to be deceived. She would not be party to a relationship that dissolved into displeasure. She might not have worldly experience, but she had experience in what she didn't want and that was a man who ruled with a strong hand and grim look, a man who put money and property first.

Henry hadn't been overtly evil.

But he didn't have an ounce of nice in him, and his controlling nature had left its mark. Seb might be like him, and he might not, but the similarities were enough to make her use caution. And right now, with a new job laid out before her, caution wasn't a bad thing at all.

Rachel hadn't only survived her first weeks of teaching, she'd excelled, and that little victory called for indulgence. She stirred up a small cake on her second Saturday in town, and as it baked in the small apartment stove, she tidied up the yard sloping from the back side of the carriage shop/smithy.

Levi had added a large barn the previous year, perfect for storing unsold carriages, and as she raked and swept, the thought of doing this for herself, on her own place, sweetened the day.

Right up until the yard filled with noxious smoke and the odor of burnt cake filled the air as dark smoke poured from the single west-facing window. "No!" She cast down the rake and raced into the small apartment, about the same time Levi and Sol burst in from the businesses facing Main Street.

Seb swooped in from the other side of the street, and between the three men, she couldn't have possibly been more embarrassed than she was at that moment.

She grabbed the cake from the oven. She used oven pads, but the thick smoke fooled her eyes. When her index finger caught the edge of the burned pan, she squealed in surprise.

"Are you all right?" Seb reached through the smoke for the pan.

Levi reached from the other side.

Only Sol was wise enough to stand back. "If you men let her through, she can get that mess outside."

She couldn't see Levi's face through the smoke, but it was easy to read the duress in Seb's expression. He moved back, and only then did she realize Eli was with him. "Did you burn it bad, Miss Eichas?"

"The cake or her finger?" wondered her brother in a wry tone.

"The cake," said the little boy in a softly troubled voice. "I didn't know you burnt your finger, too. I'm real sorry, Miss Eichas."

He sounded sweet and worried for her well-being, and Eli's gentle heart made hers feel better. She indicated the smoking pan with a frown once she made it outdoors. "I burnt it as bad as it could possibly be burnt, I fear," she told him. She set the smoking pan on the far side of the yard to cool off, hoping the breeze would take the stench in the opposite direction. "And now I've managed to fill the house with noxious smoke and not a bit of cake."

"I love cake." Eli slipped up alongside her and clasped her hand, commiserating. "I love all kinds of cake. Like white cake and not-so-white cake and fudge cake. I maybe like fudge cake the best."

"What kind was that going to be?" Seb asked the question in a low tone.

She wanted to cry. Or spit. Or maybe say bad words, really loud.

She did none of that, because in the end, it was only cake. She sighed and faced him. "Chocolate fudge."

"You never burn things, Rachel." Levi sounded worried. "You've always been the trustworthy one in the kitchen. Maybe—"

Sol cleared his throat in warning, but Levi wasn't quick enough to stop what he was going to say.

"Maybe living on your own isn't the wisest choice."

She'd wanted cake.

She'd wanted peace and quiet in her two tiny rooms and a cake to celebrate her personal victory, so to have Levi automatically question her abilities made her glad there was no weapon at hand. "Have you never mis-cut wood?"

He seemed affronted to be asked. "Of course."

"Or singed a rod too deeply?" Her brother wasn't nearly as good at the forge as Solomon, so Levi nodded again.

"Then why should a burnt cake signal the demise of my independence? You're allowed to make mistakes, but a woman isn't?"

"That's not what I meant."

"It's what you said," she told him. She crossed her arms firmly. "We all make mistakes and I was busy tending the yard and forgot the cake was in the oven. An easy enough mistake."

"That could have burnt the shop and the smithy to the ground," Levi scolded.

Sol coughed.

Levi didn't take the warning. "If I make a mistake I'm right inside to fix it. To catch it before it gets too bad."

"You're saying I should live inside the house, always?"

"When you've got something in the oven, then yes. That would be sensible. Wouldn't it?"

Rachel bit her tongue.

She bit it so hard that she had to remind herself to stop biting it as she strode off.

She didn't want Levi bossing her around, but in truth, the apartment was his and she had filled two businesses and one small apartment with thick, dark smoke.

She walked down to the creek, then along its edge, letting the crystal clear water and the thick, green leaves calm her. Back on the claim, if she put something in the oven, one of the sisters was generally on hand to keep an eye on the oven while she worked outside.

It was different in town. On her own. But different didn't mean impossible.

And yet Levi had made a good point. He'd timed it stupidly, and he should have waited, but he'd been right. An untended fire or meal could become a sorrow-filled news item and no one needed that.

A throat cleared behind her. A deep tone, already familiar. "Are you still upset? And have you seen to your hand?"

She turned, surprised and yet, not surprised. "Seb."

"And me, too!" Eli popped out from behind a tree, carrying a small box. "Miss Heidi at the hotel told me to carry this just so, and I did, but I almost dropped it once," he admitted, drawing closer. "I didn't drop it, but it might've gone topsy turvy."

"Just a little." Seb's warm voice suggested humor, but he didn't make fun of the little fellow. He put his big, strong hand on the boy's dark curls and looked down. "You did fine, son."

Son.

She heard the word, the word she'd half expected to hear, and it almost knocked the breath out of her, but she squared her shoulders and paused. *Well, then.*

She bent down. "Thank you, Eli, for being so gallant. And thank you, too." She lifted her eyes to Seb's, but this time with greater care. "It was a gentle kindness and I'm much appreciative."

"Are you a good baker?" Seb asked, then he lightened the situation with a smile and a quirked brow. "Generally?"

She laughed. "I am quite good. I've actually helped out at the inn and the new bakery. I'm going to work there over the winter when the snow's too deep to get children back and forth to school safely. As long as the trains still run, and Thelma has a clientele, we'll turn out fresh breads and cakes. Cookies, too."

"I love sugar cookies the most," said Eli eagerly. "With lots of sugar."

"I'm sure you do." She tipped her gaze down. "And Linzertortes?"

"I've never had one!" He clapped a hand to his forehead. "Are they so good, Miss Eichas?"

"Amazing. A hint of sugar, a hint of spice, just right for hungry boys. And a spot of jam for good measure."

Seb's deeper voice begged her attention, and how easy it would be to offer exactly that. "They're my favorite."

Was he just saying that to gain favor? Did a man woo women the way he cut lumber deals? And how did a man who'd lived in town for over a decade suddenly inherit a five-year-old son? How did a woman wrap her head around that?

She couldn't, of course. But she did fine with basic math, and this was adding up in all the wrong ways. "I think they've got a wide-spread popularity. When Aunt Ida brought Sol's kids to town last spring, she mentioned they were still a big favorite back in Minnesota."

"Your family was one of the first families to settle here from Minnesota. Levi and your father had said as much," he went on, explaining how he knew.

"My father wasn't one for talking much. Nor is my brother, at least until he took a wife, so it's curious that they shared much of anything at all."

"There was a storm several years back," he explained as they continued to walk. "Levi and Henry were stuck in town for three days. We all huddled at the hotel at night, wishing for the storm to end and the trains to run again."

"And they didn't run for almost two weeks." She remembered that storm, all right. She and her sisters, peaceful on the prairie. Minding stock, following the rope-line to the barn, using it to guide them back.

They'd baked. Cooked. They'd sang songs and hymns and sewed to their hearts content. Those three days of peace had been a hint of life without their father.

She'd felt guilty then.

She felt no guilt now, living an independent life apart from Henry Eichas's constant scrutiny and criticism. A father shouldn't be unkind, unjust or mean. He should be something else entirely. But again, how would she know? Secluded on the prairie for so much of her life, she was just now integrating into the ways of the world, and Second Chance wasn't what anyone would call worldly. She watched Eli chase after a bug. "He's a sweet child."

"He seems so. I don't want his first winter on the prairie to be filled with boredom, but my house won't be finished before winter. Unless November comes easy, and that's not usually the case."

"You're building a home." She stated it simply. Maybe there was a wife. Silent men don't always share their lives.

"I can't keep Eli in my little clutch of rooms. It's been fine for me, alone, but not for a boy. He needs to stretch and grow. To gaze out windows and think. To dream."

"As all children should be encouraged."

He returned his gaze to hers, as if in question, but then asked no question. "I need to get back. We've got the four-oh-seven due to arrive and I want it unloaded before dark."

A real consideration as October drew near. "Shorter days press the work, don't they?"

"Always have. Always will."

"Unless Mr. Edison has his way and lights up the world like he proclaims."

He'd turned to go. Now he turned back. "You know of his work?"

Leave it to a man to find a woman simple. She bit back what she thought and nodded. "I have a keen appreciation for science and industry. Watching my brother create beautiful wagons, and the work of Sol's hand to forge fine metal for strength, I see the beginnings of artistry and industry pairing in a perfect dance."

He stared at her until she felt heat rise. "You think me foolish. I'm not."

"Anything but," he told her. "I think you're incredibly wise."

"For a woman."

He made a face and frowned. "Why would I think or say that? It's not the womanliness that surprised me. It's knowing you've been here on the prairie for a long time, with little news. And yet you've learned and know so much. That's true industry, Rachel. That's true schooling, and it doesn't matter that you're a woman."

Not exactly the compliment she'd have hoped for...

"But the fact that you are an amazing woman is a wonderful thing."

Better. Definitely better. But to no good end, which seemed wretchedly unfortunate because she was drawn, for certain. But there were plenty of tales of women drawn to the wrong man. Not her. Not now. Not ever.

"Eli?" Seb called.

The boy turned.

"We have to head back."

The boy didn't complain. He glanced up the creek, as if wondering what lay ahead, but he turned and came back their way as instructed.

"Does he need to come back with you?" Rachel whispered the words so that Eli wouldn't hear.

Seb shook his head.

"Then what if he stays here with me while you unload the four-oh-seven, and he and I can share the cake?"

"It's no imposition?"

"To have an earnest, good boy around? To explore the creek, and wonder at the differences between the spring creek and the autumn creek?" She shook her head. "A lesson without being a lesson."

"Eli, would you like to stay with Miss Eichas while I work for a bit?"

"May I?" Eli reached for her hand and when he seized it, he grabbed a piece of her heart as well. She had to remind herself that somehow, somewhere, the boy used to have a mother.

"If you like. I was thinking a stroll up the creek would be interesting."

"It would be like the best walk ever!" Eli didn't try to hide his enthusiasm. "I love water and bugs and fings that live in water."

"A heart for science." She took his hand in hers and handed the bakery box back to Seb. "If you would be so kind as to drop this by my rooms, my young friend and I will share it when we're done exploring the world around us."

"I'd be glad to." He took the box, but his hand grazed hers. Just enough, yet not nearly enough. "I'll see you both soon. All right?"

"Yes. Fine." It wasn't fine. It was the opposite of fine because she was unschooled in the ways of men, but not in the ways of the world. Reproduction was part of the science she loved, and little boys didn't just snap into being. They were created by the union of a man with a woman. Which meant...

She refused to think of what it meant, because that put Sebastian in a whole other light, and for today, for this brilliant autumn afternoon, she didn't want to be ruled by that school of thought. She preferred, this once, being lost in the moment.

She and Eli strolled northwest, along the creek's edge. Leaves were turning. Not many trees took favor with the thick grass of the wide open prairie, nor the annual grass burnings some Native Americans had employed. Would trees crop up now that the prairie wasn't set on fire each year? She'd lived in the woods back in Wisconsin and Minnesota. The wide open grasslands here had seemed vacant at first.

It wasn't vacant any longer. Homes, farms, ranches... people were dotting the landscape now, spreading out from small towns and growing cities. Maturing, just like her.

"Hey!" Eli had strolled ahead. He stopped and pointed

through the waving, whispering cottonwoods. "Do you see her?"

Rachel followed the direction of his hand. Something moved through the trees ahead. A child?

A fleeting glimpse of garment and the small stature made it seem so, but what would a child be doing wandering along the creek?

Dancing branches and leaves shifted light and shadow until Rachel wasn't sure they'd seen anything. "You thought it was a girl?"

"Kind of. Maybe." Eli stared through the trees, puzzled. "But girls don't have short hair like me, do they?"

She rumpled his curls. "Yours isn't all that short, my friend, and yes. Sometimes girls have shortened hair." But not in general, and not here on the prairie. She studied the curving creek bank, then took Eli's hand. "The sun is telling us it's time to head back, and I could use a slice of that cake."

"Me, too!" He held her hand snug in his, but looked back over his shoulder as they made their way back toward town.

Had they seen a child ducking through the trees?

She'd ask Hattie. If someone was living up the creek, Hattie would know. The oddity of seeing a child alone, near the water, unnerved her. But she couldn't honestly say she'd seen a child. Maybe that unnerved her even more.

"There's a wash-up basin here," she told Eli as they stepped into the chilled apartment. The smoke had cleared, but the open windows had decreased the inside temperatures considerably. She closed the two windows against the crisp late-day air.

She'd start a small fire tonight, but then she'd let it burn out. Area families had donated for a coal allowance. One for the school, one for the teacher, but winter came early and stayed long on the prairie. The nearby tree line helped block the northwest wind, and Levi had built the two small rooms with care. The window fit snug in its casing. If she used her allotment of coal too quickly, she'd have to buy the balance out of her earnings, and every penny spent was money that wouldn't be saved for the future. She'd lived sparingly long enough to know that she never wanted to live that way again. Frugal was fine... she believed in being a good money steward.

But living cash-poor brought no comfort to anyone.

She set Eli's cake onto the small table Levi had fashioned. Then she halved the remaining piece and sat next to him.

A knock on the door interrupted them. She went to the door, half expecting Seb to be on the other side, but Chickie Barber stood there, the pastor's daughter from his first marriage. "Chickie, come in. What a wonderful surprise."

Chickie didn't need to be asked twice for anything. She hurried right in, spotted the cake and her eyes went wide.

"Sit down and have cake with us," Rachel told her. "It's from the bakery."

"Oh, I shouldn't, I just ran over to invite you to supper tomorrow night. Ma said folks should get in the habit of inviting the teacher to supper on a regular basis because we don't pay a teacher enough to feed a mouse, much less a full-grown person."

That sounded like Macy. "Well, it's always a comfort to be looked out for, isn't it?"

"I wouldn't mind being looked after a bit less from time to time," said Chickie. "I have the urge to run and explore and find new things, but my parents do not exactly see things my way."

Rachel understood that feeling well, but she also understood the dangers surrounding them and Chickie's impetuous nature. "Trains, runaway horses, accidents... A loving parent wants their child safe."

"I suppose. But I do love exploring, Miss Eichas. Don't you?"

She did, but she spoke with care as she set the last sliver of cake in front of Chickie. "Yes, but exploring is something that must be done with care. And there's really not all that much to explore on the prairie, is there?"

"And that's part of the problem," Chickie returned, bemused. "My longings refuse to be constrained."

Such dramatic words from the young girl, but Rachel recognized the sincerity. "Perhaps we can find a different way for your explorations to take shape. A way that puts no one in danger, and possibly opens a wealth of later opportunities."

Chickie's eyes lit up, and when Rachel took a small book off a shelf, the girl's enthusiasm waned.

"Look at you," Rachel scolded lightly, smiling. "You've already decided there can be no adventure within, but I promise you are wrong. Miss Hattie gave me this book to read some years back and I dare say the main character of the story reminds me much of you."

Chickie read the short title with a questioning tone. "Little Women?"

"A story of sisters."

"And now I have a sister," said Chickie, "but while babies are nice in their own way, they do constrict one's time and imagination. Don't they?"

Rachel had no way of knowing, but the girl's assertion made sense. "One needn't be trapped mentally just because one's travels are constricted physically."

"Pretend, you mean."

"To imagine and let your mind flow free."

"Do you do that, Miss Eichas?"

She'd done it all her life, the perfect self-therapy. "I do. I read and I study because there is so much to learn. And while we don't get information out here very quickly, we do get it and how foolish we would be to waste the opportunity to learn from it." She tapped the book lightly. "If this is beyond your reading level, I can read it to you. Or your Ma or Pa could."

"I can take it with me?"

Rachel nodded as another knock sounded at the door. In all her years on the claim, a dozen so far, she was pretty sure she hadn't had as many people stop by her door as she had the past two weeks in town. She opened the door, and this time it was Seb. The wind had taken a sharp turn and he stepped in quickly. "Change is in the air."

"As ever," she replied. "If there is one thing for certain, it is that change will occur."

"Seb, this was the best cake I ever had in my whole life!" Eli hopped off the chair and dashed to grab Seb around the legs. "Thank you so much for getting it!"

"And it has been kindly shared, I see." He noted Chickie's plate and the meager serving on Rachel's. "Your kind heart knows no bounds, Rachel."

His words... his tone... the approval in his gaze... and try as she would to deny it, the striking good looks of the man drew her as much as all of the above, and didn't that speak to her lack of experience? A worldly woman would probably flirt with him. Laugh with him. Have the common sense to engage in witty conversation.

She had none of those polished skills, so she answered quietly. "A joy shared grows more in the sharing."

He regarded her for long, slow seconds.

He must find her boring. Dull. Simple.

She refused to sigh because she was probably all those things, but she was keen, as well, despite her father's attempts to foil education and experience. The gift of reading and books and mental exploration had been bestowed from her stepmother years before, a gift she'd shared with Esther and Miri at the claim. Henry might have controlled their access to the world, and their dull clothing, but he couldn't control their minds and Rachel knew that had become a source of vexation for him. But no longer.

"If you inspire your students in the same manner you

inspire me, they are mighty lucky to have you in the classroom."

Heat rose to her cheeks, a most embarrassing feature. She'd never had to keep it at bay in the past because there'd been no reason to. "If I can inspire them to work hard, then I'm doing my job ably. Whereas you already work hard, Seb. No one can fault your work, all these years."

He regarded her and her words quietly.

She'd displeased him.

She wasn't sure how or why, but his eyes dimmed. "Let's head home, Eli."

"Okay." They moved toward the door, but then the boy darted back and offered Rachel a big hug. "Thank you for taking me with you!"

"It was my pleasure, Elijah."

He beamed up at her, a true smile, and she couldn't help but smile back. Then he let go and reached for Seb's hand. "See you tomorrow!"

"Yes."

Seb didn't look back. He moved forward, still quiet, and when the door closed behind them, Chickie rose from the table. "This was such good cake, Miss Rachel. And thank you for the book."

"You're welcome, Chickie. I'll see you at church tomorrow."

Silence swept in to fill the void once they'd all gone. She didn't welcome the silence. She missed her sisters, their constant chatter. And Nellie's bright personality raised the interaction to a level never before seen at their simple claim house on the wide open prairie.

The lamp dimmed. She adjusted the wick and set a small fire in the belly of the coal burner. Darkness filled the corners of the room as the night went on. She'd prepared her lessons for the week, and had done her washing. Her stack of books stood waiting, and her words to Chickie mocked.

She was tired of reading about life's adventures. Watching.

Waiting. Imagining. She—

She paused and pressed cool hands to hot cheeks.

She'd been excited to come to town, to teach, to make a bid for independence. It wasn't that her excitement for teaching had waned. It was because her interest in her neighbor waxed deeper, and what was she going to do about that?

Chapter Six

"SEBASTIAN!" CRIED A VOICE A few days later.

Seb had been unloading lumber when the familiar voice hailed him. He turned without thinking and took the business end of a planked board to the forehead.

"Oh, Sebastian!" His mother hurried his way, distraught. In the nine years Sebastian had been in Second Chance, his mother had never paid him a visit. He'd gone back to Minnesota several times, but she'd never made the ride west, nor had he expected her to. He yanked a hanky from his pocket and pressed it to his throbbing head, and wasn't surprised to find it bleeding.

"I can't believe I did this to you!" She hugged him, tsk-tsked over the wound, then hugged him again. "I should know better."

"It's fine, just a scratch, Mother. But what are you doing here? And more to the point," he went on, looking beyond her to the two finely-clothed young women walking his way, "what are Cecily and Althea doing here?"

Althea spoke right up, but there was nothing unusual about that. "I would ask exactly the same question, but was disallowed that option and simply ordered to gather things into a trunk and go along. I should be in school now. Right now, as a matter of fact." Althea pouted, folded her arms, and looked very much as she had at age nine, nearly eight years before.

"We needed time away." Cecily stepped in and hugged him, then gazed about. "I've never imagined the proper vastness of the prairie, Seb. I know you described it to me, but to see so far that the planes of earth and sky become indistinct on the horizon amazes me."

"Vast nothing is still nothing," grumbled Althea. "You can't possibly mean that, Cecily, you're just trying to placate Mother for her insistence. Which is, I will say again, ridiculous."

"Stop. Now." Seb had heard enough. "No one speaks to Mother that way. Not here, and never in my presence."

"You are my brother. Not my father. And you've been here so long, I barely know you." Althea faced him coolly. "Don't presume to take on a father's role with me. It will do you no good. And it's quite the boorish trait."

"Althea, you're such a brat." Cecily hugged Seb's free arm. She smiled up at him, her hazel eyes dancing. "Sebby, I've missed you so much. To have you gone, and Father always in a fettle or a fix, it's been a rough few years keeping our chins raised back home. I find this most refreshing, and I generally get around our sister's sour nature by ignoring her as completely as I possibly can."

"Does it work?" he inquired with a dour look Althea's way.

Seb's dry tone made Cecily laugh and deepened Althea's scowl. "Not in the least, but it's worth a try, isn't it?"

It certainly would be. His mother checked his head wound, decided it wasn't much more than a grazing, and waved back toward the station. "I had a man at the platform take our bags over to the hotel. I know there's no room here at the lumberyard, and I thought it would do the girls good to see how their brother's industry and work ethic has helped our business grow here in the west."

When Althea rolled her eyes, Seb decided that wasn't the only reason his mother had brought the girls to South

Dakota. "Let's get you guys settled and grab lunch. Unless you ate on the train?"

"Apples, freshly picked, and we brought a basket for you, too," said Cecily. "You always loved fresh apples, and you said there weren't a lot of fruit trees out here."

"Nor any kind of tree," noted his mother, "which means reforesting back east will help our families in the west. It's so very good to see you, my son." She grabbed his arm, looking wonderfully happy, and as he smiled back at her, stark realization broadsided him. *My son...*

His mother would see Eli.

One look at Eli would either lead her to believe her son was a rascal with an out-of-wedlock child or see the truth of the matter and realize her husband had cheated on her.

His heart pounded.

He glanced around, as if seeking options, but there were none.

His mother and Cecily chattered as they crossed the broad platform. He helped them down the steps, followed by an openly reluctant Althea, then accompanied them to the hotel. Once they were registered, his mother turned his way. "Seb, can you give us an hour to rest and wash up before joining us here for lunch?"

Seb grabbed the offer. "Of course. I'll be back here at one-thirty. All right?"

"It's more than all right. It's absolutely wonderful to be with you again." His mother hugged him tightly, and he returned the embrace. Through everything she'd been his example, his staunch supporter. Even in the dark days once Artie was gone, she'd held Seb and taught him to believe in himself all over again. He wouldn't let anything hurt her. He couldn't. But what could he do with Eli?

He strode back up the street, ruing the fact that he hadn't developed friendships. And just as that thought came, Hattie McGillicuddy called his name. He turned, fairly flummoxed by this new turn of events and not one bit pleased with his cheating father for thrusting him into this position.

"Seb, I've got two more shirts ready for Elijah and another pair of trousers. And I thank you for waiting so patiently while I finished the railmen's orders," she told him sincerely. "Nellie and I both love fancy work, but those rail worker shirts pay the bills around here. Everything else is the whipped cream on the pudding, if you take my drift." She studied him as he drew closer, then paused. Concern drew her brows together. "Are you all right?"

"Not in the least," he remarked. "I was, but my mother and sisters just hopped off the twelve-fifteen as if visiting me was normal."

"What a nice surprise, Seb! I don't believe I've ever met your mother, but of course everyone in the west who builds anything with wood is familiar with Ward Lumber. You must be delighted, except..." She arched a brow in question. "You don't look delighted, Seb. Flat out scared would be my guess, actually. Would you like to talk?"

"Do you mind?"

"Seb Ward, I've known you for all the years I've been here, and you've scarce done anything but nod on occasion. Since that boy hopped off that train a few weeks ago, I've heard more out of you and about you than I would have ever thought possible." She tucked a small square of material into her broad pocket and turned back, toward her shop. "I don't mind at all. I've got tea water on, but looking at you I think coffee would do better."

She set the coffee to brew when they got inside, flipped the 'open' sign to 'closed' and took a seat. "Pull up that chair and tell me what's going on."

"It's Eli."

She nodded.

"Well, not Eli exactly, but it's about him."

"I see..." She said it in a way that meant she didn't see at all.

"With my mother here unexpectedly..."

"Ah..."

He nodded. "It's beyond awkward, of course, and entirely unacceptable, and I can't believe she's being put in this kind of a predicament."

"She's an understanding woman?"

He nodded. "The most understanding woman of all. Kind and Christian and strong in her beliefs and her morals. If she's not helping the poor, she's tending the sick."

"She sounds marvelous."

He nodded. "She is. And now she's going to mosey on over to the lumberyard later today and see Eli and then—" He grimaced, imagining the look on his mother's face.

"She'll realize that you're a father," Hattie offered quietly.

"Yes." He said the word before her words registered, and when they did, he began to sputter. "Wait. No."

Hattie watched him without moving, a trick he'd been known to use himself.

"I'm not a father."

She looked slightly embarrassed. For him? Or by him? He wasn't sure but this only grew worse when she spoke softly. "We all understand how things happen, of course."

His neck swelled against his collar.

"And even though this is a modern age, folks have been having children at inopportune times from the beginning. Are you worried that she'll be disappointed in you, Seb?"

Was this what the entire town thought? The idea had occurred to him, but no one said a word. Of course, he didn't talk all that much himself.

The collar grew tighter and he hadn't thought that really possible. "Eli isn't my son."

Hattie's forehead creased as if embarrassed for him.

"He's my brother, Miss Hattie. My father's son."

Her expression changed, but it wasn't just her expression. It was her entire profile. "Your brother?" A new wave of understanding widened her eyes.

He nodded. "Sent here, without a word, after he lost his mother."

"On my word, Seb, this is a pickle."

"You're telling me."

"And your mother's surprise visit..."

He grunted.

"And that precious child."

"Yes." He folded his hands, disgruntled. "How do I do this? The little fellow looks like me. Like my father. One look at him and she'll assume one thing or the other, and I don't want my mother hurt."

"Or your own reputation sullied," she supposed.

He brushed that off. "A man who knows his own heart stands strong, despite loose talk. No, it's my mother I'm concerned for. She's withstood a lot. She doesn't need to face more."

"How long is she in town?"

He raised his shoulders. "No idea. I didn't know she was coming, and no details were shared in the few minutes we had together. But I'm sure her reasons for coming west are more than wanting an autumn vacation in a prairie town."

"You said your sisters were with her?"

"Another awkward surprise. Cecily has a kind heart, but Althea isn't easy to get along with, nor does she find favor with frugality. Our small town will unwittingly provide irritation which she'll return in earnest."

"Then perhaps there are lessons to be learned all around, but I see the conundrum," Hattie said. "But how about this? What if Eli was to stay with me for the duration?"

"While they're here?" The thought made his heart jump in relief. "That's a generous offer, Miss Hattie."

"Kindly given, Seb," she assured him. "You've worked long and hard for the betterment of this town and South Dakota, much like I've done," she added frankly. "If folks don't stick together in times of trouble, it doesn't matter that they do it in times of ease. We can simply tell Elijah that you're tied up with work for the short term and he'll be staying at my place. This is a small town, though."

Smaller than small.

"They're bound to run into one another."

"But there would be no reason for my mother to make the association," decided Seb.

Hattie didn't look quite as certain. She stood, moved to the cook stove and poured them both a cup of the freshly perked coffee. "Mothers are keen beings, Seb. But you're right, if Eli is with me, and in school during the week, the chances are minimized."

"You'd really do this, Miss Hattie?"

She handed him a sturdy cup of coffee and met his gaze. "I enjoy having young ones around." She seemed quite agreeable, but sadness lurked behind her look of acceptance. "I'd do it. Eli and I will get on just fine. I've got an extra cot set up in the back room, put there for the current assistant, but they've all gotten married. They're close enough to work, but have beds of their own now, leaving me plenty of room for a sweet boy. And that puts me in mind of cookies, which means..." She stood again, sipped her coffee and moved back toward the stove. "I can whip up a tin of cookies while he's still in school. If you can slip him over here at dismissal time, fresh, warm cookies will help bridge the gap."

"It would work for me," Seb assured her. "Hattie, I—"

She brushed him off swiftly. "No thanks needed. Finish your coffee. Bring me the boy's clothes, I'll tuck them onto the shelves in the back room. And Seb..." She turned his way. "You're a good man to have such a kind heart."

A good man.

Her words stabbed and soothed.

He hadn't thought much of others' opinions for many years. He'd learned to live apart a long time ago. Coming to Second Chance hadn't been a hardship for him. It had been an opportunity to build his own business, apart from his father's cold heart and misdeeds. He'd done it, too.

But as he hurried back up Second Avenue to retrieve Eli's belongings from his apartment, he realized Hattie's approval made him feel good. And that felt like a step in the right direction at last.

Rachel tugged the key from the school's lock and thrust it into the pocket of her skirt. The children had left minutes before, scattering in multiple directions like dandelion fluff on a brisk west wind.

She had a couple of needy youngsters in the class, but the rest were robust students, eager to learn. Of course, those big boys from Cutter's Crossing hadn't come back as yet. Maybe they wouldn't bother. Maybe they'd keep their distance and avoid a confrontation.

Do you fear them? Or fear failing them? And what do you know of them, other than old news and loose talk?

She feared both, she admitted to herself as she walked home. And what was there to know? A group of rowdy ruffians, disrespectful and rude. That had been last spring's reality.

Perhaps that had changed.

She hoped so. With a new sheriff in town, the boys might not be as bold. A man with a badge and a gun might be a deterrent. She scanned the north side of the wooded creek as she crossed the walking bridge, wondering about the child she'd spotted, but a loud voice drew her attention toward the lumberyard.

"We commissioned you specifically, Seb." Frederick Whimple, one of the older members of the town stood in front of Seb, just off the road's path. "We need that bridge to cross the creek, and I wasn't sure you were the man for the job and I still ain't convinced because I don't see a lick of work being accomplished, and that's all I'm saying."

"The contract was for fall. Which, as you know, has just

begun and goes until mid-December," replied Seb in a cool, even tone. "As I cited in my bid, I had to order the supports from Minnesota and they've only just arrived. Rome didn't get built in a day, nor does a bridge, Mr. Whimple."

Eli was by his side, gazing up. He looked worried and his gaze darted back and forth. He bit his lip as if fighting back tears, and his little hand clung to Seb's in a grasp of desperation.

Rachel crossed the road, surprising both men, and stooped down. "Eli, just the person I wanted to see," she exclaimed warmly. "I've got something in my rooms that cries out for a boy's help, and here you are." She smiled at him and took his free hand. "Come with me, we'll get it squared away, and Seb can retrieve you when he's done talking."

Eli didn't argue. He grabbed her hand right back and tucked his wee face in the folds of her skirt.

"Thank you, Rachel. I'll be by shortly."

"We've plenty to do, Seb." She nodded to Mr. Whimple. She didn't know him well, but Levi had business dealings with him from time to time. He paid a fair price and liked quality work, which made him a good man in Levi's book.

Their voices softened as she and Eli moved away and the boy relaxed. "I don't like loud voices, either," she told him as she opened the door. She left it propped open to let cool, clean air into the stuffy rooms. During the cold weather, she'd appreciate the tightly fitted doors and windows, but right now a soft west wind bathed the apartment with freshness.

"I'm loud sometimes." Eli looked back, over his shoulder to where the two men faced one another. "But not mean loud. Just pesky loud."

She laughed. "Did your mother tell you that, Eli?"

His chin quivered. "Yes." His voice dropped to a cracked whisper. He dropped her hand and grasped his hands together, remembering. "But then she would hug me and tell me I was the dearest boy in all the world. The very dearest, she would say."

"Oh, she was right, sweet fellow." Rachel wrapped him in a big, warm hug. "Absolutely right. She knew her son well. Elijah, have you ever made a button string?"

He shook his head.

"I brought a button sack from home." She crossed to a group of shelves Levi had installed to help organize the small cooking area for his new wife the year before. "Look here. Buttons add a whole new dimension to life."

He watched, unconvinced, but when she handed him a piece of knotted thread and the sack of buttons, he amused himself by threading and unthreading the various discs until Seb appeared at the door a quarter hour later.

She sensed his presence without turning. Awareness made the tiny hairs along the nape of her neck stand upright. Goosebumps dotted the skin beneath her sleeves. It was a silly reaction when she should be well beyond such schoolgirl antics. She smoothed damp palms against the soft cotton of her dress as she turned. He stood, framed in the door, looking...

No. She wouldn't go there. She couldn't go there. She appreciated a good work ethic. Any wise person on the prairie understood the necessity of that. But there was no joy when ethic turned to vice and people forgot to make time for ordinary things.

He regarded her from across the room, and she wished his gaze didn't undo her inside. But it did. He indicated Eli with a glance. "Once again, I am in your debt." His voice, deep and resonant. Calm. Commanding.

"Not in the least," she assured him. She moved toward the door, determined to stay neutral. "No one needs small children around while trying to do business, and I know that the bridge construction is important before the weather turns. You hear more about these things, living in town."

He acknowledged that with a quiet grimace.

"I was glad to have my young friend come visit." She noted the bag in Seb's hand with a glance. "Have you been shopping, Seb?"

"These are Eli's things." He gripped the bag a little tighter. "Miss Hattie has graciously offered to let Eli stay with her for a little while. The supplies have arrived and I need to get the bridge done, but I can't do it justice with a divided mind, so he's going to stay at the sewing shop for the duration."

"You don't want me?" Eli stared at him from across the small room. He gulped hard and dashed two small fists to his eyes. "You don't want me with you, Seb?"

The boy's words grabbed her heart, but Seb's reaction did likewise. "I can't watch you and build a bridge, Eli. It wouldn't be safe. It won't be for long. I promise."

The tears that threatened before came in earnest now. The boy sank onto the seat he'd been using and wept.

He didn't carry on like a naughty child would, wanting his own way. He wept as though all the sorrows of the world lay heavy on his narrow, five-year-old shoulders.

Seb looked no better. If anything, Rachel was pretty sure he might cry, too. She crossed to Eli, sat down and took him onto her lap. "There, there. You have a good cry, I think you've been needing this right along, and it's certainly all right to cry and mourn and grieve. And then it's good to have fun and learn and play, then cry again. You've suffered a loss, my little friend, and we understand that. So you cry when you need to, and we'll hold you and tell you that it will all be all right in the end. Because it will," she whispered softly against his curly hair. "I promise you, darling child. It will."

Chapter Seven

H ER KINDNESS.
　　Her profile, holding the boy.

Her gentleness, her womanliness, the shape of her, coming down the road each day.

Seb Ward hadn't ever been infatuated. He'd never allowed himself the thought of being smitten. He'd spent his grown-up years building a business on a rigid foundation, and all of a sudden, in the space of a few weeks, he was raising a child and found himself enchanted by a woman.

His heart beat harder in his chest.

He crossed the room, squatted down next to Rachel and Eli, and longed to hold them both. Assure them that everything would be okay, and if his mother wasn't due to come up the road any moment, he might have done exactly that, but the west-bound train had changed things again. "I want you to think about being at Miss Hattie's as an adventure."

Eli sniffed, eyes down.

"She has stories to tell, and Dory and Clifford Montrois live just around the corner from her shop."

"Clifford scolds people all the time."

Seb didn't know that. Oops.

"But Dory is nice and she likes frogs."

"A kindred spirit," said Rachel softly. When Eli furrowed his brow, she snugged him a little closer. Just a touch. Just enough to make Seb wonder what it would be like to hold and be held by Rachel Eichas. "That's a person who matches us well. Who likes what we like, and appreciates us just the way we are."

The church bell began to toll five. His mother and sisters would be making their way up the road. He'd promised them a tour of the lumberyard once the day's work was done, which meant he needed to get Eli down to Hattie's place quickly.

"Can you walk with us?" Eli asked Rachel, and he looked sad when she shook her head.

"Not this time, but another. I've got to get a few things done here for classes this week, and the light fades quickly at night. You go with Seb, and I do happen to know that Miss Hattie makes the very best cookies around. And she rarely burns them," she added brightly. She kissed his forehead and set him onto the floor. "I will see you tomorrow in school. Okay?"

"'Kay. But I'm kinda scared of bein' at the sewin' shop." He scuffed his toe against the floorboard. "I could just stay here, Miss Eichas. And be so good." He stressed the words into a childlike promise, but Rachel refused gently.

"I have to work at night, and I'd be scarce company for a busy boy like yourself. Let Seb and I get through these busy times. He needs to get the bridge done, and I need to prepare lessons. But I would love to go nut hunting with you this weekend. I saw a few likely trees up the creek and we could put some nuts away for winter."

"I haven't gone nut hunting since I was a boy," said Seb. "They were plentiful enough back in Minnesota. Hickory nuts were my favorite. But they don't grow here."

"You could join us," she told him, "Although these were walnut trees, and not too many of them. But if your work doesn't allow that, then Eli and I could hunt together and share our spoils."

"Spoils?" Eli looked from one to the other, confused.

"The nuts," said Seb. He nodded, and set his hand on Eli's head. "I'll be too tied up for a few weeks I'm afraid, so if you waited for me, the gophers would get them all."

"We mustn't let that happen," declared Rachel, smiling at the boy. "Because I love nut cookies, especially at Christmas."

She bent and hugged Eli. "Have fun with Miss Hattie and remember to study your letters. Do you have your slate and slate pencils?"

He nodded.

"Put them to good use before you go to bed, all right?"

"I will." He yawned and leaned his head against Seb's leg, looking like a miniature of the big man at his side.

The sight sobered Rachel. She'd been raised to believe in the sanctity of marriage. The carelessness of lust for pleasure's sake, and a woman's reputation on the prairie... and in a small town like this... must be guarded.

If Seb's past produced this beautiful child, then his choices went in a different direction from hers. Perhaps she was wrong, but looking at the pair, she knew better because the remarkable resemblance couldn't be denied. "I'll see you in school tomorrow, Elijah."

"Okay." He'd swiped the tears from his face, but tiny traces remained. If he was her child she'd wash his face, fill him with homemade bread and fresh jam, and tuck him into bed with a story.

That was the kind of childhood she'd longed for.

But he wasn't hers and she closed the door snugly as they walked away. And an hour later, when she went outside for a quick walk before the angled sun set, voices drew her attention to the lumber yard. There was Seb, with three women, walking through alleyways created by perfectly stacked boards.

Rachel hadn't meant to be seen.

She'd completed her lesson planning for the upper grades, and wanted some physical exercise before the light grew too dim. At the farm, her days had been filled with movement. From house to barn, room to room and field to field during the growing season. There was always something to do.

In town, the work day consumed much of her time, but it wasn't a physically challenging job and Rachel liked movement. Lack of physical activity was something else to get used to.

Seb spotted her.

He smiled.

Even from across the road, and two sections of planks, she saw the smile. Read the joy. And couldn't help but smile back.

The group moved her way. As they grew closer, the exquisite detailing of the women's clothes became more apparent. Fancy stitching, cloth-covered buttons and finely tooled shoes marked these as women of means. She was glad she hadn't changed from her new teaching dress, but Rachel was nobody's fool. Hattie's seamstress skills were second-to-none, but simplicity ruled the prairie. As they drew near, she locked one hand with the other. These women, with their classic clothes and smooth, silky hands, were a breed apart and she didn't need sophisticated experience to see that.

"Rachel, I'd like you to meet my family." Seb drew closer first, then he reached out to draw her forward by taking her hand. "My mother, Elizabeth Ward. And my sisters, Cecily and Althea."

His mother? Rachel longed to smooth her hands against her gown, but one hand was held snugly in Seb's. "Mrs. Ward." She dipped a slight curtsy, then felt silly for doing so. What must they think of her? No one curtsied any more. She pushed back embarrassment and found her voice. "It's a pleasure to meet you."

"Mother, this is Rachel Eichas. She's teaching the grade school here." Seb indicated the school up the road. "And her family was one of the first successful homesteaders in the area. She and her sisters have been running a most capable farm."

"An amazing accomplishment." His mother didn't seem dismayed by the oddity of women running a farm. "You must be skilled in all sorts of things to manage a farm, my dear. It's an absolute pleasure to meet you." She reached out to take Rachel's hand, then beamed up at her son. "What a fine spot of industry you've helped accomplish here, Sebastian."

"If by fine spot, you mean dot on the map existence, then it's marvelous." The dark eyed sister sniffed with purpose. "Seb, is this all you do all day? Lift and move boards? Buy and sell? Doesn't it grow dreadfully boring in quick fashion?"

Seb didn't seem surprised by her rudeness. "For those who find ambition anathema, I suppose my days might appear too structured."

"Althea, don't be a toad." The other woman reached out a hand to Rachel. "I'm Cecily, and I think this little town is marvelously romantic."

Seb coughed on purpose.

Althea fussed. "There is nothing romantic about dull and dust and plainness, Cecily, and even you can't spin a proper fairy tale to pretty up this place. The lack of shops and opportunity must stifle even your imagination."

"We find that the greatest opportunities lie right here, on the prairie, ours for the taking," Rachel corrected her. "Where else on earth can one acquire a quarter section of land as a trade for hard work and industry with no money required? Where else can families build a new dream, a new place, a new hope? I lived in Minnesota when I was young," she explained. "I'm no stranger to the busyness of Minneapolis and St. Paul and we have family living

there still, but when one comes west, the landscape holds
a certain freedom. The soil. The broad, rolling vista. A land
where grass grows free and cattle and sheep thrive. Different from the city, yes." She acknowledged that with a slight
nod of concession. "But grand in its own right."

Althea scoffed instantly. "If one envisions grandeur in
cotton and muslin, then yes, I see your point. All things
being relative, perhaps pleasure in little things begins to
shape one's day. I prefer a grander presence, myself."

"Althea." Seb's tone held warning. "The people out here
aren't afraid to work for a living and there's great satisfaction in that."

"We wouldn't be where we are if our father and grand-
father hadn't espoused that very thing," added Cecily.

"My point, exactly." Althea drew her cape closer. "Their
hard work and forward thinking afforded us greater opportunity without back-bending effort. That's the beauty of a
free nation, isn't it? To rise above, generation by generation."

A spoiled brat.

Rachel had to bite back words of reprisal, and it took
concerted effort.

"Althea, you've much to learn." Seb's mother scolded
her daughter with her tone and expression. "Hard work
brings its own rewards, intrinsic to the person. It's a lesson
to be learned and respected."

"According to the woman with a housemaid and a cook."
Disrespect darkened the young woman's sarcasm. "Obviously I'm not the only one content with gazing from afar."

"You're such a brat, Althea." Cecily's affronted tone
matched her facial expression. "At some point you'll learn
that being disagreeable doesn't suit. And I hope you learn
it sooner rather than later, although I believe we're too late
for that." She smiled at Rachel. "It was very nice to meet
you, Miss Eichas."

"Rachel, please." Rachel took a step back and slipped

her hand from Seb's. "And you, as well. Are you staying long?"

"We're unsure of our plans at the moment," Seb's mother replied. "Our arrival was a surprise, and I'm sure that my son isn't exactly sure what to do with us, but it's an absolute pleasure to see part of the great west at last."

They'd surprised him. And he'd tucked Elijah out of sight, out of mind, around the corner at Hattie's place.

Bitter emotion rose within her.

Yes, Seb was needed to oversee and build the bridge that would allow families to cross the creek and park closer to the church and school during rough weather, a plus for the growing town. But that wasn't why he'd tucked the bereft child aside. He'd placed him away so that his family wouldn't see the boy, and recognize one of their own.

She stepped back.

She looked at Seb, but then turned her gaze away. She couldn't meet his eyes, because the rise of anger and revulsion would show. The thought that he would cast Eli's feelings aside to maintain his status with his family, to keep his pristine image polished...

Shallow. Deceitful. Self-serving.

She backed up another step. "Enjoy your stay, ladies."

"Weren't you going for a walk?" Seb glanced from her to the stone walk leading to the small apartment behind Levi's shop and the smithy. "I didn't mean to interrupt your plans, Rachel."

"My plans are quite flexible." She walked away, going in the opposite direction, and kept walking.

She'd come so close to falling for him. So close to letting her feelings take over, lead her astray.

Her conscience had niggled right along, and she'd come close to ignoring it. Was that a plight of living in town? she wondered. When temptations appeared, did one succumb more easily because they were more prevalent? It made sense, in a way. She loved the science of numbers, the absolute answers supplied by mathematics, so perhaps the greater the chance for temptation, the greater the chance for the fall.

She walked brisk and hard until fading light forced her back, and when she re-approached her rooms, Seb and his family were nowhere in sight. They were probably off enjoying sweets at the hotel while a small boy lay tucked in yet another strange bed, crying himself to sleep.

She'd almost been duped, but no more. From this moment forward she was forewarned. She'd come to town to gain independence and a paycheck, yes. She had no intent, then or now, to sully her reputation.

Guilt kept Seb walking the floor that night. He couldn't push the image of Eli's tear-streaked face out of his mind. How much rejection should a small child have to endure? How much sorrow?

He went to the window and stared at the moonless night. His mother couldn't mean to stay long, and she still hadn't said what brought them here. Spur of the moment train rides weren't part of her typical profile, but she'd done that today and brought the girls along.

Was she running from something? Or to something? Someone? Him?

He'd talk with her tomorrow, he decided. He went to bed, wishing he could will himself to sleep, to no avail. Images crowded his brain. Eli and his father. Artie, so small and earnest. His mother's grief upon learning her little boy had died.

And then Rachel, backing away. She hadn't looked up at him once she'd met his family. Realization had tightened her gaze when she understood the timeline of his family's surprise appearance and Eli's stay with Hattie.

He clenched and unclenched his hands.

He had no choice. Rachel didn't know that, and couldn't

understand it. Most likely she shared Hattie's opinion, that Eli was Seb's son from an illicit relationship. The fact that he hadn't had time for any kind of relationship, illicit or otherwise, offered genuine irony.

Whatever drove his mother and sisters to Second Chance wasn't good. And to find an illegitimate child, the girls' half-brother, waiting for them wouldn't make things better. For now he'd stay the course. Silence and keeping himself apart had worked for a long time. If necessary, he'd go back to that, but those options thinned for a man with a child. Keeping to himself wasn't only difficult, it was pretty much impossible. And with Rachel as Eli's teacher, and their near neighbor, putting thoughts of her out of his head ranked in similar fashion.

He'd schooled himself in independence of necessity. He'd dealt with Cedric Ward's cutting coldness, his utter disregard for his sons, and his harsh manner. He'd risen above and beyond then. He would do the same now. And once his mother and sisters were on an east-bound train, Eli would be treated to all the love a little fellow deserved. Seb knew the lack of a father's love first-hand. He'd make sure Eli never had to deal with that again.

"Rachel!"

Macy Barber's voice rang across the cool autumn morning as Seb approached the loading docks the next morning.

"Let Chickie help you with those books, she's all ready to go. Morning, Seb!"

He acknowledged Macy's exuberance with a nod as she waved from the stoop of the small parsonage. He didn't want to glance toward Rachel, but couldn't help himself.

His throat went tight. Nerves along the back of his neck thrummed a jig of anticipation.

She was beautiful. So beautiful. Her brown hair, pinned up at the nape of her neck. A perfect neck, pale and pristine. Althea had scoffed at the material of Rachel's gowns the night before.

Althea was a fool.

The molded simplicity of Rachel's white top and deep gray skirt showed the womanly strength within. Beautiful curves, and a bright smile for Macy and Will's precocious daughter.

None for him, though. She didn't glance his way, nor look up. She'd branded him the evening before.

Singularity. Privacy. Work.

His old rules had held him in good form for years. He acknowledged Macy with a quick wave and continued his way into the lumberyard. Here, amid the scents and sounds of sawn boards being cut-to-order, he could simply be the man he'd been for so long. Seb Ward, lumberyard owner. It had been enough before Eli arrived. It would be enough now.

Chapter Eight

"RACHEL, I'M SO GLAD YOU'VE come home for the weekend." Esther hooked up a team on Saturday morning, preparing to cut the last section of fall hay. "I'll catch up on news from town later. The dew's dried off, and the cutting should go easy."

"Did you pack a lunch?" Nellie called from the house.

"Sure did!" Esther cringed as she led the team away. "She's mothering all of us, Rachel. It's quite stifling."

"Getting in practice for the big day." Rachel mused.

"One can only hope that once the baby is born, he or she receives the bulk share of Nellie's skills and the rest of us will toddle on as we've been doing for years." Esther paused the team momentarily. "But she's got such a good heart and a hand with lace trims that I'm not about to make a fuss or bother."

"Having someone care about us should be neither fuss nor bother. It should just be love."

"You are waxing sentimental after just a few weeks in town." Esther studied her intently. "Which means we should talk later. I must cut hay."

"And I'm helping Miri with cheese." Rachel crossed to the nearer barn, half-buried in the side of a curving bluff. The submerged section stayed cool through the hottest days of summer, allowing Miriam and Rachel time to tend fresh and aged cheeses to sell in town. "Miriam. Are you in here?"

"In the cool room."

The original barn was L-shaped and they'd cleared out the far side for the dairy work rooms once Levi and their father had built an animal barn downwind. They could cart the pails of milk across the yard to the cheese-making side, and keep the cheesing area crisp and clean, separated from the growing herd of cattle. Rachel eyed several new cheesecloth-covered rounds and whistled softly. "You've been busy."

"And missing you!" Miriam set down a milk pail and hugged her. "How do you like living in town? Is it so very different? Do you gad about and talk with folks every minute you're not teaching? Levi says he barely sees you, but he also said the parents are quite satisfied with their new schoolmarm thus far."

Rachel pulled one of the big muslin aprons over her work dress. "There is a lot to tell." And some she'd keep quietly to herself. "Yes, town is different. It's actually lonely."

Miriam had been bending over a crock of curd. She looked up, surprised. "That cannot be."

"And yet, it is. There's none of the sisterly love, the work-ing together, the back-and-forth." Rachel began straining and rinsing curd from a second crock. "I see people now and again, but with lesson planning and grading, I don't venture out too much."

"Not at all what I envisioned these past few weeks, but I can understand it." Sloshing the curd, Miri drained them off, then rinsed them again with fresh, cold water from the well. "When is the first board meeting?"

"Next Sunday. It's easier for them to meet when folks are in town for the Sabbath, rather than try to gather people at harvest time."

"The race against the clock is tangible this time of year." Miriam laid out her curd onto the thick muslin towel and began squeezing. "We feel your absence here, but Nellie is such a good cook that you may have lost that task forever."

"I won't deny I'm hoping for a home-cooked meal tonight. There's little inspiration in cooking for one's self, and little appetite for supping alone. A family donated a small basket of apples, and I treat myself to that and two biscuits nightly."

"And a nice treat it is," exclaimed Miriam, but when she turned Rachel's way, she paused. "That is what you meant, correct? You can't possibly mean that you're dining on an apple and a couple of crackers every night?"

"It's hard to keep any kind of meat, and with only one person, there's no pleasure in cooking it. And the time factor weighs in."

"But surely you could eat at the hotel now and again. And Hattie would be affronted to have you working long hours and not eating properly when she's so close at hand."

Rachel laughed. "It's proper enough, I assure you, just somewhat tedious. I don't think we realize how nice it is to have a small ice house and the occasional fresh meat. I saw a picture in a catalog of a box made to keep things cold. It was a fancy cabinet, lined with tin, something Levi could make with his skills. Ice was stored on one side and food on the other, so the ice kept the food chilled. Imagine going to a box and opening it to get fresh food."

"It would be a wonder and not something we're likely to see here for a time, but if you nip a catalog picture, share it with Levi," Miriam instructed her. "Once winter hits there's plenty of ice and long, dull days for harvesting it. Will your rooms in town be warm enough for the winter?"

"They'll suffice. They did well for Levi and Nellie last winter."

"Newlywed, a different dynamic," Miriam pointed out.

"True enough. I've got my coal allowance from the school board. I'm going scant now so I'll have plenty as needed when winter bears down."

"And how is your neighbor faring?" Innocence heightened Miriam's question. "Mr. Ward?"

"I expect he's fine." It took effort to keep her tone nonchalant. "There's little time to visit with neighbors, although Macy sends her best regards and a cinnamon cake."

"Both are welcome." Miriam retrieved a new length of muslin and began drying the curd again. "Nellie said that Mr. Ward's little boy seems to be adjusting."

Mr. Ward's little boy... Obviously she wasn't the only person recognizing the resemblance.

She wasn't sure if Miri was fishing for information, or making small talk, but her words opened the flood gates. As they readied the new batch of cheese, she told Miri the entire story, ending with little Eli being shuffled off to Hattie's house while Seb's family was in town.

Miri's frown mirrored hers. "A small child who has already lost so much..."

"As we well know." Rachel had been five when their mother died. Miri was newly three and Esther a newborn.

"The thinness of humanity does not always shine brightly on children, does it?"

It didn't. Rachel stirred salt into the dried curds. Without the salt, the curds were fairly tasteless. But with it, the flavor sprang to life in a perfect balance. "Perhaps the trials are the salt of life, teaching us to bend and flow. Perhaps these challenges help shape us to be better people."

"Wise words, whereas I'd prefer giving your Mr. Ward a nice slap right about now, because being a cast-off child is an act bestowed by careless adults." Miri had great patience for animals and little for callous humans. "Certainly nothing an innocent child asks for. How he has the nerve to just gad about town with the boy, but then, what else is one to do? So there's that." She huffed and crossed the room for cheese pans. "How are your classes going?" She removed scalded pans from a shelf and began lining them with cheesecloth. "You have a gift for patience. I know this because you strove to teach me lessons for a long time, although barely older."

"My knack stands me well in the classroom. But I'm dealing with the younger children right now, and they're more easily challenged. If those big boys come back after harvest, I may be telling a different tale."

"It's a wonder the board would allow them re-entry," said Miri. "I can't understand why that would be approved when they accosted Ivan Blount that way. An education is an amazing thing, but there's no reason for violent eruptions to be overlooked. Perhaps they'll block them from coming?"

Rachel couldn't deny she'd hoped the same thing, but she shook her head. "Their parents contributed to the school fund and larder. I don't think they'd have done that if they weren't intending on the boys' return. However it goes, I won't be afraid to send for help as needed. And yet I'd like to be able to solve the problem without intervention. Perhaps they've matured."

Miri began layering curds. "Maybe. But if they're just plain mean, a year older won't make much difference. Have you met the families?"

She needed to do that, Rachel realized. She would schedule a ride to Cutter's Crossing.

"I haven't," she said as she sloshed cheese curds repeatedly. "I hope to soon. It's hard for people to bring kids into town during harvest. Even for church services."

"I understand the fall push to get things done, although it seems easier now that we're older, doesn't it?" Miri swiped a hand to her forehead lightly. "Still as much work, but as if it's part of the plan."

"My being gone hasn't left you with too much to do?"

Miri finished her round with a casual speed that Rachel envied. "With Nellie around?"

Rachel laughed. "She moves quickly."

"And tells the best stories. Rachel, she's brought such joy to Levi that he rarely grumps anymore..."

"A major relief because he grumped plenty before," Rachel noted.

"And if he does, she sets him straight without mincing words. She's taught me a lot," Miri admitted. "I've always been careful with my thoughts and words. After dealing with our father for so long, opinions were not made welcome."

That was certainly true.

"So what a delight it is to see that women can not only have opinions but share them and Levi seems as taken with her as ever. She's been good for him." She set her round on a curing shelf. "I'll wash the pans while you finish."

"I'm slow. Perhaps slower than I was before moving to town."

Miri laughed as she shifted the used pans to a washtub outside the door. "I'm more at home in the creamery or the barn, so we're both using our talents. And I'm glad you came home to help us today. It's nice to have the help, but nicer yet to have your presence."

The day flew by. Nellie had stewed an ornery chicken that had been wreaking havoc in the hen house. Rachel had set bread dough rising before helping in the small creamery, then helped wash and hang bed linens. Once the weather turned, there'd be no time for drying thick quilts and little room to hang them in the house, so this would be their last washing until spring.

They gathered herbs and flowers to dry in bunches, and then Rachel stood on a small ladder to hang the tied bunches from ceiling beams.

"I love feeling prepared for winter." Nellie settled her arms around the growing curve of her abdomen and indicated the shelving with a nod. "This was all new to me when I first moved here, and you girls have shown me so many things. Growing up in the city with little to call my own and even less of a good example, I wouldn't have known how to do any of this."

"Nellie, darling." Esther had come back from helping a neighbor mend a shed attached to her small barn. She grabbed a slice of bread and spoke between mouthfuls. "You came to us with a wonderful knowledge of ribbons and lace."

"Don't forget tucks," added Rachel.

"And gathers," added Miri, laughing.

"Which means we get to share our full till of talents," Esther continued. "I'm at home on a ladder, with a hammer and nails by my side. Less so with a treadle sewing machine."

"And this is the best thing about being women together," said Rachel. "We share knowledge, stories, work and fun."

"I wish you could stay here during the week," Esther admitted. "I know it's easier for you to stay in town, but I miss your wisdom."

"Miri's not smart enough for you?" teased Rachel.

"Nor am I, I gather," added Nellie. "But this stew is quite good, so I must be good for something."

Esther made a face at them, but she tucked her arm through Rachel's purposely. "You are both quite wonderful, but Rachel helped raise me. Us," she added, looking at Miri. "I didn't realize how much I took her counsel for granted until she was a wagon ride away."

"Which is also a horse ride away, a task you've taken under your wing fairly often, I hear."

Esther blushed. "Levi thinks me brazen, but I'm not. I just don't want to be tied to convention when it's so much easier to saddle up and get on my way. And it gives the younger two horses exercise they sorely need. You're right, I could ride to town to visit, but not this time of year. Harvest and planting are all about two things: Harvest and planting."

That was true across the prairie. No one dared dawdle in preparation for winter. Unprepared people could perish on the wide plains, separated from one another by miles of snow-swept land. Some winters were softer than others, but in Rachel's experience, those were few and far between.

"But what about this?" Nellie smoothed her hands over the loose drape of her maternity top. "I've never birthed a child. Nor have any of you. And being due so close to winter, we're not likely to have help on hand."

"Ann helped others in the past. She's mentioned it to me," added Rachel, "although she doesn't claim to be an actual midwife."

"It's an inexact science," added Miri. "I know I have no human experience at my fingertips, but I've brought many a calf and foal into the world, with only occasional intervention needed. Generally the course of nature needs no interruption or assistance."

"But how can we know?" Nellie watched their faces as she asked the question. When she realized they had no answers, she sighed. "While I've put it into God's hands because it is a natural occurrence, I won't deny the fear within me."

"Fear of what?" asked Miri.

"That something might go wrong and I'm helpless to help my child. Or help myself," she added. "That's a daunting concern when graveyards bear such testimony to mothers and infants lost in childbirth."

"Then we must learn," Rachel decided.

"Just like that." Esther stared at her. "We just suddenly become midwives? I don't think that's how it works, big sister."

"It is." Once she'd decided, Rachel saw the path clearly. "I'll order a book through the catalog at the general store and in the meantime, I'll talk with Ann and others to gain advice."

"How are you going to find time to do that with teaching?"

Rachel frowned because for a moment she'd conveniently forgotten her long days and short, clipped evenings until the light was gone.

"But it is an excellent idea," Miri continued. "And I shall do it. I've got the most hands-on experience with birthings, and folks out here have been talking the need for a midwife. Rachel, can you order the book and send it to me as soon as it arrives?"

"I'll give it right to Levi to bring home that day."

"And Esther, didn't you say Claire Higgins was due this month?"

"And concerned for how she was going to handle all of this with her husband passed on and two young children running about."

"I'll go see her first thing," declared Miri. "The best learning tool is experience, and that means I'll be leaving you two to handle things here, but with our harvest almost done, and your quick ways, that shouldn't be a problem."

"Not if it gains me someone who has a notion about bringing a baby safely into the world," Nellie told them. "I've seen too many of those young mother graves, and far too many innocents beside them. The more we know, the safer we are. All of us," she added, sweeping her three sisters-in-law a pointed look.

"Except our prospects of such beginnings look rather thin," Rachel said lightly. "But women should stick together in these times. We need to maintain our own safety. If the men are too busy and we don't see to it personally, then the fault is as much ours as theirs."

"True words, wisely spoken." Nellie put out her hand. "I say we make a pact right now. To love, help and support one another, and other women out here, to the best of our abilities. So help us, God."

They clasped hands in agreement. An onlooker might

have thought their pledge a minor thing, but Rachel knew it wasn't small. Their promise magnified and clarified their position on the prairie. For a long time women had ceded their well-being and care to men. While that had its place, she was pretty sure the good Lord had given women wits and brains and strength to be their own caretakers and there was no place like the vast open prairie to test that thought.

Their father would have been repulsed by such views, but grown-up Rachel glimpsed the truth beyond his tight-fisted control. The town's growing needs were opening doors of opportunity, and she intended to make use of all she could.

Levi had the team hitched to the wagon early the next morning. He helped each woman step up. Nellie was last, and as he guided his expectant wife into the front seat, Rachel saw the look on his face... pride, joy, and maybe a little fear...

Longing hit her.

Was she silly to dream of romance and love? Was it imprudent to think of marriage and family? The prairie wasn't exactly crawling with eligible men, and most men her age had married already.

Seb's image came to mind. She thrust it right back out again as she smoothed the dainty autumn-toned calico with her hands. The color and the print pleased her.

Henry Eichas would have forbade such clothing. Fitted bodices and nipped waists had no place in their home, and the plain gowns she'd worn all her life were shaped more like potato sacks than dresses. He'd kept them apart purposely, and it wasn't easy to forgive him for that. He'd stymied them, he'd driven his second wife off with his meanness, and grew gruffer still.

Now their lives were different. What would have happened if Henry hadn't taken ill and passed away? Would they have slogged their lives along those same tracks, never changing? Would they have woken one day to a world changed around them?

Now they were part of the driving force. Change might be hard in some ways, but scripture and knowledge bolstered her. She would carry both forward.

She'd discovered one thing since living in town. Temptations grew in number alongside a growing population and she'd have to measure her reactions accordingly. But there was no way on earth she was giving up her pretty clothes. She touched the fall-themed calico and smiled.

If floral fabric was an indulgence...

It was one she intended to live with.

Chapter Nine

SEB WARD WAS PRETTY SURE he might be going crazy. For a non-excitable person, these were alien feelings.

Cecily seemed far too comfortable here on the prairie. His mother showed no intention of heading back to her life in Minnesota, and Althea only stopped grumbling when asleep, which meant her grousing continued perpetually.

Miss Hattie had Eli well in hand, although how long could she keep a busy five-year-old under wraps?

And he hadn't seen Rachel since she ignored his existence on Friday morning.

That didn't suit him.

He'd growled at one of his co-workers, shushed another, and felt like taking a hammer to anything in his path.

Was he being ridiculous?

He put his head in his hands while coffee brewed on the small coal stove.

He knew the answer. Rachel saw the reality of him, but believed the supposition that Eli must be his child. If he had to let her believe that, so be it. Better he take the hit than his mother. And when the adoption process was done, he'd claim Elijah as his own for the world to see and think what they would. He didn't care.

Except for Rachel, and then he seemed to care too much.

Wagons and buggies trundled into town for services. He crossed to the small window and spotted Levi's wagon. Four lovely women climbed down from the finely-tooled seats, but he only saw one.

Rachel.

She'd braided and coiled her hair and he wondered what it would be like to unbraid that hair... let it fall into his hands, weave his fingers through it.

She turned and looked up at his window just then. She spotted him watching.

Other wagons pulled off onto the grassy slope behind Levi's building. Other people climbed down, gathered, laughed and began to make their way across the walking bridge.

Not her.

Eyes locked with his, she stood silent and still, then brought one hand to the bit of lace at her throat.

He cared what she thought. Deeply. Gazing down, he didn't want to be a disappointment to her, but as that thought dawned, Hattie came into view, with his small brother skipping along at her side.

And on the other side of the street, his mother and Cecily approached, looking quite dapper for a simple prairie service.

He was pretty sure his heart stopped.

He had to get down there. He had to intervene so his mother wouldn't see Eli. Recognize him.

And then Rachel reached out a hand to the little boy. He grasped her fingers eagerly, much like Seb would do if given the chance.

And then she glanced up again.

Disappointment shadowed her pretty face. She didn't frown, she simply turned, the boy's hand tucked firmly in hers, and walked sedately toward the church.

Others followed, including his mother and Cecily.

He didn't dare attend the service. Eli would call him out instantly. Nor could he work on the bridge on the Sabbath. He picked up his worn Bible from the desk beneath the window. He let it fall open. He'd done that often as a boy, then a man, letting chance or Providence guide his readings and today the Good Book fell open to Psalm 86. One line jumped out at him. One line made him take notice. *Teach me thy way, O Lord; I will walk in thy truth: unite my heart to fear thy name.*

A believer in truth should live the truth and he'd done that all his days. Was his urge to protect his mother the right thing to do? Or had the human-knows-best mentality swayed him?

He turned his lamp higher and worked on recordkeeping until a quiet knock at his door interrupted.

"Seb? It's Mother."

He hurried to the door and swung it wide. "I saw you walking up the road for services."

"And they were so well done," she told him as she slipped her gloves off. "I was hoping to see you there, but you've always liked to pray on your own."

"That hasn't changed." He noted the well-worn Bible resting alongside his chair.

"But other things have, haven't they?"

"As expected." He smiled at her. "I think we all change as we get older, don't we?"

"Oh, Seb." She reached out and laid her head against his chest, hugging him. "You are such a good man. A wonderful son. But it's not right to place the sins of the father on the shoulders of the son."

He frowned.

"The boy, Seb. The dark-haired little boy that looks enough like you to be yours and isn't."

"Mother, I—"

"Don't you dare apologize, I know exactly what you were trying to do." She leaned back and gazed up at him, scolding with the gentleness he'd always admired. "You were willing to risk your reputation to give solace to mine."

"I care nothing for my reputation in the sight of others."

She contemplated that for a moment before replying. "Not as a general rule, but I believe there are occasions where you would care, Seb. And this is one of them." She crossed to the window. "Believing the boy is your son might be difficult for some people in particular." She indicated the small apartment that stood diagonal to the lumberyard.

"So I should cast out three reputations to save mine?" He drew his brow down. "Yours. Cecily's. Althea's."

Her expression saddened and he realized why they'd come. "He's already scandalized you? And the girls?"

"Let's just say his misdeeds have caught up with him and therefore us. This sweet boy is not the only one, Sebastian," she added softly. "I brought the girls west to have a chance to avoid the rumor mills thrashing every little detail of your father's escapades. Going anywhere in the city has become most difficult at present, and the girls don't need to live beneath that cloud."

"Will you take them east?"

She crossed back to him. "I won't. I won't go off to where Althea can become even more entrenched in herself and thwart Cecily's dreams of independence. I want to move here, but only if it doesn't put you in a worse situation."

"How could you being here be bad for me?" It was a preposterous notion.

"It could anger your father," she reminded him. "He supplies your wood. And he's a miserable person once angered."

The thought that his father could end up being the wounded party to this debacle was ludicrous. And totally accurate. Cedric wouldn't recognize the actions that put change in motion. He'd only see the backwash on him. "There are other suppliers that would be pleased to get my contract, Mother. And there's nothing Father likes more than a secure balance sheet, firmly in his favor. But." He motioned toward the window. "Are you all right being here with Eli?"

"That's his name?"

"Elijah. I've already filled out the paperwork to adopt him but it will be a while before the judge comes through."

"Oh, Seb." She clutched his hands. A sheen of tears brightened her eyes. "You have such a heart. Such a very good heart. And yes, I think now that your sisters have dealt with the initial shock they'll adjust."

She must have read his look of doubt because she changed that statement slightly. "Cecily, quickly. With Althea, we'll have to see. She's got more of her father in her, but I believe there's hope. If she's away from him, perhaps we'll see progress more quickly."

His mother and sisters, living here. In town. It would be different, yes. But nice, too. As long as Althea stayed quiet, and that was an unlikely occurrence.

She must have read his expression. "Give her a chance, Seb. She's only sixteen, there's time for her to grow straight yet. And learn to put her hand to a task."

"Are you sure you'll be okay with the boy close by? He'll be a reminder of so much that's gone wrong." He hated to pose the question, but Eli didn't deserve to be the object of anyone's wrath, no matter how understandable it might be.

"He looks very much like you and Artie, doesn't he?"

Seb nodded and waited for her response. She didn't disappoint him.

"A child is a true blessing from God," she answered. "Boy or girl, no matter how they come into this world, they come with the miracle of life. I will be his Grandma and I will look beyond his conception and focus on the joy he'll bring to you. And possibly to a certain kind-hearted young lady."

Seb understood the unlikelihood of that. "I'm pretty sure I've lost Rachel's good opinion of me. I think she shares the belief of many, that I tucked Eli with Hattie so you wouldn't be aware of my love child."

"But once the truth is known..."

He grasped her hands and raised his brows. "There's no reason for the truth to be known to anyone. You and Eli shouldn't have to bear the weight of any of this. There's no law that says people have to know our business, is there? And for the girls to deal with this on top of Father's current indiscretions would be dreadful No." He shook his head. "I'm glad you know. Not because I wanted you hurt, but because you've always taught me to be truthful. But the rest isn't anyone's concern, Mother. It shouldn't be public knowledge. Let them surmise what they may and we go along, paying our bills and living our lives. That should be on our terms, as always. Not resting on the wagging tongues of others."

She didn't look convinced, but she didn't press, either and he recalled another truth about his mother. She was incredibly patient. "I'm going to talk to that land broker. There's no time to build something this year, and we may find ourselves in diminished means when your father realizes we intend to stay. But perhaps there's a home for sale in town or at least near it."

"Mrs. Devereaux has gone back to Ohio to live with her daughter," Seb told her. "Her son-in-law works for me. He invited her to stay with them once her husband passed, but she was determined to go back east."

"And he won't keep her house?"

"He and his wife have a place a mile outside of town. He says that land is going to be worth a fortune someday, even if he's not around to see it so they'll sell her house to give her a stake back east."

"I've had my share of fortune," replied his mother in a dry voice. "I'll stick with 'good enough' from now on."

He understood her meaning, but if his father tried to write off his wife and daughters financially, he'd be dealing with Sebastian first. Bad enough he'd sullied their lives with his recklessness, but to deny them the money needed to live would be despicable. The fact that Cedric Ward was fully capable of that made a sad situation worse.

"I'm taking the girls to the hotel's dining room for Sunday dinner," Elizabeth went on. "I'll send a letter to your father tomorrow, witnessed by the local lawyer and if you could show me the Devereaux house, that would give me an idea of what's available."

"Not much because we're small," he told her. He slipped on his coat and put on his hat. "Conversely there's always someone coming or going out here. We can build a house for you ladies come spring, so anything for this winter could be considered temporary."

"My thoughts exactly." She preceded him out the door. "And there is always a brightness that comes with the spring. Isn't there?"

She was correct.

That didn't keep him from wanting to thrash his father. He felt better that his mother understood about Eli, but angry that his father thrust them into this situation. The selfishness of Cedric's actions galled him. And yet it was better for the boy so his focus should settle there. "I'm going to get Eli and join you for dinner. All right?"

"Please do. Sitting at a table for too long will tax him, so that might spur the girls into something more creative. A ride into the country, perhaps?"

Levi had a buggy Seb could borrow, if he caught him before the Eichas family headed back to the prairie. "I'll see about a ride."

He left his mother to walk back toward the hotel as he turned in the opposite direction. Many of the wagons had left the small churchyard and the adjacent schoolyard green, but Levi's was still parked toward the back of the school. A group of people stood talking. The Eichas family, and Reverend Barber. Or Dr. Barber, two titles the man wore well.

"Seb, good morning." The reverend stuck out a hand in welcome. "Nice to see you."

The reverend never jibed him about coming to church or not coming to church. Seb liked that. He grasped the reverend's hand. "And you. Levi, I don't mean to interrupt, but would it be all right for me to borrow a buggy for the afternoon? My mother and sisters might enjoy a ride into the countryside and once the weather turns, that's less likely to happen. Although I expect I'll need a sled with the girls in town, because they'll like stepping out with the horses."

"You might want to hold onto your money," Nellie advised with a grin. "There will be no shortage of young men to invite your sisters on sledding parties once the weather turns," she continued. "Do they mean to stay, Seb?" she went on. "Because I would love that. I was trying to sketch your sisters' gowns so I could duplicate the drape. That will be so much easier if they're here!"

"I believe they'll be settling here," he confirmed, but left it at that. He started to turn toward Levi, but his words caught in his throat when Rachel, Hattie and Eli walked out of the schoolhouse and locked the door.

Hopes and dreams.

He'd never bothered with ideas like that. There was no need. He had a good job and a sound business. It had been enough until now.

Need filled him as she turned their way.

A need so desperate and raw that he wondered how it came to be as he neared thirty with scarcely a thought about it before.

"When it's right, it's right." Chin down, Levi uttered the words softly so he wouldn't be overheard. "But it's a delicate thing to hold another's heart in your hand. Big or small."

He meant Rachel and Eli's hearts. Their feelings.

"Seb!" Eli raced his way and hurtled himself into Seb's arms. "Hey, Seb! I missed you like th-this much!" Eli buried his face into Seb's shoulder. He didn't cry, but his unconstrained joy was emotional enough. "I l-l-like Miss Hattie, but I want to come home, okay?"

It wasn't much of a home. Three small rooms alongside a lumberyard and a train depot.

But Sebastian understood the boy's meaning. He wanted to be with him. With family. Even though it had been unspoken thus far. "I think that's a great idea as long as you don't mind being with someone else now and again while we finish the bridge this next week. I don't know what I'd do if anything ever happened to you, Eli."

The boy clung tighter.

That was answer enough. And when Seb turned and met Rachel's calm, cool gaze, his heart longed to go home in a very different way, but grown-up problems couldn't be swept aside quite so easily. "Rachel. Hattie. Good morning." He reached up and tipped the brim of his hat slightly. "Hattie, would it be all right with you if I have Eli back at my place except for directly after school? I've still got a nanny posting up, but with harvest on us, there's been no interest as yet."

"Folks have so little time," noted Hattie, and she sighed. "I find myself in the same boat because the order for the railway woolens has just been sent my way and it's going to have Ann, Nellie and me working whenever we can which means I'm not going to have time to have Eli with me. I know it's only for a week or so, and you know I'd never say no unless absolutely necessary."

He understood.

He couldn't leave Eli with his mother. Not yet, anyway. The situation was too raw to rub salt in the wounds and have her watching her husband's love child. Nor were his sisters skilled in the ways of children. He was about to say he'd manage, when Rachel spoke up.

"Would you care to stay after school with me, Eli? Help me tidy up and then walk me home?"

Hope filled the boy's eyes and Seb's heart. "May I?" Eli looked from her to Seb and back again.

"Are you sure, Rachel?" He asked the question quietly, as if it wasn't weighted in so many different ways. Her heart. His. The boy's. Her mistaken opinion of him. And yet, he wasn't at a point to share Eli's true parentage with her. Maybe someday. But not yet.

She lifted those calm hazel eyes to his. "I think it would suit."

Eli grinned. "It would suit me as long as you don't burn any more cakes!"

That drew her smile. She gazed at the boy with such a look of affection that Seb wanted, no... make that *needed* her to turn that same look to him.

She didn't, and why would she? A proper young woman should shy away from a philanderer. How could he wish her different when he would advise his own sisters thus?

As she bid goodbye to her family and walked toward her meek apartment, he had to fight the urge to chase after her. Tell her the truth.

Something stopped him and as he watched her go, he knew exactly what it was.

Pride.

Ward pride, the same thing that tripped his father up on a regular basis. The same kind of pride that came down through the ages.

When Christ appeared in that upper room to visit his beloved apostles, Thomas doubted their stories. He wanted proof, plain and simple, and without that proof he refused to believe.

The good Lord rebuked him the next week, reminding him that those who believe without seeing are blessed.

A part of him wished Rachel saw his true colors. He wanted her to know he would never father a child and then deny that child, and he wanted her to believe that without him saying a word. If she cared, and he thought she did, he wanted her trust.

He understood that his situation looked bad, but he was a lumberman. Lumber could look bad and still be sound. Some lumber cut nicely but couldn't be trusted for the long haul.

He wanted her to believe in him without evidence. He would probably never get his wish. He understood that.

But that didn't stop him from wanting it.

Chapter Ten

RACHEL HEARD SEB AS HE led the team out of the nearby livery and hooked them to Levi's open wagon. It would be chilly in the wagon. She knew that. But it was the best choice for seeing the wide open plains surrounding them. The lakes, pristine blue, as ducks and geese landed briefly before heading south.

He was keeping Eli with him. Did that mean he'd explained the boy to his mother?

He must have.

And did she willingly forgive? How would a mother handle such a thing? She wondered as she sewed linings into the curtains to help beat back the coming cold.

She'd spent her day on the claim making cheese and drying herbs. Now some of that cheese and clutches of herbs lined her shelves, next to jellies and jams, a crock of pickles and small barrels of beans and dried peas. She'd brought back a well-smoked ham. A piece shorn off the end would flavor a pot of soup on many long, dark winter nights.

Loneliness gripped her.

She wanted to chase down Sebastian and go for a ride. Hold Eli on her lap and point out the farms and pastures and plains that stretched as far as the eye could see. Sit with her sisters on the claim and talk, laugh and muse.

She heard Sebastian park the wagon alongside the shop nearly two hours later. She'd finished the curtains and re-tacked them. She'd cleaned her lamps, trimmed the wicks and filled them with oil.

She could read with both lamps lit.

She could sit and write stories of her week with the children. Her week in the town, and the surprise arrival of wealthy women.

Neither idea tempted, and when a knock on the door startled her less than five minutes later, she jumped.

Sebastian.

She smoothed her damp palms across the skirt of her everyday gown and moved to the door. She sucked in a deep breath and pulled it open.

Not Sebastian.

Macy.

And when Macy caught sight of her face, she drew her brows down. "You were expecting someone else." When Rachel started to deny it, Macy waved her off. "Don't try and get 'round it, it's fine, Rachel. He's sneaking peeks this way, you're gazing from afar, the whole thing is too utterly romantic for a pragmatic person like me, and yet I'm as caught up in the drama as any nearby neighbor could be."

"There is no drama, Macy." Rachel shut the door quietly once Macy came through.

"Clearly a figment of my vast imagination," claimed Macy. Then she paused. "Oh, wait. I have no imagination, but I'm quite skilled at assessment and I know what I see right before my eyes." She gave Rachel a look of sympathy before she added, "I'll leave it for now because we have more important things to fuss on."

Rachel wasn't sure she was right, but she had to get her mind off of romance and onto something worthwhile and practical. "What is it that requires our fussing?"

"The annual Thanksgiving dinner served by the church, but done at the school. With your permission, of course."

"Macy, you don't need my permission," Rachel exclaimed. "It's the town's school. As long as the school board is fine with it, of course it's fine."

"Boards are all well and good for the signing of this and that, but when it comes down to the basics of a situation, they're mostly run by men who have no idea what kind of skill and industry it takes to run a school of five or six classes," Macy replied. "So while they're sure to say yes because not one of them will be cooking, cleaning or setting up a town dinner, the person most affected should have a say. And that's you," she finished. "We'd need to set up on Wednesday and that would mean classes out on Wednesday of Thanksgiving week and then we'll clean up on Friday."

Rachel winced. "Three days of missing classes is too much, Macy. How about this? We let the children out at half day on Wednesday. We enjoy Thursday as we all should, giving thanks to God, but then reconvene on Friday. If we take care to have several volunteers to help on Thursday, we should be able to return desks to their proper places by evening. Don't you think?"

Macy shook her head. "It sounds plausible, but with the likelihood of rain we could be in trouble. Or even snow by then." They'd had fall blizzards before. They both knew it could happen again.

"Let's plan on the Wednesday half day and let me think on Friday. I know it's just one day, but it takes time to get children into the habit of learning and much less time to break the habit."

"We can work that out, of course. And if we appeal to the men, I expect we can have a crew for hauling and moving and stacking stuff in and then stuff out. That's one good thing about pioneers and mountain men. They stay to muscle because there really isn't any other choice. Of course some are more muscular than others." She indicated the two men lost in conversation by the new boardwalk.

Her husband Will Barber, doctor and preacher... and Seb Ward.

Will was friendly with Seb. He didn't seem to mind that Seb wasn't a church-going man despite his proximity. Will respected the somewhat reclusive lumberman. It was evident in the way they talked to each other and about one another.

Will couldn't be blind to the situation, could he?

But if ye forgive not men their trespasses, neither will your Father forgive your trespasses. The verse from Matthew's Gospel nudged her.

If ye forgive not men...

Macy touched her arm. "Life comes with questions. Let me simply say this. You were out on the prairie when I rolled into town nearly two years ago with a newborn child."

Rachel had heard rumors, but it wasn't her place to ask prying questions.

"What if Will hadn't been able to overlook my past? What if he'd banished me because I left my own little Will on his doorstep, hoping the pastor would find a good home for my baby son?"

"Oh, Macy." Rachel covered Macy's hand with hers. "It all worked out in the end, didn't it?"

"Because forgiveness and compassion are part of God's wish for us." She sent the two men a quick glance through the fading light outside. "Everyone makes mistakes. If we own them and move on, that brings more power to us as His followers. When Jesus spotted that woman who was about to be stoned in the street, his wisdom saved her life."

He'd instructed the sinless man to throw the first stone. And not one of the angry men in that crowd fit that description. Slowly they'd dropped their rocks and walked away. "It's a lot to think about."

"And pray about," Macy agreed. "But I know it can be done for I am living proof that when two hearts are meant to be together, it's a gift from the Lord above. So I have your blessing to put together this dinner for the town..."

"Just the church congregation or will everyone be welcome?" asked Rachel.

"Receive one another as Christ received us." Macy said. "I think an open door and a good hot meal is the best way to draw folks back to church and back to God. Nothing like the kindness of a sharing heart to go a long way."

"Count me in for helping," Rachel told her. "We were kept away from town and church a long time, and Will was so welcoming when we finally started coming to town on Sundays. It was a grand surprise to find so many worshipping together."

"And look at you now." Macy took Rachel's hands in hers. "A school teacher, living in town, making her way in the world."

Macy was right.

She'd been sitting in half light, suffering doldrums when she should be dancing in the streets. Instead of ruing what she missed, she should be celebrating all she'd gained. "Macy, you have given me the new hope of simple wisdom. I'm so glad you came over."

"And I'll have to hurry back because Chickie's good with either Little Will or the baby, but the pair of them are a lot for her to handle. We'll talk soon." She went through the door and hurried across the short space of scrabbled yard, then the narrow street to the parsonage.

Will and Seb looked up, then Seb glanced back, toward Rachel. He saw her there. His hand started to come up, as if to wave, then didn't.

But hers did.

Gazing out, watching him, she raised her hand in a gentle salute.

Let him make of it what he would, but Macy was right. Forgiveness was Christ's instruction on earth. If one acted pious every Sunday but failed in their daily life, was that faith? Or simply a show of faith?

She took a warm shawl from the hooks inside the door and sat down at her small desk. The words she'd spurned an hour before poured out of her now. By the time she was done weaving the tale of her past week, dark had fallen. She got ready for bed, grateful for the warmth of hand-quilted covers, knowing she'd need to start the coal stove in earnest soon. In thick-forested Minnesota they'd burned wood, but here on the plains there was little wood to burn. Coal worked as long as the trains ran, so making her bin of coal stretch seemed prudent. But she couldn't deny her longing for a warm house someday. Warmth and food went a long way toward easing a rugged winter, and she knew the truth of that.

Both bridge abutments were now securely moored into the bedrock on either side of Lawson's Creek. The braces were built and needed to be lowered into place. Then the stringers and the cover boards. In ten days the bridge would be done, the town board would be happy and Seb could put this chapter behind him.

"Whatever possessed you to bid on the bridge project?"

Seb frowned as Levi and Sol Eichas came his way. "It seemed like a good idea at the time. But that was before we had a record-breaking year of lumber sales."

"That's why we stopped by," said Sol. "I got word from my uncle in Minnesota that Harley Lumber is looking to buy land near the depot to open a competing lumber yard."

Of course they were looking now because sales had finally gone up this year. "One good year and the sharks start circling." Seb pondered their information and his frown deepened. "I did well this year, but it's just breaking even plus a little if you look at the five years before that. I don't want a lumber war."

"And Harley was involved in that price setting scheme

a few years back."

They were, but so was Ward Lumber. Not Seb, but his father. "My father did his share of that, too, and it's made them rich men. Is your uncle certain of this information?"

Sol nodded. "As certain as he can be. He drew up the purchase offer on the plat of land where the Schultz lumber yard used to be, plus a section just south of that."

A solid-sized space for lumber holdings, but the only spot of land close enough to the depot to be sensible right now. Philip Dickinson and his wife lived north of De Smet. He'd inherited family money several years before and he'd used a share of that bequest to buy Schultz's land. "I appreciate the information."

"We welcome business and industry," Levi said straight out. "But we also appreciate that established businesses have stuck with this town through the thick and thin of these hard years. That shouldn't be overlooked."

Their gratitude touched something inside him. Sol clapped him on the arm before they turned and headed back to the wagon shop.

They'd treated him like a friend. They'd given him important information. He hadn't given much thought to how good that would feel until it happened. His men would be busy laying stringers for the next several hours and their next delivery wasn't due until Tuesday morning.

He had Jake Tucker draw up some quick paperwork, then saddled his horse and took a ride to Phil Dickinson's place outside DeSmet. Ninety minutes later, with an impromptu lunch offered by Phil's wife Grace, he'd struck a deal for the land. He was back in town by mid-afternoon, with the deed in hand. He'd file it quickly to become owner of record and that should put the brakes on Harley Lumber. He hoped.

The men had fastened the stringers into place. They were placing cross supports now, with the very best lumber. A bridge needed the skill of industry and the vision of science to deal with weight, movement and Mother Nature. He'd made it wide enough for even the biggest wagons to get through and enough space between the boards to allow for spring run-off and summertime heat expansion.

He'd just gotten his horse put up when Rachel and Eli came his way. Eli took one look at the bridge's progress and jumped in the air. "Wow! Seb, look at that! It's almost finished!"

"This part goes quickly with good men." He tipped his hat to Ben and the two men he'd hired on as bridge crew. "It's getting things secured at the edge that takes time, but a bridge is only as secure as the land holding it. How was your day, Elijah?"

"So good." Eli leaped into his arms as if he belonged there. "I was a big helper with the erasers and I picked up all the chalk sticks after I spilled them..."

Rachel raised an eyebrow in constrained amusement when Seb looked her way.

"And then I was a really good sweeper even though the broom is too big for me. But maybe we can get a smaller broom and I can help Miss Rachel every single day, like forever!"

The boy's words echoed Seb's sentiments. The thought of helping Rachel every day held great appeal. When he shifted his attention back to Rachel, she sent the boy a skeptical look. "I expect that sounds good at age five, but there will come a time when hanging with the teacher is no longer the fun it is now, my boy. And you and I have a mission," she reminded him. "We were going to go for a walk along the creek bank and pick up leaves, remember?"

"For our leaf box!" Eli turned and put his hands on Seb's surprised cheeks. The feel of those small, trusting hands... his chest ached with the goodness of it all. "We're going to make a present for you, Seb. A really, really nice one!"

"Well get to it," Seb instructed as he set the boy down. "I love presents."

"Do you, Seb?"

Ah, her voice. Her gaze. The look of her, after a long day of teaching other people's children. Still beautiful, and the wisps of hair that escaped the knot at the nape of her neck only made her more so. "I expect most people appreciate gifts, don't they?"

She regarded him quietly. "When was the last time you got a present, Seb?"

He couldn't remember, actually. The question stumped him.

She caught his expression and took Eli's hand. "Then it's high time we rectified that situation. Come, my friend. Let's grab a bucket and go walking before it gets too dark."

"I'll be by for him around five-thirty," Seb called as they moved toward her set of rooms.

Rachel waved. "You know where we are." Minutes later he spotted the pair as they trekked out back. The creek was low, and while cloudy, it was light enough for a short walk. Watching them go, a niggle of worry jabbed him.

There was no reason for concern, so why did he find himself darting looks that way every few minutes? He didn't know, but when they hadn't come back within the hour and the light was growing thin, he called two of the men to come with him to go searching.

He didn't take time for lanterns. They hurried along the brushy creek bank as his concern grew. "Let's spread out. If we're bunched together, we could walk right by them in this fading light."

The men did as he asked.

They might have looked at him funny, but even that was obscured by the long shadows of the creek thickets. He'd heard a wolf howl a few night's back. It was in the distance, but wolves traveled creek beds. What if—

"Does old Bruce Hutch still call the creek home?" asked Tom as they moved farther north.

Seb hadn't hear Bruce's name in over a year, but the old

recluse kept himself apart so that wasn't exactly unusual. "I don't know? Should we care?"

Tom ran a hand across his chin. "I heard someone say he'd gotten a might secretive out here, for his own doin's."

"Which are?"

"His own, I reckon."

Great. Add strange, secluded old man to the list of possible hairy predators and—

"Hey! Hey! Look what we found, Seb!"

Seb's heart accelerated. He turned. There were Eli and Rachel, bundled against the growing cold and carrying a bucket full of creek bank treasures. They stood at the crest of the bank where walking was much less cumbersome.

Tom coughed lightly. "'pear to be all right, I think, Boss."

They certainly seemed that way.

"We'll head back then." Ben nudged his co-worker and winked. "See you in the morning."

The two men went back toward town as Seb climbed the last few feet of the brush-filled creek's edge. "So you're fine? You're both fine?"

Did he sound gruff?

He didn't care.

Did he sound upset?

That's because he *was* upset. Anything could have happened to them, a woman and child, off alone.

Rachel nailed him with a teacher-type look of displeasure which meant she probably didn't take well with being scolded. Well being scared to death didn't rank high on his list of preferences, either.

"You can't look, Seb." The boy put his two little hands over the top of the bucket. "Not when it's a s'prise, okay?"

He endured this worry for a child's surprise? He bit back a growl because maybe— just maybe— he'd over-reacted.

Rachel met him at the edge of the brush. She smelled of pine cones and leaves and the beauty of autumn. "I believe the surprise is that you came searching us out."

He faced Rachel, half ready to keep scolding... or kiss her. And right now both felt right.

She held his gaze and he was pretty sure he flushed. That made him glad the dim light would make it tougher to see. "It was getting late."

"And?"

She wasn't going to let him slough this off easily.

"I was concerned that you might lose your way."

"With a creek within thirty feet of us to guide us back?"

"My concern was valid. You could have strayed from the creek bed."

"Which would be rash on my part as the hour grew late."

She had him. He was either accusing her of being daft or foolish, and neither one was likely to raise her estimation of him.

"Except." She reached out and grasped his hands. Both of them. She was wearing lightweight gloves, but it felt like she was holding more than his hands in hers. More like his heart. "I think that's the nicest thing anyone's ever done for me, Seb. To come looking for me, just to make sure I'm all right. Thank you."

He gazed at her. He squeezed those hands lightly. He shifted his gaze from her eyes to her lips, then back.

What would it be like to kiss Rachel? To hold her from this day forward? To win her heart? He, who had never given a real thought to winning a heart, longed to win this one.

"Can we have supper? I think it's time for supper, isn't it?"

The thought of caring for Eli with a fine woman by his side, made Seb straighten his shoulders. "It is and I'll happily treat you both at the hotel. After we drop off your treasure at Miss Rachel's place."

Forgiveness and moving ahead was all well and good in theory, but Seb's offer unnerved Rachel.

Eat at the hotel?

The hotel where his mother and sisters were currently lodging? The hotel where folks saw him dining with his little look-alike friend on a regular basis?

Rachel pulled her hands free. She tucked them together and faced him but it wasn't easy. "I have dinner waiting at home, so another time, perhaps?" She put a smile on her face as if she turned down handsome men every day.

"Dinner is waiting?"

He called her out and she held tight to her story. "I did a baking yesterday and you know how quickly bread goes stale. Best to eat it fresh."

He picked Eli up into his arms and settled the boy on one side, then hoisted the light bucket with his other hand.

"Don't peek, okay?" Eli turned Seb's face toward him with a little hand to his cheek. The effect was totally sweet and absolutely engaging.

"You have my word."

"All right!" Eli grinned up at him with a smile so much like Seb's that she wasn't sure where one left off and the other began.

If ye not forgive men their trespasses...

She didn't know Seb's story.

He didn't know hers. Levi wasn't one to talk. Neither was Seb, so the fact that they worked in close proximity for years meant little.

She was willing to explore these feelings, but only a silly woman risked her reputation in a small town. Her heart wanted to be a little silly.

Her head knew better. "I think it would be very nice to invite the two of you to have supper with me next Sunday."

Seb paused. The look he gave her set her pulse racing once more. "You mean it?"

"I wouldn't say it if I didn't mean it," she assured him. And then she smiled. "I've got a nice ham bone for soup and we can have fresh bread—"

"Yes." He didn't wait for her to finish. He smiled down at her and when she felt the heat climb into her cheeks because the thought of asking a man to supper in her apartment seemed almost scandalous, but Eli would be there. And taking this step made more sense to her than being seen in the public hotel dining room right now.

Sure, folks could make something of it, but they shouldn't. And maybe Esther would stay after church and play chaperone.

"I'd like to have you get to know my mother, Rachel."

He wasn't looking at her now. They'd started walking again, and she wondered if he had a free hand, would he hold hers? Would he wrap his fingers around hers and give her the feeling of beloved safety she'd never known?

"I think she'd like to get to know you, too."

"For what reason, I wonder?"

She spoke quickly and when he slanted a look at her, the heat in her cheeks increased.

"She's one of those astute women. Smart and intuitive. And kind beyond words."

His description sounded so nice. Her mother had been like that, what little she remembered of her. Or maybe she'd fabricated the image in her head to comfort three lost little girls. That was entirely possible. "Has your mother settled her plans?"

He shook his head. "We are looking at renting a property for her and the girls. They can winter over, then decide what to do in the spring."

"And how is that for you, Seb?" She posed the question quietly.

"A surprise, and yet, not unexpected." He aimed a look she didn't understand at Eli. "But I'll gladly help my mother with anything she needs. She's lived her life doing for others."

Rachel stayed silent.

"It sounds odd, I know, a rich woman being sacrificial, but she is. She's done more for benevolent societies in Minnesota than most groups of do-gooders. She's always said God blessed her with time and money, so why not use both to his purpose?"

"Those are beautiful sentiments and a mark of strength. Did your father join her in these pursuits?"

He replied as the yard abutting her rooms came into sight. "He did not. He had a business to run. Little things like a wife and children rarely made it into his daily schedule."

Her father was much the same way. Not rich, like Seb's, but coldly withholding gentle emotion. "Then your mother did quite well to raise such fine children."

They were approaching her door. He paused while she reached for the bucket, then the door handle. "We are flawed. But yes, she tried her best in some rough circumstances."

Rachel tried to imagine rich and rough circumstances in the same context. Austen posed it well in her novels, but after a decade of eking a living on the prairie, rough took on a whole new meaning for Rachel. Still, they now thrived as the farm and profits grew. "Then that is a good example for us all." She pushed the door open and set the bucket on the small table.

"It's freezing in here." Seb set Eli down and pulled his coat tighter. "You didn't start a fire before your trek?"

"No reason to warm an empty house, is there?"

"There is when your comfort and health are at stake, Rachel." He stopped then. Studied her. His expression changed. "You don't want to spend extra money on coal."

"Frugality being a virtue," she reminded him.

"Not if it makes you ill. There are children counting on you. Every day."

"I don't want you to get sick, Miss Rachel." Wide-eyed, Eli gazed up at her. "Then we can't do fun stuff together."

"I shall take care to build a fire more quickly next time. Will that satisfy the two of you?"

"And be toasty warm? Yes!" Eli grinned up at her. She put a hand on his head and turned toward Seb.

"Safe and warm are good things." Voice soft, he gazed at her with such tenderness that she didn't think her heart could stand it. But then she wondered if he was simply skilled at these things, and her, naïve. Eli was living proof that Sebastian had charmed at least one heart before hers.

"They are, and I will take your concerns under advisement. It makes sense and a good teacher shares sensibilities as well as knowledge."

That didn't quite satisfy Seb. He peeled off his coat, and didn't leave until he'd gotten a fire started. And when he stoked the fire with an extra shovel of coal from the scuttle, she bit back a wince. She understood the value of warmth and held it dear to her heart, but she also comprehended the old saying of a penny saved is a penny earned. The more she could put by this coming winter, the greater her choices in the spring that followed. A man of means might not recognize the value of a dime here and a nickel there.

Rachel had grown up where warmth was scarce the first years and thrift was considered a true Christian quality. She bit back concern over the amount of coal as Seb pulled his coat back on. "Thank you, Seb. That was a lovely thing to do."

He locked eyes with her.

Did he read her concern? She hoped not, but when he grimaced slightly, she knew he did.

"It's the least I can do. You did take Eli on an adventure." He took Eli's hand in his and the boy offered him an ardent smile. "I thank you for that."

"And you made great progress on the bridge, which means we've all had a good day."

Eli yawned, a sure sign that dinner should be hurried. "We'll see you tomorrow." He held her gaze long enough to say more with his eyes.

She pretended not to see the intensity. "I will look forward to it, gentlemen." She closed the door and had to admit the added warmth felt good. So good.

But she'd laid out a savings plan and while it might be all right for a well-heeled businessman to throw coal around like it was a cheap commodity, she knew better.

Chapter Eleven

"L EVI." SEB HAILED RACHEL'S BROTHER as he rode into town the next morning. "A moment when you've put your horse up?"

Levi nodded, and when he came out of the back shed, he moved toward Seb.

Seb wasted no words. "I have a sincere interest in your sister Rachel, Levi."

Levi didn't look particularly surprised. "Does Rachel return this interest?"

"I believe she does."

"And?" Levi stretched out the word as he unlocked the door to the wagon-building shop he shared with his cousin Sol.

"I wanted you to know."

"Are you seeking my permission to court her?"

Seb was doing no such thing. "Hardly. Rachel's got a mind of her own. Hers is the only permission I seek."

Levi burst out laughing. "Then the two of you will suit because she would say much the same thing. But there is talk of you lately, Seb. And while I don't put my nose into Rachel's business, nor do a lot of talking myself, I've vowed to protect my sisters. Getting involved in any kind of scandal isn't something we take lightly."

"Nor I, but I may be related to people who aren't so

fastidious."

Levi locked eyes with him. "There are no scandals in your past, Seb? Nothing that could be mistaken for one?"

He meant the boy, of course, but Levi would simply have to trust Seb's words. "None other than a few customers who may have wanted top quality lumber for low quality prices."

Levi studied him for a few seconds, then replied, "Your word has always been good with me, Seb. Today is no different. So what can I do for you?"

Seb handed him a spot of cash. "I want Rachel's coal bin filled so she can stop worrying about every shovelful she uses. And a full jug of lamp oil to be delivered to her. While I admire her care with finances, having her come down sick from cold or tired from long nights of darkness would be dreadful. We've got several months of short days before things turn back our way. I want her comfortable, Levi. But I don't want to spread rumors or inspire loose talk."

"And that is the mark of a true gentleman."

Seb wasn't sure he was a true gentleman, but where Rachel was concerned, he wanted to be. "So you'll take care of it for me?"

"I will, but if Rachel asks, I will be truthful."

"As you should be. I don't mind Rachel's gratitude or affection. What I mind is gossip. For myself, I can brush it aside. But for her..." He splayed his hands. "That's a risk I don't care to take."

"Consider it done."

"Thank you." Seb left the wagon shop as Sol was coming in. He offered him a quick greeting and crossed to the hotel. He had arranged for his mother to look at two houses. One in town and one outside of town. When she met him at the hotel door, he pointed toward the center staircase. "The girls aren't coming?"

"Althea has studies she is reluctant to pursue and Cecily is overseeing them."

"An adversarial relationship, doomed from the beginning."

She laughed and tucked her arm through his. "Like oil and water, those two. If nothing else, living away from the Minneapolis gentry will offer Althea an alternative viewpoint."

"You are being generous, thinking the plight of normal people means something to my youngest sister. She loves being cossetted. It suits her."

"And that's been a problem for many years," Elizabeth agreed. "But every stone that touches the water produces a ripple that eventually licks the sand. So maybe a glimpse of normalcy will give her more to think on as she matures."

Seb couldn't envision it, but he wasn't about to argue the point. He'd been gone a long time. Maybe Althea had more generosity in her soul than he'd seen thus far. He could only hope that was the case. He took his mother east on Second Avenue, then turned left onto North Prairie Road. In town it was almost a road, but it turned into a north-bearing trail not far out of town, and there was talk of building another bridge further up the creek to allow for easier access to town for those whose claims were northwest of Second Chance. He hadn't intended to bid on the project, but now that the first bridge was nearly complete, his confidence had grown. Maybe he would bid on it, after all.

He showed her to the house and when she looked a little taken aback, he settled an arm around her shoulders. "It's quite different from what you've become accustomed to, I know."

She brought her chin up and squared her shoulders. "It looks well-kept, Seb, and that's the important thing." She said the words courageously, but he knew what she'd left behind in Minnesota. A lovely home. A terraced yard. A circle of busy but gossipy women who probably loved sharing stories of his father's philandering. A good reputation wasn't something easily given up and his mother would pay the price for his father's self-interests.

"It's in very good shape," he told her. "Mrs. Devereaux wasn't one to cut corners, so it's a solid home. But keeping it up, even with Ben's help, overwhelmed her. She's not in the best of health herself, so when her daughter invited her back to Ohio, she decided to go."

"That is a concern out here, isn't it?" noted his mother as the climbed the three steps.

"Not if you stay healthy." He grinned down at her and she batted his arm.

"Fortunately I am quite robust."

"Have you given thought to a trade for the girls?"

She answered as he unlocked the front door. "Not until recently, of course, and that's a flaw on my part. But yes, Cecily has a fine hand with a needle and can operate a sewing machine, so she's got potential. And the voice of an angel, so teaching young ones to sing or play piano could also offer opportunities. What she would like to do," she added with a slight note of disapproval, "is open her own newspaper, but I discouraged that instantly."

"Why?" he asked.

"The unseemliness of it when there are more cultured pursuits available."

Seb didn't like to disagree with his mother, but this instance required it. "The town's been longing for a newspaper of its own, or at least an informational," he told her. "I expect Cecily would have a quick clientele if she moves forward with that idea. There's something fortuitous about being the right person at the right time with the right ambition, isn't there?"

She turned toward him, surprised. "A woman running a business like that? Dealing with all kinds of people, dealing with men?" She paused, read his expression and sighed. "You think it's a fine idea and here I am, clinging to old-world thoughts and ways while a brave new pioneering spirit surrounds me."

He laughed and hugged her shoulders. "It is different here. Hattie McGillicuddy was one of the first settlers and she began a sewing business that has not only clothed the rail men and the West, she's brought in many an apprentice to work with her. I'd send Cecily right over there to talk because winter is a fine time to be practicing new skills. And Ginny runs the General Store now while her husband oversees their claim out near the Eichas claims. Women take on a lot of jobs out here, Mother. First, by necessity, then by choice."

"Rachel, the young school teacher. She's an Eichas, correct? So that must be the farm you spoke of."

"Yes. They have three adjacent claims and the sisters run the whole thing while their brother builds wagons here in town."

"Industry and effort. When did those become alien to me, Seb?"

"It's hard to worry about industry when there is a lot of money," he reminded her. "You've put great effort into child raising and philanthropy. Don't sell yourself short, Mother. I won't hear of it."

"You see me through the eyes of a loving son, Sebastian."

"Understandably, I hope." He winked at her. "Come see this kitchen. I'm intending on modeling my kitchen after this one because Henry Devereaux said his wife and mother were well pleased with it."

She crossed to the doorway and looked genuinely happy. "It is charming, Seb. The Hoosier cabinet, the built-in shelving, and a broad space for working dough or turning things out." She ran a hand over the long wooden work space and smiled. "A woman could have a lot of fun in this kitchen. And look at that." She sighed at the sight of the large Glenwood cook stove. "That's a high quality stove right there."

"I'll take your word for it because I get most of my meals

at the hotel. A habit which will change once my house is built."

"And you don't mind having the boy live with you, Seb? Because it shouldn't be expected, should it?" She searched his face as she posed the question.

"I can't imagine turning a child away," he answered mildly. "A trait I get from you, I believe."

She squeezed his arm, checked out the upstairs and faced him. "This will do nicely, Seb."

"You don't want to see the house out of town?" That house was also well built. The owners had moved on to Washington and needed to sell their home here. "It's a beauty."

"But then I have to deal with being out of town, harnessing up to come to town, and the girls being secluded. While there is a promise in that, I think being in town over the winter is much more to our liking. And that way we can see about Cecily working with the seamstress and I can keep Althea busy with something."

Seb doubted that.

"Three bedrooms upstairs and the stovepipe runs right through to bring warmth in the winter. And an additional parlor stove to even out the warmth. Necessary in a home this size."

It probably seemed small to her compared to their home in Minneapolis, but she gave a brisk nod as they moved outdoors. "It is a sweet home and it buys us time to consider our choices. I don't know what your father will decide to do. A part of me doesn't much care," she confessed as they exited the house and re-locked the door. "My concern is to keep the girls away from the worst of the gossip. It was bad enough when they were young, but youth was in their favor. Now that they're young women on the edge of adulthood, they're more understanding of what their father's done and that puts us all in an awkward situation."

Disdain rose up within Seb. "His weakness brings pain to the people he should love the most. He's a selfish, egotistical monster."

"Who is also your father. And theirs." She indicated the hotel where his sisters were staying. "If we wallow in anger, are we any better than the person who sinned against us?"

He knew the truth in her words. He thought he'd put aside anger at his father long ago. Eli's arrival, and now the scandal that brought his family west brought it gushing back, so maybe he hadn't put it truly to rest at all. "Shall I see to the arrangements for leasing the house?"

She shook her head. "I'll handle them myself. With so many women doing things on their own here, it's the perfect time for me to follow along. And I'll send Cecily to inquire with Hattie. If there's work enough, that would be a good enterprise for her."

"And Althea's schooling?"

She grimaced slightly. "I'll oversee the final year. She's quite bright but equally obstinate. In her mind a good catch of a husband is the answer to all her future needs."

Was he that rash at her age?

Seb knew he wasn't, but then he'd held his little brother in his arms as Artie cried for his mother with his final, strangling breaths. Seb had no choice but to give up childish thoughts at a very early age. "A year of maturity and seeing Father's true colors might fix that."

"I hope you're right."

He walked her to the agent's office, then moved on to the lumber yard in time for the ten-oh-three to arrive. And when Cedric Ward strode down the platform, looking like a bulldog after a bone, it was all Seb could do to keep from punching him.

"Where's your mother?" Cedric demanded loudly when he caught sight of Seb approaching the lumber cars.

Clearly he didn't care who heard. Seb did. He jumped to the platform and met his father face-to-face. "You came here, demanding to see the woman you humiliated throughout the streets of her hometown? To see what further havoc you could wreak on the daughters you treat like favorite pets until they discover that you're a lying cheat of a man and they should have nothing to do with you?"

Cedric threw a quick punch, but Seb was a head taller and had him by at least thirty pounds. He dodged right and the punch missed. But just in case his father wanted to throw another, Seb grabbed him by the front of his shirt, and it wasn't a loose hold, either. "Don't start what you can't finish, Father. I'm not the boy I was, not that you ever cared. But while you've been wining and dining simpering women to the dismay of your God-fearing family, I've been throwing lumber. Trust me." He held his father's gaze tight. Really tight. "The last thing you want to do right now is test my patience further." He released his father's shirt, but not his gaze. "And if you came to town thinking to make more trouble for them, me, or Eli, you'd better get right back on that train and head back to Minnesota. You've done enough harm already."

"You think you're someone?" His father snarled the words in a voice Seb remembered like it had been ten days. Not ten years. "You think I can't squash your little lumberyard between my hands like a pile of dust? Because I can, boy. Don't forget who sends you all this lumber to build your precious prairie."

"Everything that comes my way is bought and paid for and there's no small number of suppliers who would vie for this contract. I've already contacted two others," Seb replied smoothly. "We'll be negotiating prices quickly."

"You think it's that easy?" His father pierced him with a cold, hard look. "You think you can snap your fingers and others will jump on board? They won't, Seb. Not if I tell them not to. And that's exactly what I intend to do, after I've collected your mother and sisters."

He'd come to get them.

Not to apologize or woo their return.

But to gather them up like stray cattle and re-fence them. "You intend to make a scene here, where they at least have a vestige of self-respect remaining? Because you certainly negated that option for them back in Minneapolis, didn't you?"

"That's none of your concern."

"You made it my concern when you sent my new brother here," Seb corrected him in a cold, hard voice. "When you made me complicit with your back door dealings. But better that Eli be with me, where he can be loved and raised, than shrugged off into an orphan asylum. At least you had the decency to do that."

His father's flat expression gave Sebastian a clue.

"It wasn't your choice, was it? Someone forced your hand to find a spot for the boy."

"Doesn't matter how or why. He's here with you and out of my hands."

"Which is so much better than being with you, Father." He spoke softly but directly because no child deserved to be raised under Cedric Ward's iron fist and casual disregard. "There's a four-ten train coming through this afternoon. I suggest you get on it and head back where you came from. There is nothing for you here."

"We'll see about that." Cedric pushed by Seb.

The men had paused their work. They stared at his father, but when they shifted their attention back to Seb, genuine sympathy marked their expressions.

He said nothing.

What was there to say?

He followed his father toward the single hotel. Would the lumber baron have the decency to keep things civil?

Probably not, but he'd be there, by his mother's side, if things got out of hand. It was the least he could do.

Chapter Twelve

RACHEL TOOK ONE LOOK AT Seb's face that afternoon and sent Eli back into the school on a meaningless mission. "I need four slate pencils from the can on my desk. Would you be a darling and get them for me?"

"Sure!" They were half-way to her place. She handed him the key and he sprinted back toward the white-washed school as Seb drew close. "What's wrong, Seb? Is it the bridge?"

He shook his head. "The bridge is progressing. No, I had a surprise visit from my father."

"First your mother and sisters. And now your father." She set her hand on his arm. "It's always hard when there's strain in a family, Seb."

His expression darkened. "Well he's gone back to Minneapolis and my youngest sister went with him."

"And your mother and Cecily stayed?"

"There's nothing for them there, Rachel." He looked sad. So sad. But resigned, too. "Except for loose talk and speculation. There's no reason my mother should be subjected to gossip and ridicule because of my father's actions. Cecily understands that. Althea only sees the difference in comfort levels from their lives there to a winter here and would trade anything to be back to her life of gilded leisure."

"This must be so hard on your mother. Oh, Seb."

"My father tried to use Althea as reason for my mother to return."

Rachel understood the strong arm of an unloving father. "And still she stayed."

"After assuring Althea that she would always be welcome here."

A permanent separation. A willful young woman. "How can I help?"

He stared beyond her, then shrugged. "You already have. By being here. Helping with him." He indicated Eli with a shift of his chin. "Keeping him safe and sound is my first priority."

"And I am happy to help with that in any way possible."

Eli raced their way. His happy face glowed with success as he handed her the slate pencils. "One, two, three, four. Just like you said, Miss Rachel!"

"Exactly right, clever boy. Now let's get back to my place and put a few things right before it gets dark. And I expect a slice of bread with jam would taste good right about now, wouldn't it?"

"I am so hungry!"

"And delightfully normal, I'd say." Eli skipped off ahead of them. She reached out a hand to Seb's arm once again. "Seb, I will pray for Althea's wisdom and her safety. A headstrong girl left to her own devices without an ardent guardian is trouble in the making."

He considered her words as they fell into step together. "Althea thinks her road to a good life is in a good match. A rich husband will keep her in the style she's grown used to. And then there's Cecily who wants to learn the sewing trade from Hattie. One filled with industry. And the other..."

"Time will tell," she reminded him. "At sixteen we're all a little crazy, aren't we?" The look he gave her said no, so she amended her statement. "Well, most of us, Seb. Such a time of change and growth and yearning. She might grow to be quite the different person in a year or two."

He didn't look convinced. "I'm afraid she is too much like my father. The rest of us were different. Perhaps kinder is the word I'm looking for. But Althea is her father's daughter, through and through."

She caught one phrase in particular. "The rest of you? Are there more siblings than you and Cecily?"

His look sobered. Pain darkened his gaze. He dipped his chin slightly. "There was, once. A brother. Younger than me by four years. A good, solid boy with a heart of gold. His name was Artie and he counted on me to look after him."

"Oh, Seb." She took his hand in hers and didn't dare think of how natural it felt to hold this strong man's hand in hers. "I'm so very sorry."

"He died at the lumberyard in Minnesota. He was eight years old."

No wonder the thought of Eli around the lumber and the rails made him a little crazy. "What a tragedy for all of you."

"He shouldn't have been there. Neither of us should have been there, but a Ward son was put to work early on to learn the business. Except by the time we were youngsters, the business had grown and danger lurked at every turn. I tried to tell my father to let Artie stay home. He was little and he couldn't keep his head wrapped around things, but my father thought he was soft. Molly-coddled, he called it. And then..." His voice trailed. He gazed off, looking heartsick. "He was gone."

"We shall be extra vigilant with Eli and any of the local youngsters when it comes to the busyness of the rails and the lumberyard. We'll work to keep them safe," she promised. "All of them."

He watched as Eli chased a field mouse, darting to and fro through the grass. "Accidents happen. I know this." He

spoke softly, as if he'd come to terms with this reality long
ago. "Life doesn't come with guarantees. But to deliber-
ately put a child in harm's way isn't of God. It's the evil of
man that treats a child's life with careless abandon."

She'd thought him hard-working and overly ambitious.

He was industrious and ambitious, but the compassion
that colored his gaze and tone painted a very different picture, one that reflected his care for Eli. Seb Ward would be
a fine father. The kind who provided for his family and
loved them, unconditionally. How could she have thought
otherwise?

Because you are quick to assess others by your own experiences.
Maybe you need to broaden your views as well.

The mental scolding held truth.

"I'm heading back to the bridge to work with the men
for ninety minutes. That is, if you don't mind keeping Eli
with you?"

"Not at all."

"Thank you, Rachel." He placed his other hand over
hers, and gazed down. "You have no idea what that means
to me. To us." Eli's shouts punctuated his statement.

"To me as well, Seb." She lifted her chin and locked eyes
with him on purpose. "It means a great deal to me, too."

His gaze brightened. A smile softened his jaw. "Well,
then." The smile grew. "That is good to know. I must go."
He squeezed her hand lightly, but he didn't want to leave
her. Leave them. She saw it in his face, but duty called.

She took Eli to the house, started a fire, and when she
opened the coal bin from the trap door inside, she stopped
and stared.

The bin was full to capacity.

And there, on the shelf to the left of the hanging hooks,
was a freshly filled jug of lamp oil. Two commodities that
went a long way to ease the dark and cold of a prairie winter had been put up for her.

She crossed to the wagon shop through the adjoining

door while Eli practiced his 'at' words on a slate. "Levi, you filled my coal bin? And my lamp oil? How kind of you, but that wasn't expected. You know that a teacher gets an allowance of both."

Sol looked up from the blacksmith side of the shop. He said nothing, but quirked one brow, then went back to work.

"A small allowance, I believe," Levi replied, but he kept his gaze down and went right on sanding a lovely piece of hard maple.

"Yes, but frugality is a virtue, isn't it?"

"Frugality is. Freezing isn't."

"It was kind of you, brother. Most kind. But I really want to make this happen on my own, without—"

Sol cleared his throat, nice and loud. This time the eyebrow went up and he folded his arms, gazing at Levi.

"What's going on?" She looked from Sol to her brother and back. "You're acting oddly. Both of you."

Levi paused his work. Then looked up. "It is possible I was simply a middleman for another's purpose. Someone who wants you healthy and warm throughout the winter."

Seb.

The heat that rose to her cheeks made them plenty warm. "Levi..."

"Rachel, the rest is up to you. I was simply following the instructions of a kind gesture. But it was one I happily followed because he was right. Safe and warm are two things we should all be able to count on with winter approaching."

Sol dipped his head back to his work, but not before she read his smile.

Men of few words surrounded her, but maybe showing their emotions with action instead of words was a better portion in the long run. "I've got to get back to Eli. And maybe I'll have a surprise in store for his guardian when he finishes work."

"There is the matter of reputation involved here," Levi said softly. It was a prudent reminder. "Loose talk is just that if the fire isn't fed."

He was right, of course. She could risk her job just by being kindly and she didn't dare do that.

"I think watching the boy is a noble thing. But after seeing the tempest on the depot platform when Cedric Ward rolled into town this morning, I'd take care, Rachel. Care enough to let things simmer down," he went on. "Seb's a good man. But his father makes our father seem easy by comparison. And he wasn't afraid to use very loud threats to make his point be known."

So Cedric Ward had made a public scene? What a shame for his family. "You are a good and dear brother and I'll take your words to heart." She kissed him on the cheek. The move surprised him. They'd been raised in an unaffectionate home and while the sisters often embraced one another, Levi had never been one to show emotions. "And thank you for sparing my reputation by being the go-between. I shall think of both you and Seb as I work on lessons each evening in a warm, snug set of rooms."

She went back to the two-room apartment, fully expecting Eli to be seated at the table, working away.

Eli was nowhere to be seen.

She called his name.

Nothing.

She hurried out back to check the necessary.

No Eli.

She stared off, into the wooded creek bank where they'd walked to gather leaves and nuts and fallen items to make a present for Seb. Would Eli have gone off on his own?

No.

She winced as realization set in.

Of course he might. Any youngster might, when unattended, right after she'd made a solemn pledge to help guard his safety.

Her heart sped up. Her hands flexed. She stared at the darkening creek. Shadows had grown long and deep in the scant time she'd been inside. She turned to scan the road. A short distance away the sound of bridge building echoed through the late-day quiet.

Where would he go? Would he follow the hammer's sound and run to Seb? What would a little boy do?

She started for the creek, then spied a light diagonally across Second Avenue. A warm light that spilled onto the narrow boardwalk lining the side road. A light that beckoned.

She headed that way and when she opened the door to Hattie's sewing shop, there was Eli, happily seated on a stool, munching a biscuit from Hattie's green tin. "Eli. What have you done, coming over here without permission? And without telling me?"

Guilt lifted his brows in surprise. "Uh oh."

"Uh oh doesn't begin to describe how worried I was," she scolded as she closed the door against the evening chill. "I came back from the wagon shop and you were just gone, without a word. You can't do that, young man. Ever."

Bright tears filled his eyes.

Be strong. Better they cry now than you cry later. Wise words from her grandmother, long years before. She hardened her resolve against his winsome show of emotion. "What have you to say for yourself?" Arms folded, she stood her ground when what she really wanted to do was grab him and hug him, happy he was safe and sound.

"I had to go to the necessary."

She stood silent, waiting.

"And I came out and saw Hattie's light and she told me I could come by for a cookie anytime." His gaze flew up to Hattie on the far side of the sewing counter. "So I ran over and beminded her about the cookie and she said as long as it didn't spoil my supper and it won't, Miss Rachel. I promise!"

"Oh, Rachel, I had no idea he'd come across without permission." Hattie said, bemused. "I knew you were watching him this week and simply went with the proximity of a boy and a cookie."

"This isn't your fault, Miss Hattie." Rachel assured Hattie in a kinder voice before she turned her attention back to Eli. "But Eli needs to know that when a grown-up gives a direction it is to be followed. That's what keeps children safe in a world fraught with danger. Runaway horses, trains, workmen and laborers, none of which are expecting a child to dart forth."

"You are absolutely right," Hattie told her. She sent a more silent message with her eyes. "And the next time Eli darkens my door, I shall ascertain that he's got permission to be here."

"I am certain his family and I would both be gratified by that extra note of caution," Rachel replied.

"Oh, Miss Rachel!" Eli slipped off the stool and raced her way. He wrapped his arms around her and clung tight, not just to her dress... but her heart. Such a dear, precious child. "I didn't mean to make you worry, okay? I'll try to be good every minute. Every single one. I promise so much!"

She bent low and wrapped her arms around him. "I need exactly that. Grown-ups have much to do and disobedient children put themselves in danger. I don't want anything to happen to you, Eli. Neither does your—" She stopped herself before she said the word 'father', but when Hattie lifted a sympathetic brow, Rachel knew she understood. "Neither does Seb. Or Miss Hattie. We all want you safe. Is that understood?" She drew back, staying stern and hating every single minute of it, but Seb was right. A loose boy was a danger to himself and maybe others.

"Yes, ma'am."

"Good." She hugged him again, and breathed a silent 'thank you' to Hattie. Hattie had lost her family years back.

She'd come west because living in Massachusetts with the pain of lost children had taken her down a dark and lonely road. Here, as one of the first settlers in Second Chance, she'd led the way for others to begin anew. "Say thank you to Hattie for the cookie, then head back to my place where a very lonely slate lies waiting a scholarly effort."

He nodded, glum, but thanked Hattie and criss-crossed the street a few moments later.

Rachel turned to Hattie. "Thank you for your kindnesses to him."

"Well, I can hardly resist that sweet face and his circumstances. And seeing Seb torn by his father's antics and what that elder Ward has put his family through in Minnesota makes me realize that the sanctity of a small town, a bit removed, is a wonderful buffer zone."

Obviously the news of Cedric Ward's scene and shenanigans traveled, even in a tiny place like Second Chance. "Levi mentioned a fracas on the platform."

"More than one, with Sebastian's sister having her say about a wretched little town with nothing to offer anyone of substance."

Rachel grimaced as she reached for the door handle. "Hattie, there are some folks who think of Sebastian as prideful with the way he keeps to himself. These scenes could add fuel to an already smoking fire."

"Straight to simmering now, I'd say, but good folks won't jump to conclusions and those that will are best ignored. Of course that isn't always possible in a town this size."

It wasn't.

"I heard that your sister is taking tips on midwifery," Hattie added in a quick change of subject.

"I had a book sent and she's avidly studying. She and Ann both, I believe."

"We could use that kind of service here now, with so many new folks coming into town. A midwife would be a wonderful thing and I was glad to hear that the Eichas sisters had taken initiative."

"Dear Hattie, I'm not so sure it was initiative or simple fear of the unknown. Either way, we women need to take care of one another, don't we?" Rachel hugged Hattie goodbye and hurried back to the apartment where a chastened little boy copied letters onto his slate. She wanted to hug him. Tell him how glad she was that he was safe.

She didn't, though, because she didn't dare make light of his cavalier choices to chase off. Grandmother's words about crying made perfect sense.

A few tears now might save a lifetime of anguish later, so Rachel turned up the lamp and brought out her sixth grade planner. She took a seat near Eli and together they worked for nearly a half-hour before Seb came to the door. But when the little fellow turned and hugged her legs... then peeked up and apologized again... she knew she was right to stand her ground. And just as right to fall head over heels in love with this boy and maybe... just maybe... the handsome guardian at her door.

"Thank you for the gift of warmth and light, Sebastian."

He looked surprised, then a tiny bit uncomfortable. "Your brother said he'd have to tell if asked. Which means you asked."

"Let's just say that Levi is not exactly the kind to cover things well. It was a kind and thoughtful thing to do, Seb, and I'm grateful."

He took her hand.

Oh, her heart...

It sped up, and when he raised her hand to his mouth in the sweetest of gestures, her pulse hitched a beat. "I want you safe and warm and happy, Rachel. Knowing that you are makes me content."

"I can't think why," she whispered as Eli came their way.

"Can't you?" His eyes twinkled into hers. His left brow lifted ever so slightly. And the tiniest smile tweaked his mouth. "I expect you can. Given significant effort," he finished, teasing, and she felt heat rise to her cheeks. "Thank you for watching my little friend."

His friend.

Her heart cooled.

Eli deserved to be who he was. What he was. To call him a 'friend' minimized the relationship and the trust, didn't it?

She withdrew her hand quietly. "I am happy to help with Eli anytime. He is a delightful boy."

Eli peeked a guilty look her way. She ruffled his hair and didn't speak of his escapade. "See you tomorrow."

"Okay!" He grabbed Seb's hand. His tiny fingers were dwarfed by the big man's hand, and Seb held tight. That meant the child mattered, but not enough to be forthright about who he was?

That disappointed her because in the end, the truth did set one free. Pretending a life was living a lie, wasn't it? And what good could possibly come from that?

None, she knew.

She closed the door snugly, then thwarted the west wind by tucking a thick piece of old flannel along the bottom.

She didn't like family discord. She and her sisters had grouped together as a defense against her father's autocracy. They'd kept each other sane, if truth be told. Seeing the unrest in a rich family like the Wards simply proved that money didn't buy joy. Joy comes from the Lord, the gift of faith, hope and love.

And yet Seb's love for his family was evident, so wherein lay the truth? And was she being impatient?

Yes, because her heart was involved and this was the first time her heart had ever been tempted in such ways.

I will lift up mine eyes unto the hills, from whence cometh my help. My help cometh from the Lord, which made heaven and earth.

The sweet words of the 121st Psalm came to her.

She didn't need all the answers at this moment. She

needed faith and hope and the sweet industry of her hands. She was in no huge hurry to give up the independence she'd dreamed of for long, hard-working years on the windswept prairie. She'd learn how to take care of herself here. Become experienced. And then make decisions.

That's what she told herself, but as she climbed into bed and doused the light a short while later, the thought of Seb's gaze... and his hand, holding hers... stirred a different kind of longing.

She repressed it purposely.

She had a job to do, at least for a full school term. For the first time in her life Rachel was a free, independent woman and that wasn't a post she'd give up lightly.

Chapter Thirteen

ORDER REFUSALS AND A DIMINISHING supply of lumber had Seb boarding a train for Minneapolis ten days later.

His father had been true to his word and three major lumber suppliers refused to ship him lumber. But despite the weight the lumber barons carried, there were smaller mills along the rail lines and the great Mississippi, and Seb intended to find one to suit his needs and fill his orders.

"Seb, I would be happy to watch the boy for you." His mother had come across Main Street early to see him off. "It's silly to send him elsewhere."

"Whereas I was thinking prudent," he replied, then kissed her cheek. "You've had enough scandal of late, Mother. Hattie is happy to watch him and this way he can go to school with Rachel and come home with her."

"She is an amazing woman, Seb."

"She is, and if she's as wise as she is beautiful, she might be smart to maintain a distance." It wasn't what he wished, but it might be what a smart woman would do. "No one walks willingly into Cedric Ward's crossfire."

"You give your father too much credit and yourself too little." She gripped his hand. "It's good to be aware of him. But not good to fear him for the Lord, our God is on our side. And I pray daily that your father will someday have a change of heart."

"For your sake, I agree." The likelihood of his father having a change of heart was slim, but his mother didn't need his negativity. She needed his strength.

"Not for my sake, dear son." She reached up and kissed his cheek. "But for his. Damnation is a long and fearsome choice."

"He's free to choose kindness or valor, but he's disinclined toward either," he replied. "I'll be back as soon as I can."

"Go with God, Sebbie."

The old name made him smile.

She hadn't called him that in a long while. It sounded right, coming from her. It took two days of travel and the inspection of five smaller mills before he found one that matched his standards and pricing. And when he did, he inked the deal on the spot. He had four hours before the westbound train, so he took a quick turn around the town. The General Store wasn't the small operation Ginny ran in Second Chance. It was a large store, taking up three building lots with a generous upstairs for family living, and the store was well-stocked with all kinds of provisions. He ordered a barrel of apples for his mother and sister and one for Rachel, then sacks of nuts as well, two things he couldn't buy in Second Chance. Then he added twin sacks of raisins and barrels of milled oats and cornmeal to his order. And when an ivory calico dotted with pink and gold flowers caught his eye, he had to buy it for Rachel.

She might think him forward, but the thought of her wearing the joyful pattern pleased him. He wanted to bring joy to her life. Unfortunately, joy wasn't a strong suit in the Ward family dictionary of late. When the savvy clerk cut a dress length of the calico, she held a beautiful handmade shawl against it, done in a slightly deeper shade of rose. A shade that would look lovely against Rachel's soft brown hair.

The shawl got packaged right along with the dress goods, and it pleased him to do it.

He bought a hat for Eli and a warm coat, too. And some lined pants, the kind little boys needed to run outside and play. Eli would need boots, too, but Seb had no idea how to figure out what size so he decided to have Ginny order them.

By the time everything was packed and sent to the train, he'd lightened his wallet and his heart. He'd found a supplier, stocked up on goods to please his family, and a couple of new shirts for himself.

When the train pulled into Second Chance, and his purchases unloaded, he felt good. Right up until a young prairie man hopped up onto the wooden deck and spat at his feet. "Stinkin' no good price gouger. You Wards think you control everything. Well you don't. And you never will. No matter how much money you've got to throw around or where you settle in the West. You're disgusting."

Then he strode off.

Seb stared after him.

He'd seen the man months before, a new settler who acted insulted by Seb's prices and the lack of competition. Was he still angry over that, six months later?

As he gathered his small bag and hoisted one of the wooden barrels, a woman passed by. She nailed him with a scathing look, averted her gaze and stomped by as if passing a despicable creature from a Dickens novel.

He toted things to the lumberyard.

Old Ben met him right off, with Tom not far behind. "There's trouble brewin', boss, and folks are up in arms."

He didn't want more trouble, but that didn't seem to be an option. "What's happened?"

"The town got wind that you bought that property along the rails."

Seb frowned. "It wasn't a secret."

"No, but the reason they found out was because Bill

Harley showed up and complained to the town that you blocked his business venture and that you were exercising some kind of influence over the town because you had money and no one else much did," Tom explained, "there-fore creating your own little monopoly."

Scorned for investing in the town. Scorned for protect-ing his business.

"We knowed you weren't meanin' no harm, Seb, but some folks don't necessarily see it that way," added Ben. "They think you're bein' all proud because you're a Ward, so you're throwin' your weight around."

Anger pierced him. "The same weight that stuck it out during horrible years when we all wondered how to put food on the table and keep our businesses going?"

"And that's what they need to hear, boss, about loyalty and standin' ground," the older man said frankly. "There's a council meeting tonight. I'll stand with you. No one in this town's got a gripe with Ward Lumber exceptin' Bill Harley and a few folks always lookin' for somethin' for nothin'. And Harley's just mad that he got outfoxed and rich enough to make trouble about it."

"I'll help take stuff up the stairs, Seb." One of the younger workers eyed the barrels and sacks he'd unloaded from the train.

Seb pointed to a few items. "If you could grab a hand cart and take these over to the old Devereaux house, I'd be obliged. My mother and sister will be staying there for the winter. I'll have one of them run over with a key."

"Sure will." He loaded the things onto a cart and hauled them off.

"And this stuff, boss?" Ben noted the other barrels and sacks and one well-wrapped package sitting on top.

"Those are for Rachel." He indicated the assorted bar-rels and the other things he'd purchased for her. "I'll run them across the road. But this lot stays here." He handed Ben the wrapped parcels of clothing for Eli and him and a few other items. "If you don't mind putting them upstairs, Ben."

"Glad to."

He hauled the apple barrel to Rachel's door first, then took a couple of trips to and walk the additional items across the street. Will Barber met him as the pastor crossed toward the church. He looked at the barrels, then Seb, then the packages.

And then he grinned.

That almost got him punched because Seb wasn't in a grinning kind of mood. When the top package began to slip from his grasp, Will reached out and caught it. He righted the package and faced Seb. "There we go. No harm done."

"Except that the whole town is angry over a simple real estate transaction and wants me tarred and feathered for protecting my business."

Will lifted one brow. "The whole town you say?" He glanced toward the parsonage, then Rachel's door, and then the wagon shop. "Perhaps an exaggeration because I know of no one in town who feels that way. And you can stop this in its tracks by going to the meeting tonight and saying your piece."

"I've been saying my piece by my actions for over a decade, Will." Seb set the packages atop the barrels and crossed his arms. "Good solid lumber, at a fair price. Isn't that evidence enough?"

"Growth brings competition."

"Says the pastor of the only church in town," Seb noted drily.

"There's a Lutheran church in the planning now," Will answered. "They plan to break ground on Pearl Street next spring."

Seb hadn't known that, but it didn't make a difference. Or did it?

"You did nothing wrong, Seb," Will counseled. "I know

that. But the appearance of wrongdoing can be just as damaging as the deed, and that's something to consider. Don't let a few hotheads change your focus. You're an asset to this town so swallow your pride, go to the meeting and state your case."

He didn't want to state anything of the kind. Mostly he wanted to be left alone to run his business and live his quiet solitary life but that all changed when a scared little boy climbed off the train long weeks back. "I'll show up but my pride will be quite intact, thank you."

"And I'll be there to support you. As well as others, I'm sure."

The last thing he wanted was a town spectacle, but there appeared to be little choice in the matter.

Ben called to him from the lumberyard. School would be out soon, so he left the supplies on Rachel's step, then re-crossed the road. He checked two orders, discussed the new supplier specs with Ben, then went up the road to check the final workings on the bridge base. Once the base was complete the final rails would be installed and the bridge would be ready for crossing.

The fresh wood slats gleamed in the late-day sun. He'd based the design on Howe's patent and the finished product was a solid work of human hands, a bridge that would span decades. He'd brought in chemically treated wood to withstand hot sun, heavy winter snows and long, cold spring rains, believing the longevity justified the expense.

And yet people doubted him.

The shouts of children drew his attention as school let out.

He walked that way. He wanted to see Eli.

You mean Rachel, his conscience scolded.

Both, he decided. And when he spotted her closing up the school, he increased his speed.

He'd missed her. He'd missed the boy. He'd never much missed anything before, not since Artie died, but these last few days had been filled with sharp longing.

She saw him coming and paused, on the top step. The autumn wind puffed her gown and wisped her hair into tiny, feathered ringlets around her cheeks, and the urge to tame that hair and kiss those cheeks and then her mouth...

Her sweet, beautiful mouth...

Swept over him.

"Seb!" Eli raced his way and launched himself into Seb's arms. He caught the boy up, tossed him up, onto his shoulders, and laughed when Eli shrieked.

"How's that for a ride, my friend?" he asked Eli as he moved toward Rachel.

"It's so fun! I want to ride up high on your shoulders all the time I think!" He screeched the words. His little fingers clung to a mix of Seb's collar and his hair, but Seb didn't mind. The boy's joy invigorated him. Somehow, someway, God had given him a second chance to look after a child. To be the protector and steward of a boy's well-being, so when the pinch of his collar and tug of his hair sent a jab of pain, he welcomed the opportunity that came along with it.

"You're back."

"I missed you."

She blushed and dropped her gaze, but he brought it back up by tipping her chin gently with one hand while the other kept hold of Eli's feet.

She lifted her eyes to his, and if it wasn't broad daylight in the middle of the street with a boy riding his shoulders, he'd kiss her. And he might just go on kissing her, which meant he better make a proposal and get that house built because a woman like Rachel deserved a warm house. Cozy rooms. And a fine husband. Right now, gazing down, he wanted to be that husband.

"I missed you, too! I fink I missed you like this much!" Eli went to throw his arms wide, messed up the balance, and began to topple off of Seb's shoulders.

"Whoa, buddy!" Seb caught him with one arm and managed to spin him around before the boy landed face first on the ground. He set Eli onto his feet and cupped his chin. "Gotta remember to hang on up there, okay?"

"I forgot!"

"You did. But next time you'll remember," Seb promised him. "That's the way of learning, I suppose."

"Did you know I'm so fast? Like super fast, Seb?"

"I did not know that," Seb admitted. He shared a smile with Rachel. "Am I to get a demonstration of your speed?"

"Yes!" The boy laughed as if Seb's guess was the most wonderful thing, then he took off running.

His hat went flying, but Eli didn't stop until he got to Rachel's door. The sight of packages and barrels made him dash right back. "You've got stuff at your door, Miss Rachel! A lot of stuff!"

She saw the items as they drew closer. "Seb Ward, what have you done? You'll have people talking and there are a few who do more than their share of that already."

"If they're talking about us, and about what a fine match we'd make, then it's all right."

She stopped dead. Looked up at him. And when she swallowed hard, he knew he didn't want to hear what she was about to say. "I'm not comfortable being the object of others' conversations, Seb."

"Nor am I," he admitted. "But it seems I have little choice of late."

She looked at him, then Eli as he examined the packages on top of the big, broad barrel. "We always have a choice. It's living with the choices we've made that can be hard. But doable." She smiled Eli's way. "He is a beautiful child, Seb. A true gift from God, as is every baby born."

She thought Eli was his.

It was on the tip of his tongue to blurt out the truth, but his sister's voice hailed from down the road.

"Seb! You've returned." Cecily came his way with hurried steps. "And no doubt heard all the scuttlebutt around town about your land purchase."

Rachel looked at Cecily, then Seb, puzzled. "You've bought land?"

"A piece near the railroad for business expansion."

"Except that's not how some folks are seeing it, and Mother is fit to be tied," Cecily continued. "She doesn't like hearing your name abused at the hands of others and she's become quite protective."

"I think I'm old enough to handle myself," said Seb, but the disappointed look in Rachel's eye offered warning. "There's no reason for people to be upset in any case."

"Then you'll be explaining that to them because the talk at the General Store hasn't gone in your favor, Seb." Cecily sounded upset and defensive. "But then who pays heed to those types? Not us, certainly."

Pride laced her voice and Will's words came back to Seb. He'd advised humility earlier, and Seb had thought him wrong. Cecily's haughty tone showed him otherwise.

Rachel noted it, too. He read her expression. She faced Cecily. "It is mostly those types who make up the prairie, of course. Who build the homes and the farms and stake the claims. Simple folks, like those the good Lord brought to his side as disciples."

Cecily looked affronted, then embarrassed. "I'm sorry. I didn't mean harm, it's just that hearing people talk about Seb as if he's cold-hearted makes my blood boil because he might be a private person but he's got the biggest heart there is."

"Then your blood needs to cool down," Seb told her. "My customers are my bread-and-butter. They're what keep this town going. And I'll go to the meeting tonight and see what the fuss is about."

"Do you need me to watch Eli for you?" asked Rachel, which meant she wouldn't be coming to the meeting. Was that to avoid the tumult or to distance herself from him?

Either one, possibly. "I'd appreciate it. Hopefully the meeting won't go overlong."

It was then that Cecily noticed the packages at Rachel's door. Her eyes went wide because the barrels on Rachel's stoop matched theirs. She slid Seb a knowing look, then took his arm. "I'm helping Mother get settled in the new house, but we both intend to be at the meeting."

"And make it a bigger deal than it needs to be?" Sometimes less was better, but it was a Ward trait to go bigger and bolder.

"I prefer to think of it as supporting someone we love."

"You cannot fault that." Rachel spoke softly.

She was correct to a point. "Cecily, I appreciate your defense. Mother's, too. But I'd prefer that you and Mother stay away tonight. Sometimes the least said is soonest mended and if we treat it lightly, perhaps others will realize that's how it should be. More people can add more fuel to a smoldering fire and that's exactly what Father wants to happen. Let's not give him the satisfaction."

"How about if I keep Eli here for supper and then you can gather him up once the meeting has run its course," suggested Rachel.

"But I wanted Seb to have supper wif me." Eli had been off chasing after a pair of mallard ducks that had paused by the nearby creek. "I've been missing him."

Seb gave the boy a stern look. "Do not argue with grown-ups, young man. If Miss Rachel is kind enough to mind you while I conduct business, then you need to follow the directions she gives you. Is that understood?"

"Yes, sir." Eli sighed, then tucked his head against Seb's upper leg. "I just was missing you so much."

Seb's somewhat reclusive heart inched wider. The love of a child was something he hadn't planned or expected, and here it was, his for the taking. And no matter what people thought of the situation, he was blessed to have this boy in his home. "And I, you." He stooped low and took Eli into his arms.

He'd never been hugged like this by his father. He'd never ridden on Cedric's shoulders or run around the yard or thrown a ball back and forth, so hugging Eli was a new and wonderful thing. The kind of thing that made a man stand taller and work harder because someone small was counting on him. "I'll see you later, all right?"

Eli nodded, and when Rachel asked him to carry the lighter packages into the apartment, the boy took the task with eager hands.

"I'll see you tonight, brother. And nice to see you again, Miss Eichas." Cecily gave Rachel a polite nod, then noted the apple barrel. "I expect you're a good baker?"

Rachel eyed the barrel of apples as well. "I am, and apple desserts are among my favorites. Now if only there were raisins to go with..." She lifted a waxed sack and smiled when she spotted dark, sweet raisins inside. "I see apple strudel and bread pudding in the future. And cinnamon raisin bread is always a Sunday treat."

"Recipes we'd love to try," Cecily assured her. "My mother hasn't baked in a lot of years. She's anxious to begin again, but recipes are scant."

"Then I will gladly share ours," Rachel told her. "It's always more fun to share, isn't it?"

"It is."

Cecily pulled her wrap tighter and headed toward North Prairie Road.

Seb hoisted the apple barrel and brought it into Rachel's rooms. Then he did the same with the smaller barrels and packages.

She set Eli to work on a number chart while Seb started a fire, and when he straightened, she was watching him.

What did she see? he wondered.

The hard-edged businessman who secured available property to thwart competition? Or the smart entrepreneur who knew there wasn't enough business for two lumberyards as yet and wanted to protect his hard work and investment?

Two accurate, yet diverse opinions.

"I thank you for the provisions, Sebastian."

She'd never said his full name before, and his heart melted when she did because she didn't say it the way a mother would.

The way those three syllables rolled off her tongue was quite different, indeed.

"You have taken great care to make sure your neighbor has light and heat and now food."

"Perhaps because my neighbor is a touch too careful with her funds and I want nothing bad to ever befall her. Not hunger." He took her hands in his and wished he never had to let them go. "Not darkness." He kissed the back of each hand, gently, and let his mouth linger just a little. Just enough. "And not the chill of winter."

"I'm feeling quite warmed at present," she told him, but she drew her hands back with purpose. "But your generosity will not go unnoticed by others and my position here is on approval. What will the school board think? And the parents, too?"

He had other ideas about what she should be doing. Marrying him. Making him the happiest man in the world. Having babies that would toddle after Eli, trying to keep up with their big brother. "Anyone who disapproves of donating food to the teacher is a selfish person deserving of no regard."

"A simple stand when one has money," she reminded him mildly. "When one is frugal by necessity, a hard stand is not as easily embarked upon."

She was right, and he had angry people to face. He kissed Eli goodbye and when the little man showed his affection in a fierce, sweet hug, Seb was pretty sure he could face anyone. Then he saw Rachel studying him and Eli, and his confidence waned.

He knew what she thought about his relationship to the boy. What they all thought. But why would people think it was their business at all?

It is her business if you're intending on courting her. You want her to blindly trust you and disbelieve her eyes, but what is marriage based on if not love and trust?

Are you testing her, like you've been tested? Because that doesn't seem fair.

He walked to the meeting, head down, pondering that thought.

She wanted to trust him, and yet he hadn't trusted her enough to be truthful about Eli. About his parents. Rachel would keep the knowledge to herself. She had a heart that cared for the weary and she wasn't one for idle gossip.

But he hadn't yet told her the truth, and maybe that meant he was the one with the problem after all.

Chapter Fourteen

HE STRODE INTO THE CHURCH building when Will opened the door. A dozen men followed. Five were members of the town council.

Others showed up quickly. He recognized the man from the train depot. And the angry woman, too, although he didn't recall their names.

Mr. and Mrs. Martin came in alongside Baxter Smith. Ben sidled in, not the kind of man to get involved, which made his presence even more important. Tom was on the board. He'd already taken a place up front. Silas Pritchard came in, and Ginny and Red from the General Store filed in, too.

By the time the meeting was slated to begin at six, the church was half full.

He'd had no idea there were that many people to stand against him.

He stood in the back, shoulders squared while seven separate people angrily addressed the council.

They accused him of price-fixing. Of sabotage, forcing his former competition out of business four years before. They cited buying the adjacent property before Harley could close the deal as a continuing pattern of thwarting free enterprise.

And then the angry woman stood to address the council.

"We're God-fearing people in this town," she began, and she had the nerve to turn and face him head on. "We're church-goers with families. We don't let things get out of hand and we follow the Good Book."

Several people nodded agreement.

The woman pointed a finger at Seb. "Your life is your own, Mr. Ward. I'll give you that. But when your sinful ways come to fore in our sweet town, then the time for your free ride is over. Not only do you take advantage of your singular place of business, holding landowners hostage, but you've defiled the sanctity of family, first for yourself and now by your attentions to Miss Eichas. I made no approval for putting a woman in the slot of schoolteacher to begin with, but to have her dalliance with a known womanizer in front of the whole town, and in particular the town's children, is reprehensible."

Seb's neck caught fire.

His palms itched.

Was she seriously impugning Rachel's good name in front of this group?

"I move that we advise the school board to remove Miss Eichas from her position immediately, and that the school be closed until a suitable replacement can be found."

"You can't be serious." Seb moved toward the front as he spoke. "This meeting isn't about Rachel Eichas or what she's doing. Ostensibly it's about me protecting my business by buying a piece of property. One has nothing to do with the other."

"Seb makes a good point, Mrs. Johnson," noted a council member.

Johnson...

Seb's brain made the connection at last. Mrs. Johnson was part of the small enclave of families just northeast of town. Not as far out as Cutter's Crossing, but not close, either. "This is an informational meeting. Not an inquest. We're convened simply to see if matters of business were conducted in a way that is detrimental to the town's welfare."

"Funny that the council never held a meeting during the rough years when Seb Ward, myself and others squeaked by with nothing to show for it and not much in the larder, either." Hattie McGillicuddy had been sitting quietly in the back of the room, knitting. She didn't set the knitting aside, nor did she stand, but her quiet words commanded attention. "No one held meetings to commend the local businesses for their combined efforts to stay afloat when Western commerce ground to a halt after bouts of bad weather and plagues of locusts and failed enterprise. Doesn't anyone here see a correlation for how this all came about at the same time Cedric Ward stormed into town, yelling about this, that and the other thing?"

Several council members exchanged looks.

"This council sits to oversee the town," she went on, "but heaven save us from a town and a council that ties a business owner's hands by needing to negotiate and/or inform the council of every little thing."

"Thwarting business investment isn't a little thing, Hattie." Sam Hirsch ran the livery stable not far from the hotel and had sat on the council for half-a-dozen years. He clasped his hands and leaned forward. "But you make a valid point."

"A point because they're in cahoots!" Mrs. Johnson crossed her arms over her chest and glared at Seb, then the council. "When we needed lumber for our barn, it was either pay Ward prices or not build. When folks tire of living in a soddy or a dugout and want to build a home, it's Ward lumber or nothing. That's a monopoly if ever there was one."

Seb's head ached, but her thin-skinned words almost urged a smile. He faced her and the council, trying to stay calm when he really wanted to throw something. "One business in one small town isn't a monopoly, ma'am. It's an enterprise. And when there were two lumberyards years back, we both suffered. I bought them out and like Hattie said, it's been a juggling act ever since."

"Bought them out with Daddy's money, you mean." She sniffed as if insulted by the thought, but she was wrong. He'd never used a penny of his father's money except to stake his original investment, and he'd paid that back many years before... with the interest his father required.

"My father has no financial interest in my lumberyard. None whatsoever. But he is my father. That part is correct."

She glared at him. "Having money doesn't make you above reproach, Mr. Ward, and anyone can see that you're going around town, parading a boy that just happens to look like you. Anyone with a lick of common sense knows that children don't just suddenly appear. They come into being in the usual way, I expect, but for the Wards of the world, common decency has few restrictions, it seems." She whirled back to the council. "And that is why it's your duty and responsibility to examine the issue of Mr. Ward and the school teacher and the effect upon our children."

"I'm not sure when courting a woman became a law-breaking act," noted Hattie from her seat. "Seems to me if no one courts anyone, pretty soon there'll be no need for a school because there won't be children to teach, Myrt."

"All well and good for you, Hattie," the woman shot back. "You live in town and your business is well-set. For those of us eking a living out of prairie soil, things are a little different."

"Are they?" Hattie aimed a look of steel at Myrt Johnson. "For a five year effort you'll be awarded the ownership of one-hundred-and-sixty acres of prime prairie farm land. Now that's a mighty tough task, and I know this because I gave up my claim years back. A woman alone can't keep a claim and run a business in town, but your family now has two claims and your son Leon has started his own carting service for folks, taking them or their goods here or there. It seems to me like the prairie's been good to you. I paid my way for my town property, I paid my way for my shop and my rooms behind it, and I paid my way for the goods I carry and my sewing machines, so I am unsympathetic to your stand. Women in business or education still have the right to conduct their lives, and last I looked, romance was part of that life. For most," she amended with a smile toward old Ben who'd never been married.

"Your opinion has been noted, Hattie, but Myrt's raised an important question as well," noted Sam. "We've had men teachers in the past, and there hasn't been a problem before now."

"There is no problem." Seb stared at them, aghast. "Rachel Eichas is doing a marvelous job with the children, and everyone here knows it."

"What we know is that there *was* some misgiving allowing a woman a job that a man couldn't handle last year, and with harvest over, this could be a problem," said a second council member. "In any case, it's not our place to do much or say much, but we can recommend that the school board meet soon..."

"Three of you are on the school board." Now Seb rued his chronic decisions to stay uninvolved in town politics. "Which means—"

"That we'll take Mrs. Johnson's concerns under advisement at our next meeting which is scheduled for the second Sunday of November."

"I say we have an emergency school board meeting tomorrow night," Myrt demanded. "I've got a granddaughter in that school and I won't be sending her along to school as long as the situation is in such disarray. Three weeks out is too long to wait."

"There is no disarray," said Seb. "And no reason to even bring this up at a meeting. If your problem is with me, then fine." He faced Myrt Johnson and her son. "But please leave Miss Eichas out of this. She's done nothing but good work since coming into town."

"We'll see about that." Myrt huffed to punctuate the sentence. "In the meantime, Lucy Johnson will not be attending school." She strode out, making as much noise as she could with the clomp of her shoes, and Leon followed her lead.

Will Barber waited until things were quiet, then addressed the rest of the council. "I propose that we table the matter of Seb Ward's purchase of land and take it up at our regular November meeting, but I'll add this caution." He looked up and down the small table set up for council and school board meetings. "If we start punishing the businessmen and women in this town for being smart, then we set ourselves up for failure. Now maybe another lumberyard would succeed, and maybe it wouldn't, but I'm not ready to hang one of our own out to dry because he had sense enough to invest even more money into the town he's supported for over a decade. Do I have a second to this motion?"

"I second it," said a second councilman. "My Kate's got a pot of stew waitin' and I've been digging potatoes all day. I'm ready for some food and some quiet."

"All in favor?"

Will's motion was passed by a unanimous vote, but it didn't solve anything. It just put things off for several weeks, which meant Rachel's job and reputation would be the object of discussion through no fault of her own.

"Don't let this get too far under your skin, Seb." Hattie moved up alongside with her knitting bag slung over her shoulder. "Folks have their say, they cool off, and things move on. Happens all the time."

"In big cities, yes. But here? Where I've worked for so long to do the right thing?"

"And stayed on the outside edge, keeping your own counsel."

"Being a private person doesn't make me bad."

Hattie began walking toward the door. He fell into step with her as Will approached them from the far side of the church proper. "Not bad, but it is a separation. Folks can take that any way they please, of course, but there's something to be said for being of the town and not just in the town."

"I think having Eli around will take care of that in the most natural way possible," Will offered as he withdrew the church key from his pocket. "Nothing like having a youngster to pave the way. They do drag us into the most interesting situations. Mine happened to include finding me a wife, so I'm quite on your side in this." He aimed a grin at Seb as he locked the door. 'Where no wood is, there the fire goeth out:'" he quoted easily. "So where there is no talebearer, the strife ceaseth.' That Proverb has been included in many of my Sunday lessons, Seb. Less talk, more work, and things have a way of evening out."

He knew Will was right. Hattie, too. But how would he face Rachel with this news?

The only way he could. With an apology and a pledge to keep his distance. His father had ruined people's lives by careless self-indulgence. How could he do the same to a woman so dear to his heart?

He couldn't. Not and live with himself, so when he picked up Eli a few minutes later, he asked Rachel to step outside a moment.

And when she wrapped her thick shawl around her shoulders and did as he asked, the last thing he wanted to do was set her aside and yet...

It was the only thing a decent man could do, under the circumstances.

Chapter Fifteen

"LET ME GET THIS STRAIGHT." Rachel locked her gaze with Seb's and if she scowled some, well, who could blame her? "A few angry people realize that you bought property another lumberyard was interested in and that somehow threatens my position in the school?"

He winced because it sure did sound stupid. "Yes. Basically."

"That is absurd," she declared. "One has nothing to do with the other, and I expect that the people complaining might be some of the same people who opposed a woman teacher in the beginning."

Myrt Johnson had said as much. He'd had no idea because he'd paid no attention to town agendas that didn't affect the lumberyard or him directly. Now he rued that lack of involvement for multiple reasons. "Rachel, I'm sorry."

He looked sorry. He looked downright penitent, but how could something so nice go so dreadfully wrong?

"I know how much this job means to you." Concern deepened his tone, and she was pretty sure that Seb wasn't accustomed to being thwarted. He was a fixer and this current problem didn't come with any obvious solutions.

And her position in the school did mean a lot. It was more than a job. It was a mission. It was something she did well, but she also believed in fairness. Threatening a person's livelihood because of hearsay was grossly unfair. "I won't deny it," she answered. "I love my job. I love being able to have a job, this is a dream come true for me but it's not my only dream, Seb."

His gaze softened. "No?"

"No," she told him. "But I'm not about to let someone chase me out of it for no good reason, so I'll be at that school board meeting next month. I will stand on the merits of my work, which should be the only thing that matters."

"You are correct, of course. But that's not always how things happen, Rachel."

She pulled the shawl tight against the rapidly chilling air. "Then we'll give it our best shot. You with the council. And me, with the school board. But it's late and Eli needs to be tucked in for the night. He's been a gallant little helper, but he's tired."

She opened the door and stepped back inside. Welcome warmth swirled around her, warmth provided by the man on her small stoop. Both oil lamps gleamed, chasing shadows into abeyance, a light afforded by the same generous person. Were they in such Puritan times that simple gifts of a man for a woman took dark undertones?

As Seb helped the tired boy shrug into his woolen coat, she faced him. "How is it that many of the Western territories declared women's rights to be the law years ago, but our town frowns on women working? Women forging their way? And to have women calling out other women is galling, isn't it? When we should be supporting one another."

Seb lifted Eli into his arms. "People fear change."

"But isn't that what the good Lord brought with the birth of His son? A voice of change and truth and light? A new commandment to love one another? To forgive? And those women who followed that cross, who stood in its shadow when men had run in fear, those are my exam-

ple, Seb. Those are my standards of behavior," she declared.
"And there was nothing small-minded about them."

"And yet little changed in the rights of women in these
two thousand years," he said softly. "I welcome that change,
Rachel, but I won't sacrifice your good name and reputation at any cost. A fine reputation is a precious thing and I
won't see yours ruined."

She lifted her eyes to his. Read his intent. His serious
expression said more. He would step back or even step
away to protect her.

She didn't want him to step back. Now that she'd gotten to know the big heart inside the strong man, stepping
back was the last thing she wanted him to do, but when
he leaned forward and gently kissed her cheek in goodbye,
she knew he would do exactly that. And there wasn't a
thing she could do about it because a good man should
never be faulted for putting others first. And despite his
past indiscretions, Seb Ward was a very good man.

Macy Barber and Hattie caught up with Rachel a week
later, in a rare moment when Macy wasn't carrying a baby
or gripping the hand of a tiny boy. They came her way as
she walked home from school, and the pair was a welcome
sight indeed.

"Rachel, dear, we need to talk." Hattie motioned toward
Rachel's apartment. "Do you have a minute?"

"With my lumberyard friend keeping his distance, my
sisters knee-deep in work on the farm, Nellie nearing her
confinement and most folks steering clear of me, I have
nothing but time it seems."

"This is a sour business," Macy declared when she followed Rachel and Hattie inside and closed the door.
"From beginning to end, and while Seb's father may have
started the tempest out of spite, we have too many people
ready to take up the charge. But that's not why Hattie and

I are here."

Rachel looked from one to the other. "No?"

Macy filled her in. "Anna Ingraham stopped by the parsonage on her way out of town today. They come in rarely. Like you and the Gilberts and some others, they've done well and provide much of their own needs now, but she wanted someone to know that the children from Cutter's Crossing are planning to return to school on Monday. And that includes those three teenage boys."

Cutter's Crossing had sprung up in the slew of early claims. When the railroad veered south through Second Chance, Cutter's Crossing suffered a loss of people and hadn't recovered. Rachel knew the boys' return was imminent. Now she knew when. "Then it's good that I have lesson plans waiting for them."

"You need to take this seriously, Rachel." Macy sounded like a scolding mother. "You know the history, and you know that Will and I are right here to back you up. Seb, too. We're all within a quick dash of the school."

Seb.

She hadn't seen him except in passing as Eli veered off for the lumberyard apartment each school day. He'd brought the boy to church, but sat in the back and when the service was over, he didn't linger and she spared herself the embarrassment of chasing him down although she'd been sorely tempted. "I will call if needed. I'll send one of the young boys to gather reinforcements if I must, all right?"

"You are far too calm about all of this," declared Hattie. She scowled, and Hattie McGillicuddy never frowned like that. Today she did. "I don't want to see you hurt."

"I can't think they'd hurt a woman."

Macy scoffed purposely.

"And you know what a weak-minded creature Mr. Blount was," Rachel added.

"That doesn't negate the end result," Hattie reminded her. "An injured teacher and a cancelled school term. I think we should have the sheriff come by and give the boys a stern talk. Meet them along the roadway and explain that such things will not be tolerated. Maybe have him sit right there in the school, too. A show of strength is never a bad thing."

Hattie was right, but Rachel wanted it to be *her* show of strength. Her success. "While I welcome his involvement along the road, I don't want the students distracted by him in the classroom. Although if he's in town and can come on the fly, that would be a relief to know. Knowing that part of the town is against me has me questioning so many things," she admitted. "I know that I'm a good teacher. And if these young men want to learn—"

Macy rolled her eyes.

Hattie didn't but seemed just as skeptical.

Rachel ignored their expressions and continued. "I want to give them that opportunity. I will call for help as needed. I'm hoping that won't be the case, but in that instance I won't hesitate. And remember, I am quite different from my predecessor."

"There wasn't an ounce of kindness in him," noted Hattie. "And still he was soundly defeated."

"But it may have been that lack of kindness that brought it on," said Rachel. "Purposely inciting a child to anger is going to reap disastrous results, correct?"

"So can too much innocence," said Hattie. "I don't know these boys or their families, but they've proven themselves untrustworthy. It's not up to us to offer the trust they've lost. It's up to them to regain it."

Hattie made a good point. Glad for the warning, she thanked her two friends.

When Levi came into town on Saturday morning, she crossed into the wagon shop. "I need a hand, brother."

"With?"

"I want to see the hamlets north of us. Cutter's Crossing and Helmsley, but I need a carriage. It would be unseemly to ride, even though I'm perfectly capable of doing so."

"I'd like to think what that would add to the current gossip."

"A woman riding should be of no concern to anyone, but hence the request for a wagon. I'll be back by midday."

"You're not going alone." He took one look at her face and softened his words. "I think it would be wise to have someone along. Not because we anticipate trouble, but because we understand it can happen."

He was right. She didn't like it, but she crossed to Hattie's shop and tapped lightly on the door. And when Hattie bid her in, Rachel didn't beat around the bush. "I'd like to ride north this morning and meet the folks in Cutter's Crossing and Helmsley. Just briefly. Enough to introduce myself so they know what to expect this coming week. But I'd like someone to accompany me, Hattie."

Approval brightened Hattie's eyes. "And that's the glory of owning your own shop," Hattie replied. She flipped over the "open" sign that hung suspended from a silver chain. "I can close up shop as needed. Can you give me twenty minutes?"

"Gladly."

Thirty minutes later, Rachel guided the team to the well-worn road heading north. And as they moved farther from the growing little town, her opinions sobered.

The land holdings around the crossroads marked "Helmsley" showed little improvement. Some land showed signs of being worked, but other plots lay fallow, thick with faded green prairie grass. They passed a few soddies that appeared unoccupied, then one which was clearly a home. Laundry hung on a line suspended between two thick posts, and the home was nestled into the side of a swell.

"Clever placement to keep things comfortable," noted Hattie. "Snugged against the hill, good insulation from winter wind and cold and summer heat."

"We lived in a soddy the first two years," Rachel told
her. "It wasn't horrible, but it was dark. And the darkness
would close in around you. You couldn't light enough
lamps to chase the shadows, and of course there wasn't
lamp oil enough for that, in any case."

They passed another empty sod house a few minutes
later, but off to their right, a small cluster of buildings
came into view. They were small and tucked together like
a town, but there was nothing left or right to make it seem
like a town.

A square, hand-painted sign saying "Cutter's Crossing"
stood near the wide path. A black arrow pointed to the
right.

Rachel took a breath and urged the horses into the turn.

A woman was hanging laundry outside the first board
building. She watched them with a puzzled expression as
Rachel pulled the horses to a stop. She set the brake and
waited as the woman approached the buggy.

"Are you looking for Bancroft?"

Bancroft was the small town to the north. A rail spur
had gone through there recently, and they were reputed to
have their very own post office now.

Rachel shook her head. "No. Cutter's Crossing. I'm
Rachel Eichas. I'm the new school teacher in Second
Chance and I wanted to take a ride up here and meet
people."

Nerves and appreciation mixed on the woman's face.
She waited as Rachel and Hattie climbed down. "I'm Dee
Lief. My boy Ivan and his little sister will be coming into
town starting Monday. As we're able, of course." She gazed
north. "Once storms settle in, it's a hard trip to walk twice
a day and it's not always possible to drive in."

"Blizzard snows have interrupted many a child's education here on the prairie," Hattie agreed. She reached
out her hand. "I'm Hattie McGillicuddy. I've got a sewing
shop in town."

"I've seen that shop." Dee seemed almost embarrassed about that. Her next sentence explained more. "I've always thought what it would be like to walk into a dress shop and order a dress."

"I'd never done it, either," Rachel told her. "When I was given the teaching job, I realized I'd need a couple of dresses to wear, so I visited Hattie. It's funny how one thing feeds another in an economy, isn't it?"

"Or doesn't," said Dee. She glanced around the small collection of worn buildings. "We waited for a railroad that never came. Then most folks left, but we hung on, hoping for improvements in land or prices. Maybe we hung on too long. Or not long enough," she mused in a quiet voice. "We thought ourselves fortunate that the locusts haven't troubled us, but maybe bugs weren't the only problem with settling here."

Stuck in the middle between two towns on rail service, and a long walk from either in good weather when bad weather was the norm half the year. "Such beautiful farmland, though. It seems it should come into its own in time, doesn't it?" Rachel posed the query gently.

"But do times match?" The woman scrunched up her face. "There's the puzzle with no easy answer."

"Mama! Come quick! The ash pan!" A boy's face appeared briefly at a side door to the plain-fronted building. Home? Business? Both?

Rachel couldn't tell but the woman hurried off, hustled the boy inside and firmly shut the door.

Nothing and no one else appeared on the cold, dusty street. No merry curtains hung at windows. No lamps hung outside the five narrow buildings. No boardwalks connected them. They stood as separate entities on a yawning prairie.

"Well, then." Hattie took Rachel's arm to climb back into the buggy.

A cat dashed by just then. Cats were welcome to help

control the inevitable mice on the prairie, and when two kittens followed the cat, Rachel got back down from the wagon and walked to the side door. She knocked lightly and waited.

"Yes?" Dee cracked the door open. Reluctance shadowed her features. "Did you need something, Miss Eichas?"

"Kittens," Rachel replied.

The woman's brows shot up.

"We have a need for kittens in town and on farms and I just spotted some. Can I convince you to sell them?"

The woman's eyes went wide. "Sell them? To you?"

"And then I'll pass them on to families in need," Rachel explained. "Unless you're in need of all of them?"

"We've got a nest in the back," said the boy. He looked about twelve or thirteen years old. He offered her a sweet smile. "I'm Ivan," he went on. "I'll help you catch them!"

"I'd be beholden, Ivan."

"Cora, watch the baby." Dee gave the order into the dark room behind her. "And pay attention this time."

"Yes'm."

They moved toward the back of the building. A lean-to shed stood open, and Ivan cautioned her back with his hand. "They scare easy, miss. Best let me."

After witnessing the kittens' mad dash across the road, Rachel believed him. "I'll act as a doorway deterrent," she told him.

One cat darted left.

Ivan ignored it and made a quick grab for one on the right.

Success!

He handed the scrawny cat over as his mother appeared with a wooden crate. "Something to make the trip easier," she told Rachel, but when Rachel went to tuck the small cat inside, Dee held up a hand of caution. "I'd wait. Once in, they're easy to keep in, but lift the lid—"

"Good point." It took Ivan a minute to coax the other

kitten out of hiding, but when curiosity got the better of it, he nabbed it quickly and tucked it into the box, then followed by adding the kitten in Rachel's hands in through the narrowest slit he could.

He let the lid fall into place and dusted his hands against his pants. "Done."

"And well done at that." Rachel reached into her pocket and handed over four dollars.

The boy's eyes went round.

So did his mother's. "This is far too much."

"It's not," Rachel assured her. "That little calico is a female and we need all the help we can get to reduce the numbers of rodents out here. Folks will be happy to pay me back my investment."

Dee seemed amazed. So did the boy.

"And what about getting your grain to the new granary that's being built?" Rachel motioned toward a wooden silo up the road. "Are there wagons enough to haul it in?"

"That's Daniels' grain, their place is just out of town, and he doesn't trust middlemen. He'd rather go load by load and take his chances."

The Daniels boys had been last spring's troublemakers.

"They live straight out this road?"

"Yes."

"Then I think I'll swing by there and introduce myself before we take our furry friends back to town." Rachel took Dee's hand. "Thank you for chatting with us. And for the kittens."

"It was an honest pleasure to have company," Dee replied.

"I expect it gets lonesome out here," noted Hattie. "The prairie is ripe with opportunity, but a wide, vast plain for much of the year and that's a stark truth for families."

"It can wear on you," admitted Dee. "But then there's always the good Lord above, watching over us as the days go on. And I can't deny praying for good neighbors by and by. But for now, we're doing all right."

Hattie and Rachel crossed back to the buggy. Hattie settled the small crate behind the seat.

The kittens yowled their displeasure, but they'd be content in new homes soon enough. Rachel urged the horses on, and as they headed east on Cutter's Crossing Road, Hattie pulled her coat tighter. "Snow's in the air, Rachel. You can feel it coming."

"How do students out here brave the elements to get to school?" she wondered. "There aren't enough children to have a proper school here, and none in Bancroft as yet, but this is a fair piece to drive, Hattie."

A small house appeared on their left. Behind it was a narrow barn, plain but solid. Figures were visible far out in a field, and when they got to the house, no one answered the door.

Chickens chased in a slatted pen, and a handful of cows grazed old grass nearby. The place showed rugged care without a hint of gentling. No garden edged the sod-roofed building. No curtains trimmed the two south-facing windows, but the place wasn't dirty or neglected. Just woebegone, as if biding its time.

Rachel pulled out a short piece of paper, jotted a quick note, then slipped it beneath the door. And then she urged the horses into a full turn.

The wind hit them full on. Cold and blustery, she glanced Hattie's way as they neared that single turn-off to take them back to Second Chance.

Hattie had every right to protest the turn in the weather and the probable foolishness of driving that far with change in the air.

She didn't complain.

She pulled her thick scarf tighter and drew the wool blanket up snug to cover their legs and laughed. "I like your energy, Rachel, indeed I do! This is the kind of thing that builds a country, young woman. Not boards and battens and new roofs, although they all have their place. It's in the initiative of men and women to see a task and get it done. And you have that initiative, sweet Rachel. And I'm mighty glad to witness it."

"Hattie, you praise too highly, but I'm too cold and windswept to argue," Rachel told her. And then she smiled. "And who knows what good it did, but if the Lord above was willing to reach out to the most common of people, who are we to be any different on such a nice day for a little drive?"

Hattie grinned as she clutched her scarf snug around her ears. "That's a fine way to live one's life," she agreed.

A gust of wind swayed the buggy to the left. It took all of Rachel's strength to keep it arced into the wind. Her maneuver put more strain on the horses, but it kept the buggy from tipping over.

Levi met them as they clip-clopped their way down Main Street. Relief softened his jaw. He crossed over as she pulled the horses to a stop, then reached up a hand to help each woman down, one at a time. "You two go warm up. Sol and I will see to the horses and the buggy."

He didn't scold.

He didn't fuss over the uselessness of the trip the way he might have two years before.

"Thank you, brother."

He pulled his knit cap low as Sol appeared from the smithy. "Go. Get warm. The girls sent some cake and bread, both of which probably sound good about now."

They didn't just sound good.

They sounded marvelous. Rachel lifted the kittens. They set up an excited chorus and Levi looked from her to the crate, then Rachel again.

"I expect Seb's mother could use one of those if she's a mind. Moving into a house that's sat empty for a number of weeks, a cat's a mighty good thing to have."

"I'll check with her." She could have crossed to Seb's rooms and asked.

She didn't.

He was trying to protect her reputation, a reputation sullied by careless words of others, yet what right had they to offer an opinion at all?

None. If she could overlook his past indiscretions, others should mind their own business.

Hattie followed her into the cozy apartment, made nicer because Levi had added coal to her fire.

The wind howled. Sullen stratus clouds lay dark and heavy in the sky, but twin lanterns, hot tea and sliced apple cake chased the chill from their bones. Once Hattie went home a short while later, Rachel drew on her thick shawl and walked to the hotel. When Elizabeth Ward answered Ginny's bell page, she spotted Rachel in the small lobby. She smiled instantly. "Miss Eichas. What a lovely surprise."

Rachel had to resist the old-fashioned urge to curtsy. "My brother suggested it, actually. I was out in the country this morning, and I happened on two likely kittens. Levi mentioned that with the Devereaux house standing empty for weeks—"

"And prairie mice prevalent," noted Ginny from the small front desk.

"Oh, what a marvelous idea, and nothing I'd thought of," admitted Seb's mother. "I am in your debt, Miss Eichas."

"Rachel. Please."

She smiled. "And you must call me Beth. All my friends do."

It was a kind gesture. "Then I'll consider myself blessed to do so." She waited while Beth eyed the kittens through the slats.

"I think the gold one would do nicely. That calico has a busy way about her, and I think a quiet orange tabby makes more sense in town."

"We can keep them here the next few days," offered Ginny. "If the calico has no home, I'll make an offer on that one," she added.

Rachel explained what she'd paid, and neither woman blinked an eye at the sum.

"Scarcity drives demand and pricing," noted Beth as she withdrew the orange-and-white little cat from the box. "But until this land is settled, I'll take whatever help I can get to outwit invasive critters. I'm so glad you thought of me, Rachel."

"Me, too." Ginny instructed her daughter to set up food scraps and a sand-filled box for the pair. "I'll keep them on the porch off the kitchen while they adjust," she went on. "If we let them out too quickly, they're likely to disappear."

"I'll gladly pay for the inconvenience," Beth told her. "You weren't expecting a kitten as part of our stay and we won't be moving for another few days."

"Nonsense." Ginny's daughter hurried off to the back kitchen as her mother set aside Beth's concerns. "Neighbors helping neighbors, that's all this is. Just what we should do."

"This is a town filled with kind hearts." Beth made the observation quietly as Ginny's daughter came back for the kittens. "My family and I are grateful for that."

"It's my pleasure, Beth." Ginny faced Seb's mother and spoke frankly. "Your son opened one of the first major businesses in this town and stuck with us through thick and thin. I'm glad to be of service to his mother."

Cecily hurried down the stairs just then. She spotted the kittens and her eyes lit up. "What a sweet baby cat!"

"He'll need a name," said Beth, and Cecily didn't hesitate.

"Pumpkin, of course, for that sweet rich color."

"Pumpkin it is."

Rachel drew her shawl around her shoulders. "I've got to get home and work on next week's lessons."

"I heard the older boys are coming back." Ginny met Rachel's gaze. "We're only a message away, dear. All of us in town."

"A message I hope we don't have to send," Rachel told her. She faced Seb's mother. "I'm so glad you've got Pumpkin for your new home, and I'm hoping he's not one bit necessary. But if he is, that he does his job well."

"Nature's way," replied Beth. "And the kindness of others."

Rachel tugged the wool shawl tighter. She hurried home, chin down, tucked against the cold, gusting wind. And when she got back to her very empty apartment, she tried not to think of Seb and Eli, across the road. She pushed aside thoughts of tender looks, gentle and maybe not-so-gentle kisses, and button strings for little boys.

She worked until eyestrain made her stop. She added coal, set the stove damper, and curled up in bed beneath a finely stitched quilt from the farm.

But sleep evaded her, at least until Seb's light winked out across the way.

Was he thinking of her? Yearning for her?

She thumped the pillow into a thicker wad and turned her gaze away from the street. From his light. His business.

But she couldn't turn her thoughts off quite that easily, and it was a long time before sleep claimed her.

Chapter Sixteen

MONDAY MORNING BROUGHT A COLD west
wind and the threat of November snow.

Rachel almost hoped for a storm. To delay the inevitable
for a day or two because of snow would buy her time...

And let fear win the day, she realized soberly.

*Trust yourself. Trust your intuition and your strengths. There
will be help close by, if needed. But how sad would it be to not
try?*

She donned her warm coat and a full scarf around her
head and neck, then headed to the school.

Someone had already started the fire. Several people
knew where she kept the spare key, but that simple act of
getting the place warm for her ignited her courage.

She put her things away, set the primary lesson on the
board, then put the older students' lesson to the right of it.

And then she set a book on her desk. A book she loved.
A book she hoped they would love. All of them.

The first students arrived red-cheeked and talking of
snow. They'd all gotten settled when the sound of bigger
feet clomped into the entry. Three boys and a girl came in.

The girl was younger, a primary student.

She took the seat Rachel indicated with a nervous smile
and sat quietly.

The boys, young teens, sauntered in. One she recognized

from her Saturday journey to Cutter Crossing. Ivan Lief, the quick kitten catcher. He spotted her and his eyes sparkled momentarily. But then he paused as if waiting to see what he should do.

The other two boys exchanged grins, then proceeded to demand certain seats.

Rachel intervened. "Gentlemen, I need your names for the roster and your grade levels. It seems that information was left unfilled from the last term."

"Harold Daniels." The middle-sized boy spoke right up. "And that's Reggie Daniels. And Ivan Lief."

"So Cora is your younger sister?" Rachel indicated the young girl to Ivan. "I'm glad you were able to bring her into school, Ivan. And I want to thank you again for your help on Saturday. Both kittens are warm and cozy and doing quite well."

The bigger boys frowned his way. Their looks disconcerted him. "Ma made me. She said—"

"No one cares what your ma said, Ivan." Harold shot him down quickly. "And I want that seat." He pointed to the seat Lucy Johnson's absence left vacant, between two smaller boys.

Rachel had arranged a long bench next to a similar table off to the left. She moved to it. "I'm actually putting you three older boys over here, near Constance." The teen girl didn't look thrilled by the arrangement, but she stayed quiet. "It's better to group like-minded students together."

Harold stared at her.

She refused to challenge him by returning the stare. She moved up front and directed the younger children to primer practice.

Eli looked nervous. He glanced from her to the teens and back. He must have overheard his uncle's concerns and his worried expression touched her. Once the younger pupils were engaged, she returned to the four older students. She handed each of them a notebook and a pencil.

Harold lifted the pencil, studied it, then her, then snapped it cleanly in two. "I don't need no pencil. I don't need no schooling. I don't need to be here."

Rachel's heart rate rose like mercury on an August day, but she hoped her face remained calm. "You are free to leave, of course."

He scowled. "My folks said I should stop bein' stupid and learn something, but maybe I don't like learning things, teacher. Not one little bit."

Rachel scanned her classroom quickly. Half the students were staring at him, mouths open.

The other half were pretending it was business as usual, poor things. She turned her attention back to Harold. "Learning can be a scary business."

"Ain't scared of nothing. And no one," he told her, and he directed that hard gaze right at her.

"A brave stance, but it's often a cover for fears we carry inside," she said lightly. She faced the other three. "Do any of you fear something?"

Constance looked like she feared opening her mouth about then. Reggie just glared at Rachel, but Ivan spoke up. "The creek, when it's up. I fell in once. My pa saved me, so I don't like taking our cows across the creek."

"And like a chicken, he goes the long way around so they can cross the old bridge." Reggie's sneer deepened the meanness of his words.

Ivan flushed and hunched down.

"Chicken or smart?" Rachel posed. "To choose the wiser path is commendable, Ivan. It will stand you well as you mature because wisdom can be even more important than education."

"It's the same stupid thing." Harold rolled his eyes.

So did Reggie.

"It's not," she explained as she drew up a stool. "The two can walk hand-in-hand or be far removed, but a wise man examines the choices around him. He then chooses with care, whether or not he's achieved an education. A wise man knows he needs to get seed into the ground while there's enough moisture to make it sprout. Too late and he has a crop failure. Too early and the seed rots."

Reggie looked up with interest, but dropped his eyes when Harold threatened him with a look. "My pa didn't send me to this dumb school to learn about plantin' seeds." Harold made sure every one of the students heard him, then glared their way. "A smart teacher would know that."

"But he did," Rachel replied. She left the stool sitting there and moved to the side chalkboard and sketched a quick diagram. "Here is the seed. Here is the root. And the sprout. What does the dry, hard seed need to take root?"

"Water?" asked Constance.

"Absolutely." She gave Constance a smile of encouragement as she drew a quick cloud and raindrops on the board. "And what else?"

"Well, they like it warm," said Ivan. He shrank to the left to avoid Harold's piercing look. "They don't grow if it's too cold."

Rachel wrote water and heat on the board.

"Sun." Reggie got a sharp jab from Harold for jumping in. He glared to his left. "Knock it off, Harold."

Rachel sketched a sun above the seed, then wrote 'sun' on the board. "What else?"

They exchanged glances. "I think that's it," said Ivan, as if embarrassed that she didn't realize it.

She opened the book in her hand to Matthew 13. "Behold, a sower went forth to sow," she began.

"Dirt!" Ivan seemed excited to have figured out what she was about to say. "Good dirt."

She smiled at him and finished the verse before pointing out the importance of placement. "The rocky soil didn't work. The thorny soil didn't work. The thin soil was strong enough to give the plants room for roots, but wasn't good enough to maintain the plant. Seed sown on good soil allowed roots and branches and leaves."

"Does that mean God knows about farmers?" asked Reggie.

Harold snorted. Rachel ignored him. She raised the Bible slightly. "Jesus picked simple laborers to be his first followers. Fishermen. A tax collector. But the Bible is filled with good advice about farmers, so yes. God knows farmers. And allowed us a great land to sow those seeds."

"From way back then?" Reggie again, looking skeptical but interested.

She nodded. "From the beginning of time." She set the Bible onto her desk and raised another book. "I have only one copy of this at the moment, so I'll read aloud to all of you."

And when she began reading about the escapades of Tom Sawyer, Harold made a show out of being bored.

Not Reggie or Ivan, though. They listened. And they joined in the class laughter when Tom bested Aunt Polly.

Were they cooperating because she was a woman? Or because she was nice?

Rachel didn't know, and when they broke for lunch, she noticed the meager crusty bread in the metal tote the Daniels boys shared. There wasn't a lick of jam on that bread and no dried meat to go alongside like some of the other children carried.

Harold gave her another hard look, as if daring her to say something.

She stayed mum.

But she noticed when he gave his younger brother the bigger bit of crust, leaving the smaller for himself.

His hard-set chin dared her to make something of it.

She didn't. She understood how pride wasn't always a bad thing. Sometimes pride strengthened one in times of trouble, and after seeing the Daniels' place north of town, she understood the challenge they faced.

At day's end, the students hustled through the schoolhouse door. Some walked to homes in town. A few were picked up by wagons. But not Ivan, Cora or the Daniels' boys. They trekked together, on foot, through the small town and beyond, until they disappeared from sight.

She locked the schoolhouse and wrapped her coat more firmly around her. She spotted Seb as he directed an order from the upper platform. She moved his way.

He looked up from the paper in his hand. Saw her. And oh, the look of longing in that man's eyes about melted her heart.

Then the look disappeared. He jumped off the platform to meet her at street level. "Miss Eichas?"

So now she was Miss Eichas again?

She ignored the change because she had to. He was trying to protect her. Safeguard her job. How sad that such a thing was necessary in these modern times. She jutted her chin toward the path east of town. "The children from Cutter's Crossing are walking north. Will they walk all the way out there? It's nearly three miles."

"Hot and dry miles in summer and bitter cold and windy in winter. They'll most likely meet a wagon on the way, coming to fetch them."

Winter. How would they make the trek in the winter? "I'm sure the big boys can handle it, although not love it," she told him. "But that's a long haul for Cora Lief's little legs. No wonder they give up and don't come into town for school."

"Some would say the value of a solid education is well worth the cost required."

She wanted to blast his cool, calm response, a response without one bit of affection shown. She couldn't, though, because he was right to be correct and keep a distance, and that only made the situation more aggravating. "A view I share, but it's still a long way," she pressed. "They can't attend until harvest is complete, and they can't come when the weather is too bad." She studied the path east of town from their higher vantage point. "I expect that means their education has been consistently interrupted."

"A problem many children share out here."

"Unless taught at home," she mused. "Or brought in by wagon as needed."

"Which is often the case, but also the problem. If a wagon can't make it, the distant students stay home." His voice was kind, and she recognized the common sense in his words. She'd spent her life living and learning on this vast land. It could be done, but only with inspiration, advice and tutelage.

"Today went well," he noted. "I was glad of it."

"You came around to see?"

"A couple of us did. You did well, Rachel."

The use of her name drew her smile. "So you remember my name, Sebastian?" She turned and aimed the full portent of that smile his way. "Because I can't get yours out of my head."

"Rachel." Chagrin deepened his voice.

"Seb, I appreciate that you're looking out for me. I do," she insisted when he frowned in disbelief. "But if God is for us then who can be against us?"

"Any number of people in a small town," he answered. "I've got to get back to work. We've talked too long already."

She began to turn, disappointed, but his next words— softly spoken, just for her— gave her heart. "And yet, never long enough, beloved."

She didn't turn. He was right, why give gossips fodder for their wagging tongues?

But when she was shielded by the high walls of Levi's wagon shop, she turned and waved slightly, to show him she heard.

And when he touched his hand lightly to the brim of his hat, her heart stirred. She could solve this whole thing by leaving her job. That would put control squarely back in her hands.

But she had every right to be a working woman and to keep company with a good man. Unfortunately, Seb's past clouded his years of fair dealings and the boy through a very different twist into the mix, and there wasn't a thing she could do about that.

Unless...

An idea struck her. A rash, crazy and possibly brilliant idea, and before she turned out the lamps that night, she wrote down a short argument to use at the school board meeting. Short because scripture already said what she needed to say, so she'd let God's word do the talking for her.

"Seb, you have been the most marvelous help." His mother set small tins of baking supplies on the pantry shelf while he leveled a bad leg on the kitchen table. "I don't know what I'd do without you." The sound of the kitten scampering upstairs made her smile. "And our youngest friend is hard at work, from the sound of things."

"Any word from Althea?"

Her smile disappeared. "None. Dotty Urtz wrote that she sees her now and again, and that your father is fairly absent so the thought of our daughter, headstrong and pretty much unchaperoned is a big worry. But there's no fighting it at the moment. Your father did exactly what he wanted to do, but Althea's not a child. She knew which decision to make, but creature comforts have governed her life for a long time. The thought of giving those up weighed heavy on her."

"Spoiled."

She accepted that with a grimace. "Yes. And I'm to blame as well for not putting my foot down and taking her to task more often."

"Would it have done any good, Mother?" He wasn't trying to be belligerent. It was a sensible question considering the circumstances. "Father would have gone on treating her like a prized pet and you would have lost her affection with no good result."

"It was a risk I should have taken," she told him softly. "I see that now. I was too concerned with keeping the peace to do my best for her, and that was a mistake. But all parents make mistakes, Seb." She set a light hand on his arm. "Learning to forgive those mistakes is a two-way street."

She was right. His pride got in the way of forgiveness sometimes, especially where his father was concerned. Maybe he'd have time to examine his conscience after the coming meetings, but right now, with his enforced separation from the woman he loved— yes, loved, he admitted to himself— and foul rumors taking root in town, he wasn't feeling philanthropic.

He set supplies where his mother needed them, and when he'd set their trunks into the respective bedrooms, he was done. "I'll get on. Eli will be out of school in a few minutes."

"Seb, we appreciate your help. And your help with the boy especially. Cecily finds your good example to be quite refreshing because few in our former circles would have made a similar sacrifice."

He kept his face averted because talking with his mother about his father's love child wasn't just awkward. It was wrong. And yet, she was the one bringing it up.

"And with Cecily helping Hattie now, folks might begin to put things together. Why I'm here and not in Minnesota."

"People should mind their own business."

She laughed softly, but it wasn't a happy laugh. "That is rarely the case, and everyone is quite adept at running others' lives far better than their own. Having a child show up out of the blue would raise eyebrows anywhere, Seb. You know that."

"Doesn't make it right."

"Well, son, what started out wrong can never be made fully right, but with love and compassion we'll make this town a place to call home. How is Miss Eichas faring?"

He shook his head. "I'm keeping my distance. The school board meeting is in five days. I don't want to cloud her reputation any more than I already have."

"You haven't clouded anything, Seb." She kept her hand on his arm and gazed up at him, worried.

"Guilt by association, and nothing I want to discuss."

"But I thought the council was simply upset by the land purchase. Seb, that's what you told me."

That was all he'd told her because he didn't want her privy to more loose talk about him and Elijah. If she was going to live in this town, he wanted her as comfortable as possible. "The council's concern is the land purchase, although it was perfectly legal and sensible in my view. The concern brought to the school board questioned Rachel's abilities."

"And her associations."

He frowned because he couldn't lie to her. "Yes."

"Oh, Seb." She hugged him. "I know what the Good Book says about the sins of the father raining down on the children, but I take much more comfort in Paul's words to the Corinthians. That if any man be in Christ, he is a new creature. His sins are washed away. And that is how you must approach all of this, my son. As the strong and clean person you are."

"I will, Mother."

He wouldn't, of course, because that would cast the shadows onto her and Cecily and he wasn't about to do that. But he didn't want her fretting over it, either.

It was a situation with no clear winner. He either spoke the truth to clear his name and take the associated burden off of Rachel—

Or he protected his mother and sister by keeping silent,

and allowing his personal reputation to be tainted.

He understood the benefits of truth. He'd lived them all his life. But when the truth laid a nasty burden on his mother's shoulders, then the lie of omission might be the better way to go.

Chapter Seventeen

IN AS MUCH AS YE have done this for one of the least of my brethren, ye have done it to me.

Matthew's words spurred Rachel into motion. Why couldn't she use words and examples from the past to secure a brighter future for local children?

She stopped by the inn and bakery when school let out on Tuesday afternoon and presented her idea to Thelma and Charles Thornton.

"Boarders?" Thelma looked surprised when Rachel first suggested keeping the Cutter's Crossing children in town through the week. Then she looked intrigued. "It's true we don't get much business mid-winter."

"And if the families could cover the cost of food, perhaps the town could cover the cost of lodging? I don't know why it wasn't thought of before, it was a common practice in New England before they had improved roads and transportation."

"Rachel, I think it's an excellent idea," Charles agreed. "And it might be possible for the older boys to learn a trade of some sort to trade for their lodging bill. The town is growing and there's nothing like an apprentice to help a tradesman accomplish more work in less time."

"That's a marvelous idea!" Levi had been complaining about the influx of work and how he wasn't sure if he could keep to his schedule, especially with a new baby due. "I'll ask Levi."

"And Seb?" Thelma must have read her expression. She frowned quickly. "It's a ridiculous state of affairs when loose talk causes a divide like this. I've never seen Seb Ward so happy or sociable in all the years I've known him. That boy drew him out of his shell and finding you put a spark in his step, and I'm not the only one who noticed."

"So it seems," agreed Rachel ruefully. "But I'm putting my trust in God to see this through. A few small-minded people shouldn't be able to influence an entire town."

"And yet we all know that one bad potato *can* spoil the barrel. I will be at that school board meeting and I'll support you and this idea one hundred percent," Ginny promised.

Rachel was not a public speaker.

Oh, she did fine in front of a classroom of children. That was different. But she'd never had the opportunity to address a group, nor did she long for such a chance, but she marched into that school board meeting and didn't sit in the back.

She went right up front, along with Hattie and Macy, Miriam, Esther, Nellie, Ginny, Thelma and three other women who worked in town. One way or another she would have her say, face her opponents and challenge their arguments.

If she didn't faint dead first.

When the board members had gone about their regulatory business from the prior meeting, Hans Wilbur addressed the room. "We have three items on this evening's agenda. The first is to take up a collection over the next six months to re-roof the school in July as planned. The sheriff has kindly offered to oversee the collection and keep the money in his safe until we have a bank in Second Chance. Is there any discussion on this topic?"

Not one person seemed to care about a roof when there

was a much meatier topic of conversation in the room: Rachel's love life. An entity that had been non-existent until a short time ago.

The board voted unanimously to collect money for the roof and then the head of the school board turned toward Rachel. "Miss Eichas, we thank you for being here."

She nodded slightly.

"Our next agenda item is for the board to present to the town the idea of boarding pupils during inclement weather to ensure their educational opportunities. The board recognizes Rachel Eichas to come forward."

"What?" Myrt Johnson stood right up, indignant. "We are supposed to be talking about her. Not listening to her!"

Rachel's heart jumped. It thumped hard first, then it raced. Nothing on the wide open prairie had prepared her for the small-mindedness of some people.

And yet, living with her father...

It had, she realized. And that gave her the courage to stand up, move forward, turn and face the room.

The room wasn't just full.

It was packed.

She hadn't dared look around once she took her seat, and a good thing, too, because facing this crowd wasn't something she did lightly.

"Go get 'em." Nellie whispered the words from the front row, and when she smiled at Rachel, it was more like a benediction. Rachel wasn't standing here talking for herself, or for Nellie or her sisters...

She was talking for that baby Nellie carried. For those students in the classroom. If no one stood in the face of narrow-mindedness and idle gossip, who would ever stand again?

She lifted her sheet of paper and faced the crowd, chin high, shoulders back. And when she saw Seb standing at the very back, looking quite wonderful and strong, the last bit of fear dissipated.

"I'm here to present a unique opportunity that could offer children from outlying areas a better chance at achieving the education we all want them to procure. After having met with the Thelma and Charles at the inn, I'd like to offer this idea up for consideration. That children whose families cannot transport them in and out of town during inclement weather be given lodging at the inn at no cost to them."

"No cost?" whooped a man from one of the middle chairs. "Well, that's mighty generous of the Thorntons, ain't it?"

Rachel smiled at him. "It would be, but I think we can defray the costs adequately in two ways: If families donate foods for the children's consumption or pay the inn a food allowance, thereby keeping it affordable for the families involved."

A few eyebrows shifted up in interest. And just as many mouths turned downward in opposition.

"Little lady, staying at a hotel doesn't come cheaply, and those of us who respect the Thorntons's' right to own a business must contend that a proposal that puts them in dire straits is really no proposal at all. Now is it?" Myrt Johnson's sister planted her hands on wide hips as she stood, and her expression showed exactly what she thought of this whole idea. Even though she hadn't heard half of it.

"Of course we couldn't expect Thelma and Charles to donate the cost of lodging." Rachel aimed a full, bright smile at Myrt's sister. "But if the older students are apprenticed to area businesses, then those businesses could defray the inn costs by paying the inn instead of the apprentice. Local businesses get the benefit of help, students learn a trade and get the full opportunity of an education, and when it's planting time next spring, the students go back to their homes just in time for the inn to host fair weather travelers."

"Thelma, you up for this?" asked Hans directly. "Because

I was kind of expecting a half-baked idea, but this makes sense to me. I wouldn't mind hiring on one of the older students to help at the livery. Shoveling snow and cleaning stalls gets tough come winter."

Levi was standing in the back, near Seb. He raised a hand when Hans finished speaking. "The wagon shop is willing to hire on an apprentice, too. So is the lumberyard."

"Well, we know there's at least one or two younger ones whose families can't get back and forth. Who's going to hire a six-year-old and an eight-year-old?" Myrt stood up beside her sister and rolled her eyes.

"Well, the littlest one is going to stay with me," announced Hattie from her seat. "I've got room and with Cecily Ward helping me keep up with orders, we've got the means to handle one mighty cute little girl."

"And Red and I are willing to board the Haney's little girl for the duration," added Ginny. "She can help me in the mercantile and she'll be company on those winter nights when Red dozes off mighty early. A woman can only do so much fancy work without benefit of conversation."

"Young lady, this is a very forward-thinking proposition," said a board member who lived on a claim west of town. "It's not something that's been done before."

"Actually, it's been done for centuries, and more recently in Eastern towns where travel was difficult," she corrected him. "That brought about the idea of boarding schools as populations grew. I don't see that as logical for here," she continued. "With improvements in transportation and roads, I expect we'll see easier ways for getting around before too long. So this idea solves an interim problem and offers children the chance for a full education at no extra cost to the taxpayer."

"I can't deny liking that part." Hans steepled his fingers. "And that you've done your homework on this and laid groundwork. That's impressive initiative from where I'm sitting."

"Except that if we vote her right out of the teaching spot, it's not all that impressive, is it?" Myrt brought them back to the primary intent of the meeting in a strong voice. "Because who's going to run the program then?"

"Now, Myrt—" Hans raised a hand of caution.

Myrt didn't let Hans finish. "Don't placate me, sir. We might as well get right on to the next item on the agenda, an item you seem to have shrugged off but I'm telling you that right-minded people who cherish God's word don't take this kind of thing lightly. When a woman takes up with a man who has gilded his path at the expense of others—" she aimed a sharp look back at Seb. "A man who totes around a child formed in his image and likeness some years ago, with no benefit of marriage, then it is clear to many of us that loose morals and shallow values can prevail if we turn our heads to such things. And that cannot be allowed to happen."

Here it was.

Her moment. Her chance to remind the crowd what the Good Book truly said.

She didn't look at Seb. She didn't dare.

Instead she directed her attention to Myrt and her sister and the small group that surrounded them. "I love our town."

Several of the women sniffed audibly.

"It's growing so nicely, and it's filled with people who want to see this land rise up to be splendid. It is truly a land of opportunity, and I can't help but admire any man, woman or child who takes that seriously," she told them. "As a woman who grew up on the prairie, I respect a person's right to grow their business. This town went through years of tough times." She made eye contact with as many as she could. "Those folks know what it took to stand tall in the face of trouble and adversity. There's something solid in that," she added, but then she reached down and lifted her worn copy of the Bible.

"But here's something more solid," she said softly. "Words to live by, and in those words we have a woman about to be stoned for an accusation. But when the Lord himself proclaimed that the man without sin should throw the first stone, what did those accusers do?"

She didn't have to answer the question because every person in that room knew exactly what they did. They dropped their rocks and walked away.

"Seventy times seven," she reminded the group. "That's how many times we're instructed to forgive. And I think that's a lesson every town could use when neighbors start minding other people's business. If the Good Lord told folks to forgive and move on, well." She faced Myrt and her sister directly. "That's good enough for me."

And then she sat down.

She didn't look at Seb. He'd never brought up the issue of Eli's existence. Nor had she. And when two people truly care for one another, they should be honest.

She had fallen in love with Seb Ward, and her virginal heart beat faster just thinking of it, but something as serious as love needed to be based in trust. And as much as Seb cared, he hadn't seen fit to speak openly about the boy. His son.

And while she loved the man, a relationship should only be based on truth. And that was something she and Seb didn't have.

"I think Miss Eichas has made a good point." Hans looked up and down the board. "My wife did mention that if the school board gets into the habit of running folks' lives that maybe we're concentrating too much on the people and not enough on the education. Does anyone here present have a problem with the education Miss Eichas is providing to their children?"

Not one person raised their hand.

"Then I propose we end this discussion. All in favor say

aye."

A chorus of ayes filled the table.

"And to the matter of hosting children over winter, with the offers of apprenticeship and food as explained by Miss Eichas, I submit we try this for the current school term and re-visit it next spring and summer. All in favor?"

Every single one of the board members agreed, and even though Myrt Johnson didn't look happy, she didn't carry on or fuss, and that was a relief.

Levi went to get the wagon while the women adjusted their coats and scarves. It would be a long, dark drive back to the homestead, and Rachel fussed at Nellie in particular. "Are you sure you don't want to stay the night? Between Hattie and me we can put up Miri and Esther. I'm sure we can get a room for you and Levi at the inn."

"With this baby drawing close, I like the idea of being home," Nellie told her. "Levi knows the trail as well as anyone, and so does the horse. We'll be fine."

"But we'd best get going," added Miriam. "The horse has stood too long already. Before we go," she added softly, and she reached out to hug her older sister. "I just have to say how proud I am of you, Rachel. You handled this like a true professional woman and I was absolutely in awe."

"Whereas I was tempted to punch someone," added Esther cheerfully. "That means I needed your talk on forgiveness most of all. Let's walk you home and we'll be on our way."

"I'll see her home," said Hattie. She smiled and tucked her arm through Rachel's. "That gives you a quicker start."

"Thank you, Hattie." Levi came in through the door just then. He faced Rachel. "You made me proud, Rachel. And you made me think hard about things. Again." He drew his brow down slightly, but without the angst he used to carry like a yoke on his shoulders. "I'll see you tomorrow."

Rachel walked back with Hattie.

She'd hoped Seb would wait and walk her home now

that the school board had made its decision, but Seb was nowhere to be found.

"I'm sure he had to get back to little Eli."

Hattie must have been reading her mind. Or caught her quick, hopeful looks. "Am I so obvious?"

"Yes."

Rachel groaned.

"Not to all, I'm sure."

Rachel didn't exactly believe that because half the town had shown up at tonight's meeting.

"But Seb's got his own trouble brewing. And he's a man who takes care on a daily basis."

"I love that about him." She spoke softly as they walked toward the wagon shop building. "But what truly draws me is that he pauses all of that to care for his boy. That's a true mark of goodness right there. Work is important, but a child is the most important."

"Henry Eichas did not put his children first." Hattie matched Rachel's low tone. "But in the end, you all turned out just fine. Why is that?"

Rachel shook her head. "I don't rightly know."

"Your faith, child. Your heavenly father, guiding you. Steering you, all four of you, into doing things together, helping one another, staying the course. Not one of you let Henry's anger become your own. Well, except for Levi, but once he saw the error of his ways, he did a turnabout. If we put our faith and trust and hope in mere mortals, we are bound for disappointment. But trusting God's word and Mary's example will never steer us wrong."

"I'm glad we're friends, Hattie."

Hattie laughed lightly and turned for her shop. "As am I. I'll see you soon. I have that last dress complete, but we need to do a final fitting."

Three dresses.

Polished boots on a regular basis.

Her own set of rooms. And enough coal to keep her

warm throughout the winter.

So many blessings, but when she saw Seb's light in his apartment window, she longed for one more. And yet—

She wasn't about to go begging for attention. Not now. Not ever. And that was that.

Chapter Eighteen

"A TELEGRAM JUST CAME IN FOR you, Mr. Ward."
Ginny's daughter handed over the cream-colored
piece of paper with the proper decorum expected of tele-
graph operators across the country. And since this was his
second telegram in two days, Seb was pretty sure he didn't
want to read this one any more than the one that arrived
the previous day. He accepted the sheet and waited for her
to leave before he pulled the flap open to read the note
within. "Due to unforeseen circumstances, Winkler's Mill
will be unable to fulfill your recent order. We apologize for
any inconvenience."

Seb wanted to crumple the telegram and throw it.

He didn't.

He'd received his first cancellation of goods yesterday
afternoon. And now his second, from the back-up lumber
supplier.

Seb didn't have to read the telegram twice. It was easy
enough to read between the lines the first time.

His father had gotten to the smaller producers and put a
stop on Seb's order.

That meant another trip, a trip he didn't have time for,
but this newest turn left him no choice.

Was Cedric hoping Seb would cave?

Most likely.

He threw the missive away and crossed to the office window as Rachel hurried home from school.

She'd been brilliant last night. She'd shined like a beacon of hope in a raw, rough land and folks had followed along, not because she was some great orator. They followed because she believed in a future they could all share.

But he couldn't share the future with no lumber to sell, and dealing with his father would be like courting the devil. Seb knew better. He refused to even consider it. But that meant he needed to find a supplier, and find one quickly, before winter sank its teeth deep into the South Dakota soil and put a hard stop on train travel and deliveries.

He threw a few things into a travel satchel, arranged for Hattie to watch Eli, and boarded a train for Chicago the next morning.

His father was unafraid to wield his power in lumber circles, but while Cedric Ward had a firm hand on the Minneapolis area lumber trade, he carried no weight in the Chicago clearing yards. Northern production had been on the increase for years. With shipping lanes open to the huge processing yards in Chicago, Seb would be able to cut a deal and stay in business.

That is if he had a business waiting by the time he got back and faced the town council.

He got into Chicago late. Meeting with lumber managers would have to wait until morning. Chin down against the tunneling west wind, he hurried past flickering gaslights to a nearby inn.

He didn't dare think about Rachel. Or wonder what she would think of the resurrected city, destroyed by fire less than two decades before, now rising in most pristine fashion along the lakeshore.

And yet he couldn't think of anything but Rachel. Her eyes, warm and brown. Her cheeks, pale and fair. The beautiful hair she pinned into a most secure fashion.

What would it feel like to unpin that hair? Let the rich brown waves cascade over his hands?

And what have you to offer her besides family scandal and potential financial ruin? Doesn't that seem somewhat selfish on your part? His conscience scolded.

It did.

And yet he wanted to extend the offer anyway.

He needed her. Wanted her. Which meant he needed to trust her enough to be honest with her. She deserved that.

By the next night he'd locked in contracts with two suppliers again, but he added a personal codicil. If they backed out of the contract for anything less than death, they'd owe him a twenty percent payment. The speed both suppliers used in signing the unusual add-on showed the strength in numbers. Clearly these two shippers had no intention of listening to Cedric Ward's bullying tactics and that was a relief.

The shops were still open when he inked the last deal, and as he passed one sparkling jewelry store, he stopped.

A man in love should have a ring in hand. He shouldn't grope around or go shopping after the fact. A real man came to the table prepared.

He strode into the store, head high. When he walked back out twenty minutes later, the tiny box in his vest pocket felt like a weight had been added and lifted. He would go to Rachel and tell her the truth, but then he'd tell her why no one would ever know because his mother's good name would be protected.

And then it would be up to her.

He hoped she'd understand, but if she didn't, he had every intention of encouraging her. Proximity was a wonderful thing and Seb Ward intended to use it to his full advantage.

"Rachel." Sol Eichas showed up at Rachel's door first

thing the next morning. "I've dropped Ann at the farm and brought the children into town." He looked white and scared as he faced her. "It's time."

Time? Time for—

Her heart thumped twice and she swallowed hard.

The baby.

She looked from him to the school. "I must teach, Sol. Although my heart and soul want to be at the farm. Leave both kids here and you go about your business."

He looked left, then right as if lost. Sol's first wife had died in childbirth a few years before. "I can't."

"Well you cannot go back there and be nervous," she told him firmly. "Stay here and be nervous. With me. We'll let Miri and Ann practice their combined skills. Come along, Sarah." She took the four-year-old's hand into hers while Ethan skipped ahead. "I'll go out to the farm when school's out, Sol."

"And I'll take the children home then."

"Good." She said good, but how was she supposed to keep her mind on fractions and sentence diagrams and European history for the older students when such things were happening at the farm?

A baby. A birthing. A whole new adventure was opening up for the Eichas clan and she wasn't just nervous. She was scared.

She set Sarah with the older students on purpose. Even a sour teen wouldn't be mean around a fresh-faced little one like Sarah. True to his word, Sol pulled up a wagon at dismissal and took her straight out to the farm.

"Being at the farm means you miss the council meeting tonight," he reminded her as he directed the horse down the prairie road.

"I was torn." She smoothed the thick blanket over her lap when the wind picked up. "But Nellie and Levi's need is immediate and Sebastian is a strong man in his own right. The council shouldn't need swaying, but if it does,

I'm sure he can handle it."

Sol didn't appear quite as convinced. "He's got some who believe in him and his ways, but he's not well-liked."

"He is the Mr. Darcy of Second Chance," she agreed, and when Sol frowned, she continued. "From a most popular novel. A man of great renown but singular in his own right."

"Well singular doesn't win friends on the prairie," said Sol bluntly. "Not when you're running the only lumber business in town because you bought out one guy and blocked the other."

"You don't see the sensibility in Seb's actions?"

"I do," admitted Sol. "But that's because I run a similar enterprise with your brother. We're the only wagon makers and metalsmiths in town, so people only have one option unless they ride back east a ways. It's the folks depending on those businesses that get riled up when trade is limited. When you pile moral indiscretion on top of shady business, folks are ripe for talking."

Was it shady business? Was she fooling herself? Sol's explanations made sense, but was she viewing them through the eyes of a beloved maiden or a practical woman? Didn't she have a tough opinion of Seb herself, initially? "He's a wonderful man, Sol. And I hope people see that. If God tells us to forgive seventy times seven, who are we to say otherwise?"

"Good words, but when it's folks' livelihoods at stake, the ability to put a roof over their heads, then there's some serious discussion to be had." He took the left fork that led toward the Eichas claims. "I'm not coming in when we get there." He set his jaw tight. "I'll take Ethan and Sarah on home. And if I'm this tied up over Nellie's baby, what am I going to do when Ann's time comes?"

Another baby. Another new life on the vast, open prairie. "She hasn't breathed a word, Sol, but I wondered."

"Losing children makes folks real careful," he said. "Ann

had hope and joy seeped out of her for a long time, but there couldn't be a better mother for Ethan and Sarah. Same goes for whoever might be coming our way as winter draws to a close."

"Then it's good we're training Miri and Ann on the art of midwifery," she declared. She jumped off the wagon when he turned the horses into a curve. "Thank you, Sol!"

He nodded and gave the horses a quick chirp as she went up the three steps. By the time she opened the thick door, Sol was urging the horses up the drive at a steady clip.

"Rachel." Esther crossed the front room and clasped Rachel's hands in a death grip. "I am about as scared as a woman can get and that's outrageous, isn't it? Please tell me how silly I am and I'll set worry aside."

Rachel did no such thing. "It's not one bit silly, it's quite smart, and when one is raised in seclusion and never exposed to such things, how are we to react?" she asked. "We trust in God and we make food."

"Food?" Esther frowned. "Nellie didn't look one bit hungry. She looked... well... dangerous."

Nellie underscored that opinion when she let loose a wail upstairs.

Rachel squared her shoulders. "At some point people will be hungry," she said practically. "I like keeping busy and it's nice to be in a real kitchen again." She tied an apron around her middle and set to work. "Do you need help with the animals?"

Esther shook her head and took up a knitting project. Then she cast it right back down and began pacing the floor. "Levi's out there. He took care of everything early. Just in case he was needed here, but he went kind of green and Miri kicked him out."

"Then be a dear and get me a bunch of vegetables from the root cellar, and a piece of that smoked ham, won't you? The wind is kicking up a storm, and nothing like some fresh hot soup to beat back the weather."

"Absolutely."

Rachel talked brave and normal, but her heart raced.

The Good Book was full of hope and cheer if you knew where to look, but graveyards across the country bore silent testimony to the plight of women in childbirth. The loss numbers were far too dear.

"Rachel, I just realized, you're missing the meeting tonight," remarked Esther as she set a basket of potatoes, parsnips and carrots on the floor, and put the generous slice of ham on the wooden block.

"First things first."

Another wail from upstairs had the sisters exchanging long, worried looks. Esther leaned closer. "I am never, ever, ever doing this. Mark my word."

"Life comes with travail," Rachel replied softly. "But for all that morning sickness Nellie endured, and now this, it does seem like a rook deal, doesn't it?"

"And of course the men puff out their chests like a rooster gone a-courtin'," noted Esther.

"Well, they're men."

"Hmm." Esther peered up the stairs to their left as they worked together in the kitchen. "For all the discomfort of it, Nellie has seemed quite happy."

"And Levi most concerned and loving."

"Which is a happy switch for our brother. So maybe it's worth it in the end?" she asked, but then Nellie wailed again and Esther ducked her chin. "Or not."

"Essie, can you bring us another sheet and some towels?" Miri called down the stairs.

"Of course." Esther gathered them and thrust them at Rachel. "You take them. I'll chop vegetables."

Rachel set the kettle on the stovetop and accepted the clean linens. She hurried up the stairs.

She'd helped birth animals. The cats seemed quite content as they produced kitten after kitten. And the horses seemed to go about this birthing thing with an air of nonchalance, pawing and circling for less than an hour before producing a fine, four-legged copy of themselves. And their cattle generally went off to a private stand of bushes or trees and returned a short while later with a calf at their side.

Clearly humans were different.

She turned the corner toward Nellie's room.

Miri opened the door, saw her and smiled. And in that moment, that smile, fear left Rachel completely. "It's going all right?"

"Just like the books said and very similar to Claire's birth three weeks back. None of the scary things the books warned of, and Ann said it should be fairly soon."

"How can she tell?" It seemed a silly question, but if Rachel was ever going to face such a thing, a little bit of knowledge was a wonderful thing.

"The waters have given way and the contractions are stronger. And quicker. Do you want to greet Nellie?"

She wanted no such thing, but she wasn't about to be branded a chicken, so she slipped into the room quietly behind Miri. "Nellie."

Eyes wide, Nellie looked her way, then that gaze narrowed to mere slits. "This is not fun."

"Oh, Nellie, dear, it's not, is it?" Rachel took her hand gently. "And not one of us with a mother on hand to comfort and console or tell us how lovely things are after. But we have one another." She swept Miri and Ann a warm smile. "And five women together can make a marvelous stand to set things right as needed. And you are still most beautiful, dear Nellie."

Nellie puffed a loose fringe of hair out of her eyes and tried to glare but failed. "Time enough for pretty later. Right now—" Her face grew more intense and she raised up. "Ooh!"

Rachel fled.

She didn't run screaming and she prided herself on that,

but she didn't dawdle, either.

And when the soup was bubbling merrily about ninety minutes later, the cry of a newborn split the air from above.

Levi jumped out of his seat.

Esther clenched her hands in joy and prayer. Moments later, the bedroom door creaked open above. All three stood, staring upwards.

Ann appeared at the top of the stairs. She held an amazingly small bundle in her arms and as she reached the first floor, she tipped her arms sideways. "Levi Eichas meet Levi Eichas Jr., and might I say, he looks every bit his name."

"It's a boy?"

"A beautiful son," Ann said softly. "A child to treasure, all your days. And now I must get him back to his sweet mama. I'll call you in a few minutes to come sit with Nellie, all right?"

Levi stared at the baby with a look of such loving intensity that Rachel's whole being went soft. "Ann." He put a gentle hand on Ann's shoulder. "Tell her I love her. Tell her I'm so proud of her and grateful and so very happy."

Ann took pity on him. "Run up and tell her all that yourself, then make yourself scarce while we tidy up. Birth is not without its downsides and we've got washing to do."

"I set up a hot water kettle like you said." Esther indicated the big round kettle on the other side of the stovetop. "One for soup. One for washing."

"You both did well." Ann offered the praise with a sweet smile.

"And I've been given reason to believe we'll be doing a similar service in just a few months, Ann."

Ann gazed down at the baby in her arms. He blinked, clutched a fisted hand to his cheek and mouth, then squirmed as if great and odd things were happening inside him. "I was scared to say anything, which is foolish, I know, for God has blessed me with so much. But yes, in four months' time we'll be doing this at my house, so Nellie has given me a good bit of practice. And three other ladies due mid-winter, which is a dreadful time to deliver, but folks aren't always thinking of that if you know what I mean."

Rachel knew exactly what she meant, each time Seb pulled her into his arms and settled her with a very unsettling kiss.

Seb.

His meeting would be over by now.

She looked at the clock, wishing she could share their joyous family news, and wondering if the man she loved had just been virtually run out of town.

Chapter Nineteen

IT WASN'T UNUSUAL FOR LATE-DAY trains to run late, but this was one day Seb hoped for an on-time run. Then he'd have time to share the truth with Rachel and maybe have supper with the boy before the council meeting, but when a herd of wayward cattle blocked their way, it was a nearly an hour of moving the cattle, and then the train, and then the cattle again when a few reconfigured a little further up the line.

By the time the 4:03 rolled into the Second Chance station at 5:32, he had just enough time to meet with Ben and Tom and get to the church for the scheduled meeting.

"I can't say I wasn't worried when that train didn't roll in," Ben told him as Seb alighted from the second car. "But here you are and just in time."

"For a hometown welcome or a hanging?" quipped Seb, but Tom brushed that off.

"People are going to have their opinions one way or another. Today and every day," he went on. "Our job is to show them that profitable business can be good for all concerned. No one benefits if you go under, boss. Were you able to find contract lumber?"

"I was. With guarantees. And with their prices being more competitive, the additional rail passage isn't the increase I thought it would be, so our prices can stay where they are."

"Now that's a piece of good news!" Ben exclaimed. "Hattie's got Eli, and she won't bring him to the meeting, but she sends her best for a good outcome."

He glanced toward Rachel's rooms as they walked toward the church. No cheerful light brightened the windows, and the whole wagon shop looked forlorn, a perfect match for the dull, gray day.

He strode up the church steps and through the door.

The church was nearly full already, and the atmosphere inside felt more like a court hearing than a simple council meeting.

He looked around as he stepped in.

No Rachel.

He'd hoped she'd stay away. There was no reason for her to hear them malign his name, but when he didn't see her pretty face in the crowd, regret stirred him. He'd wanted her to stay out of this fracas, but a part of him wished she'd stand by him. Of course she had no reason to, because he hadn't trusted her with the truth.

He didn't take a seat.

He stood at the back like he'd done before and when the preliminaries were over, Ben raised a hand from the council table up front. "We don't normally sit real formal at this council, but tonight's a night for some of that because there's no way I can vote against my boss's best interests," he told the room full of people. "If we make things difficult for Seb Ward and he moves his business, then I lose a job and that won't set right with the missus."

"You're citing a conflict of interest, Ben?" Will Barber asked in a clear, calm voice.

"I am doing exactly that."

"That will make us four voting members," announced Will.

Two of the councilmen were businessmen like Seb.

Two were prairie farmers.

Would the farmers understand the dollars and cents of

retail trade?

Myrt Johnson sat with a contingent of family and friends. They'd taken seats directly in front of the two farmers, and when Seb scanned the room, he saw a lot of familiar faces, but few he would call friends. And not one member of the Eichas family was there to stand with him. He hadn't expected Rachel to come, but Levi and Sol were as close to friends as he had. Them and Will Barber, and Will was sitting up front.

Neither Eichas man had come.

A swell of old bitterness began to rise within him, but then a different thought niggled. *If God be for us, who can be against us?*

God's love and protection was sufficient, always. His grace moved mountains. So when Myrt Johnson's son started in on unfair business practices ruining life for the people of Second Chance, Seb held tight to that verse from Romans. And if he ended up having to move his business out of Second Chance, he'd do it.

He'd hate it...

But he'd do it. Because people should be allowed to run their businesses and their personal lives in their own way, without explanation.

"The way I see it—" Will had called on Myrt after three east-side farmers spoke their piece about unfair lumber prices and being trapped by narrow choices.

"We need to open this town up to more options. We're not a sleepy little place like Cutter's Crossing. We're a rail town, and that railroad is going to bring us things we never thought possible five years back. The thought of letting people of questionable moral value stand in the way of our progress makes no sense. And like I said last week at the school board meeting." She sent a pointed look toward Seb. "Birds of a feather flock together, and when a town starts letting loose morals guide its way, it loses a little more standing each day."

Several people nodded, and when she mentioned Eli—
again— more people seemed inclined to agree.

What kind of town would this be to grow up in? What
kind of upbringing could Eli have in a place where folks
discriminated against him, not for being who he was, but
who they thought him to be? Seb's son from an illicit
romance.

He was just about to have his say, to tell them what he
thought of narrow-minded virtue, when Will called on
someone behind him.

He turned, surprised, and his mother used the side aisle
to quietly walk up to the front of the church.

"Mother. No."

She didn't look at him right off. She looked at the council, then the gathered group as Cecily came and stood
strong by Seb's side. She took his arm, smiled up at him,
and patted the wool of his jacket. "We stand with you, dear
brother. Always."

He wanted to stop his mother, but when she folded her
hands across her chest, he realized something anew. That
maybe this was the cleansing she needed for herself and
not just for him.

"Pastor Barber, I thank you for this opportunity to
address the town." She sent a somewhat nervous smile to
Will and he nodded, grave.

"My son is a good man."

Myrt Johnson and a few people in her vicinity snorted.

"He is," she told them directly. "Seb is a very good man.
He keeps to himself, he prays on his own, but his deep
abiding faith and trust are second to none."

"What else is a mother supposed to say?" grumped Myrt
in a low tone, but not low enough as to go unheard.

Elizabeth Ward ignored her. "Seb has worked lumber
from the time he was seven years old, long before he should
have been hauling boards and stacking beams. He's never
shirked a day in his life, and when his little brother was

tragically killed in a lumber accident nearly twenty years ago, it was Seb who held our sweet Artie in his arms and comforted the dying child. And it was Seb who brought respect to the name of Ward Lumber when he came west to open his own business."

"Little boys that come out of nowhere and look suspiciously like their new caregiver isn't how we see respect in God-fearing towns, ma'am." Myrt Johnson stayed frank, but then softened her words. "No offense meant."

Elizabeth locked eyes with her. Long seconds of silence stretched the moment. And then she spoke. "Except when that little boy is your brother, it is a major gesture of respect." She turned slightly to address the board as well. "My son has taken charge of a child sent by an immoral father who sees little value in keeping his or his family's reputation unsullied," she continued. "Seb has been treating the boy as his own, while trying to spare me and my daughters the embarrassment of my husband's indiscretions."

A few soft gasps rounded the room.

Looks were exchanged.

"My daughter and I are going to live in this town." She clasped her hands lightly in front of her, the image of composure. "We've rented the Devereaux place. I hope my son will remain here, too, because this is a lovely place to live, raise a family, and build a business. But when gossip and ill will wag the tongues of God's people, loose talk turns embers into flames. Cecily and I came here to escape the gossip of my husband's misdeeds. Not to immerse ourselves back into the thick of it. Pastor Barber, I'm asking the council to think carefully as they look at the arguments placed before you tonight. Are they well-thought arguments, or the discourse of a few wagging tongues? And even if I wasn't Seb Ward's mother, I'd expect the council to look at his strong and fair history and the kind heart he keeps humble. And as he raises his brother as his own son, I would hope the whole town would embrace the child," she added. "He is but a child who has already lost his beloved mother, and who never had a father to look up to. Until now."

She didn't go back to her seat.

She came and stood by her son, eyes forward, chin up.

Will Barber addressed the other three voting members. "We've heard a lot tonight, and as a pastor it pains me to see the damage gossip can have. Not just on a business, but on an entire community. As a board member, I want what's best for Second Chance and I stand by Seb Ward and his lumberyard with my vote. Gentlemen?"

Will addressed his unspoken question to the three other voting members. All three raised their hands.

"Is it aye from all three of you?"

It was and when they'd voted for Seb, Will smacked his small gavel against the wooden table top. "The Town Board of Second Chance approves the ongoing work of Sebastian Ward and his lumber yard and finds no ill regard in his purchase of town properties. This meeting is adjourned."

It was over.

Seb hugged his mother, then his sister. "And you two are all right being here? Facing this?"

"I expect people will be so busy running their own lives that they'll soon forget to run ours," said his mother. "Which means we can all get on with our lives, my son."

He'd thought that, too, but when not one Eichas showed up to offer support, he was pretty sure the writing was on the wall. Still, he would not give up. He would go to Rachel, explain the truth and ask her forgiveness. He clapped his hat onto his head. "I'm going to see you back to the hotel, then I intend to stop and see Rachel."

Will overheard him. "Rachel's not there, Seb. Nellie went into labor today and I'm pretty sure that Rachel has her hands full keeping things calm on the farm. I saw her heading out of town with Sol once school was out. I'm not sure which one looked less comfortable," he added.

"The woman who's had no experience with such things and no mother to guide her or the man who lost his first wife in childbirth."

"I'll hitch up and head straight out."

His mother laid a gentle hand of caution on his arm. "They've most likely had an exhausting day. You could wait until tomorrow."

Except he couldn't wait one moment longer. He gave her a quick hug. "Will, can you see Mother home?"

"Happy to oblige," Will answered. "Do you even know where you're going, Seb?"

"We happened to pass the Eichas claims when Seb took me and the girls out to see the prairie," said Elizabeth.

Will's smile grew. "Just happened to, eh?"

"We'll see to Elijah," his mother promised, but she was smiling too. "You go. But be careful."

Careful was the last thing on Seb's mind as he headed out the door. He hooked up the horse and buggy from the livery and was on the road quickly.

The prairie loomed black before him, but the scattered claims along the way offered hints of light. He was almost afraid he'd gone too far west when the horse rounded a curve and the Eichas house appeared on his left. Lantern light brightened several windows. As he pulled the horse up in a tight circle, the back door opened.

Rachel stepped out. She crossed a small stretch of browned prairie grass and flung a bucket of wash water onto the nearby weeds.

Then she turned.

Saw him.

Oh, the look of her!

Joyful. Excited. Happy to see him. She set the bucket down and came his way. As she did, the plaintive cry of a newborn baby broke the evening quiet.

"Rachel."

"Seb."

So beautiful. So perfectly lovely, even as she tried to swipe her damp hands against her apron.

He didn't pause. Didn't wait. Didn't ask.

He kissed her.

He kissed her long and slow and deep and if the night wasn't turning downright cold, he'd be all right standing there, kissing her forever.

"Seb." She whispered his name and drew back. "Seb, we need to talk."

"I like kissing better." Saying it, he realized how true it was.

She smiled against his cheek, but withdrew slightly. "Seb—"

"But we do need to get a matter straight between us," he interrupted her. "I should have done it weeks ago, because how can you ask someone to spend their life with you if you don't trust them with everything? Your heart? Your soul?"

"You're asking me to spend my life with you, Seb? Because this is a most interesting way of doing it."

He kissed her once more, just because. "I am, but first I have to be honest with you, Rachel. Like I should have been from the beginning."

Chapter Twenty-one

HERE IT WAS.
The confession she longed for. With the moment at hand, she almost wondered if silence wouldn't have been the better choice. And yet, she knew better. "I'm listening, Seb."

"Eli isn't my son, Rachel."

Not exactly what she'd expected him to say. "He's not?"

"He's my little brother."

"Your brother. But—" She leaned back against his arm— his very strong arm— and frowned. Then stopped frowning. "Your father sent him here so your mother wouldn't know."

"Yes, without word or warning. And I want what's best for Eli, Rachel. It's not his fault that his father is a scoundrel."

She understood that better than most. "A child should never be held accountable for the sins of the parent. And you've been trying to protect your mother. And your sisters, too."

"Yes. Except my mother came to the town meeting tonight and explained the whole thing."

"She knows?"

"From the moment she saw him in church. The resemblance is striking."

"Which got tongues wagging."

"Yes." He drew her in for a hug. A long, warm hug. "I was wrong to stay quiet about it and let you wonder. There was a foolish part of me that wanted your trust without explanation."

Hadn't she been searching for much the same thing? "Not foolish, for what is love without trust?"

"Men have deceived women in the past. I understand the hesitation. But that's not why I'm here, Rachel." He loosed her from his arms and stepped back. And then he went down on one knee...

Her heart raced. Her palms went damp and it had nothing to do with kitchen wash water.

He held out a small velvet box with one hand and gazed up at her with a look of such true love and devotion that her knees went weak. "Rachel Eichas, will you do me the honor of becoming my wife? Sharing my life and Eli's life and any precious babies that come our way?"

She would, yes.

But not with him on bended knee. She grasped his hands and gave a light tug.

He stood. The slanted light from a nearby window highlighted his confused and slightly amused expression. "If the answer is not 'yes', I will court you until it is, my darling."

She laughed softly. "The answer is absolutely yes, but I don't want you on bended knee. Well, except when you are by my side as I go through that." She tipped her gaze up to the window above them, where little Levi crowed with discontent. "I want my husband to stand with me, side by side. Through whatever life sends our way. So yes, my beloved Sebastian." She reached up and drew his face to hers for a most convincing kiss. "I will marry you. And I will love you all of our days."

"Soon?"

She laughed softly with her forehead against his. "When the house is done. I don't need a fancy honeymoon but

I will require privacy and that is an unachievable goal in your apartment and mine with a boy running around. Hopefully that will give you reason to build quickly, my love."

"The best reason I could imagine." He slipped a beautiful ring onto her finger. "I love you, Rachel."

She sighed and laid her head against the warmth of his woolen coat. "I know. And I am so glad that you do because the feeling is quite mutual. Now let's go inside and tell the others and then if you would offer me a ride back to town, I will gratefully accept. For I have a class to teach come morning, you have a dear boy waiting, and I do believe my work here is quite done."

They slipped inside hand-in-hand and when the hugs and exclamations were done, and her long coat securely fastened, her beloved Sebastian helped her up, into the buggy. He climbed in beside her and looked her way. "All set, my love?"

Her heart breathed a sweet sigh of satisfaction. She shifted closer to him, then laid her head against his strong shoulder. "All set. Let's head home."

Epilogue

"RACHEL, DARLING, WHILE THE CURRENT trend is tipping toward white as the color of choice for a wedding thanks to a British queen, I think this blue and yellow floral is perfect on you." Nellie adjusted the wedding gown's skirt as she spoke.

"Where would I ever wear a white dress again?" Rachel wondered. Then she touched the white lace trimming the tucked bodice. "This will be perfect for Sunday church services. Thank you for making it, Nellie."

Nellie finished her fussing, then stood. "I do believe I promised you a proper wedding and a gown just short months ago."

Rachel laughed. "At a time when I doubted both. Yes. You did."

"And you are a dear and beautiful bride, sweet sister." Miriam stepped forward to hug Rachel. "In all my years I never was able to envision these changes in us. In the farm. In our ways."

"We move forward, a group of women determined to claim our lives and our rights and the West as our own," said Esther.

"Essie." Levi came their way, carrying his tiny namesake. "While I heartily support your stands on these things, it's her wedding day. Plenty of time for suffragist views tomorrow, I believe."

"She's fine, Levi, she's stating no more than what I will embrace by her side, and how happy I am to hear my brother offers his full support."

"My wife's fair temper would slay me would I not," Levi replied, and the amusement in his eyes softened the deep tenor of his voice. "And since I enjoy my wife's good opinion..."

Nellie winked at Rachel.

"And see the reason behind the campaign, I will offer all the support I can."

"Well said, husband." Nellie reached for the baby. "If you give me our sweet son, I will go into the next room and feed him before the ceremony. That might gain us thirty minutes of peace."

The pudgy baby grinned up at Nellie and batted her cheek with chubby fingers.

"Oh you sweet little dumpling!" She nuzzled the baby's neck, making him laugh as she walked away.

"Shall we head over to the church?" asked Rachel.

"We mustn't risk Seb seeing you," declared Hattie as she adjusted a small white veil into Rachel's hair.

"An old wive's tail, Hattie."

"And yet it is all right to give rise to some traditions if not all. A little anticipation is good for a man's heart. And his soul."

"I'll make sure that Seb and Eli are inside the church." Levi came forward and did something he rarely did. He hugged her. "I am quite happy for you, Rachel. And for me because Seb has promised me a family discount on future lumber purchases and that's no small thing in the wagon business."

Rachel laughed out loud as he hugged her.

"Did our brother just make a joke?" asked Miriam as she set thin towels over three sugared cakes. "And a funny one at that. Will wonders never cease?"

"Since I intend to use some of that finer lumber to create an ice box for your goods at the mercantile, I'd be more appreciative, little sister." He didn't say the words in a scolding fashion, like he used to.

He said them teasingly, with the smallest of smiles and the biggest of hearts. "I will cross the road and waylay the groom. Rachel." He turned her way once more, this time quite serious. "Go with God, my sister. And should you ever need anything, please know that your brother will always stand by you. That should never be a question in your mind."

"Oh, Levi." She hugged him again, and if her dress got a little wrinkled, who would care? Not her. "You are a dear brother to all of us and we love you."

"Since that was not always the case, I am very glad that it's gone that way now." He crossed to the door in short steps. "I'll see you all in church."

He opened the door.

Splendid spring air flooded the small room. Birds, returned from their long winter trek, made a joyful noise in the trees, and the songs and sounds of rebirth surrounded them. The creek, quiet all winter, flowed with strength now. The trees, silent gray sentinels for months, bore leaf tips of honey, green and copper, almost ready to burst into bloom. And the prairie grass, long faded, was turning a vibrant Kelly green once more, it's deep roots a testimony to this new land.

Hattie finished fussing with the veil, then stepped back. "We're ready."

Miriam opened the door.

The women crossed the short distance from Rachel's little rooms to the humble prairie church. They went up the steps and through the door.

Seb had been in deep discussion about something with Will Barber. The discussion ended the moment he turned. Saw her.

Oh, his face.

That beloved strong and steady countenance, not quick to smile but fast in love and hope and passion.

He came her way quickly.

Hattie was about to fuss, then didn't. She smiled instead, and took a broad step back.

A few dozen people filled the seats of the church. Friends, family and a few of her school families had made it a point to attend. And there, tucked in the second last row, were the Daniels' boys. Reggie had spent winter weeks working for Seb while Harold worked at the livery. By staying in town, the two young men had done well with their studies, and learned a fair trade. They didn't look the least bit comfortable to be there, but they'd come on their own and what a marvelous tribute that was.

"Rachel. My love."

Seb took her hand, but what he truly held was her heart, from this day forward.

He lifted it for his kiss, and when he met her gaze and let his linger, a shiver of sweet anticipation ran through her.

He was her love and soon to be her lover. Her husband. Her trusted helpmate.

"Yes, my darling?" She smiled up at him with just enough twinkle to say she shared his feelings of the day. "Are we ready for this, Sebastian?"

His smile went wide. "Ready and willing. I would walk you down the aisle but your brother gets that right today. But it will be my absolute pleasure to do so from this day forward."

She leaned up and gave him a whisper of a kiss on the cheek. "And mine, dear husband."

Seb went back to his place at the front of the church. Nellie rejoined them, holding that chunky, smiling baby, and the girls slipped into their pew. Miriam took a place to stand as witness and when Levi took Rachel's arm, her heart jumped.

She turned. Gazed forward. Locked eyes with Sebastian and with each step she took down that short aisle she drew closer to her dream come true.

Her love. Her life. Her beloved husband.

And as Sebastian reached out and took her hand, Rachel didn't feel like she was giving up her freedom to gain a spouse.

On the contrary...

She was about to embrace a life she thought had eluded her.

It hadn't done anything of the sort.

It had come as so many things do... in God's own sweet time.

DEAR READERS,
I hope you loved this Regency-styled prairie romance. I know I loved writing it, it's so much fun to go back in time to simpler things, gentler thoughts and the old-fashioned work of human hands… but with that being said, romance is romance, and Seb Ward and Rachel Eichas were made for each other, weren't they? ☺

I've thoroughly enjoyed creating Rachel's happy ending, and her sister Miri has got a lot going on between learning midwifery, birthing cows and pigs and whatever livestock happens to be on the claims, and oh yes… making cheese! Miri has a hand in the cool room, and an eye for business. She's a savvy one, and while she thinks romance is all well and good for others, she has absolutely no thought of tying the knot and settling down anytime soon… or ever. And with her father's strictly conservative views on faith, salvation and Jesus, she's pretty turned off of in-your-face religion.

But when a new pastor comes to town, and two orphaned children come stumbling out of the brush along the creek, well— Miriam Eichas might have her hands full and she might just need that sweet commitment of happy-ever-after love, after all… if she doesn't kill the hero first.

Beau Carlisle hunted desperados before he turned his hand to shepherding a church flock, and he's pretty sure he can handle whatever comes his way in Second Chance, South Dakota.

What he didn't reckon on was the love a wonderful woman and two little kids because he'd loved a woman once. And a child. He'd loved and lost and Beau Carlisle was 100% sure he'd never love again.

Oops…

I hope you enjoy Miri's story when it releases and huge thanks for reading Rachel and Seb's beautiful romance.

Feel free to contact me at *loganherne@gmail.com*, visit my

website *ruthloganherne.com* and I love having new friends on facebook *http://facebook.com/RuthLoganHerne* on my author page or friends page.

Wishing you every blessing!

Ruthy

Rachel's Apple Cake and Whipped Cream Frosting

This is an easy recipe for a homemade cake with an old-fashioned consistency that Rachel loved to serve to family and friends throughout Second Chance. The whipped cream frosting was so much easier once Levi fashioned ice boxes for his sisters and that was a marvelous convenience on the prairie!

For this cake, you simply dump all the ingredients into a bowl and mix until smooth. Pour batter into prepared baking pan (lightly greased, then floured) and bake at 350° for about 30-35 minutes in a 13" x 9" pan.   Adjust time slightly for 8" or 9" rounds.

For cake:

2 cups cake flour
1 1/2 cups packed brown sugar
1 teaspoon baking soda
2 large eggs
1 cup sour cream
1/2 cup oil
1/3 cup water
2 teaspoons cinnamon
3/4 teaspoon nutmeg
1/4 teaspoon cloves

Mix until smooth. Pour batter into pans, bake for about 30-35 minutes until top springs back when touched lightly with finger, or when a toothpick inserted into center of cake comes out clean.... it can have a few moist

crumbs, but no liquidy center.
Cool.

Apple Pie Filling:

3 large apples (I used Crispin, a personal Ruthy fave for baking!)
2/3 cup sugar
1/4 cup flour
1 teaspoon or so cinnamon
3/4 cup water

Peel, core and chop apples. Mix sugar, flour and cinnamon. Put apples, flour mix and 3/4 cup water into pan. Mix thoroughly, cover and heat over low/medium heat, stirring now and again while apples soften. Mix will thicken with heat. When apples are fork-tender, remove from heat, cool.

Turn cake out of pan. Split in half, creating two layers. Spread apple pie filling on bottom layer. Replace top layer. Cover with lightly sweetened whipped cream, then gently spoon the remaining apple pie filling over whipped cream. Serve chilled.

Whipped Cream:

2 Cups heavy whipping cream
½ cup sugar

Beat whipping cream on high speed. Gradually pour in sugar. Continue beating until stiff peaks form. Don't overbeat or you'll have sweet butter… and then you'll be starting again!

Other books by
Ruth Logan Herne:

INDEPENDENTLY PUBLISHED BOOKS
Running on Empty
Try, Try Again
Safely Home
Refuge of the Heart
More Than a Promise
The First Gift
From This Day Forward
Christmas on the Frontier
The Sewing Sisters' Society Anthology

FROM WATERFALL PRESS/AMAZON
Welcome to Wishing Bridge
At Home in Wishing Bridge

FROM WATERBROOK PRESS/PENGUIN/
RANDOM HOUSE
Back in the Saddle
Home on the Range
Peace in the Valley

LOVE INSPIRED BOOKS
North Country:
Winter's End
Waiting Out the Storm
Made to Order Family

MEN OF ALLEGANY COUNTY SERIES
Reunited Hearts
Small Town Hearts
Mended Hearts
Yuletide Hearts
A Family to Cherish
His Mistletoe Family

KIRKWOOD LAKE SERIES
The Lawman's Second Chance
Falling for the Lawman
The Lawman's Holiday Wish
Loving the Lawman
Her Holiday Family
Healing the Lawman's Heart

GRACE HAVEN SERIES
An Unexpected Groom
Her Unexpected Family
Their Surprise Daddy
The Lawman's Yuletide Baby
Her Secret Daughter

SHEPHERD'S CROSSING SERIES
Her Cowboy Reunion
A Cowboy Christmas (with Linda Goodnight)
A Cowboy in Shepherd's Crossing

**FROM BIG SKY CONTINUITY/LOVE
INSPIRED BOOKS**
His Montana Sweetheart

FROM SUMMERSIDE PRESS
Love Finds You in the City at Christmas

Made in United States
North Haven, CT
29 March 2024

50665533R00148